Vengeance in Venice

Silver and Grey
Book 6

Mary Lancaster

ARE YOU SIGNED UP FOR DRAGONBLADE'S BLOG?

You'll get the latest news and information on exclusive giveaways, exclusive excerpts, coming releases, sales, free books, cover reveals and more.

Check out our complete list of authors, too!

No spam, no junk. That's a promise!

Sign Up Here

www.dragonbladepublishing.com

Dearest Reader;

Thank you for your support of a small press. At Dragonblade Publishing, we strive to bring you the highest quality Historical Romance from some of the best authors in the business. Without your support, there is no 'us', so we sincerely hope you adore these stories and find some new favorite authors along the way.

Happy Reading!

CEO, Dragonblade Publishing

ADDITIONAL DRAGONBLADE BOOKS BY AUTHOR MARY LANCASTER

Silver and Grey Series
Murder in Moonlight (Book 1)
Evidence of Evil (Book 2)
Ghost in the Garden (Book 3)
The Trick of the Treasure (Book 4)
Word of the Wicked (Book 5)
Vengeance in Venice (Book 6)

One Night in Blackhaven Series
The Captain's Old Love (Book 1)
The Earl's Promised Bride (Book 2)
The Soldier's Impossible Love (Book 3)
The Gambler's Last Chance (Book 4)
The Poet's Stern Critic (Book 5)
The Rake's Mistake (Book 6)
The Spinster's Last Dance (Book 7)

The Duel Series
Entangled (Book 1)
Captured (Book 2)
Deserted (Book 3)
Beloved (Book 4)
Haunted (Novella)

Last Flame of Alba Series
Rebellion's Fire (Book 1)
A Constant Blaze (Book 2)
Burning Embers (Book 3)

Gentlemen of Pleasure Series
The Devil and the Viscount (Book 1)

Temptation and the Artist (Book 2)
Sin and the Soldier (Book 3)
Debauchery and the Earl (Book 4)
Blue Skies (Novella)

Pleasure Garden Series
Unmasking the Hero (Book 1)
Unmasking Deception (Book 2)
Unmasking Sin (Book 3)
Unmasking the Duke (Book 4)
Unmasking the Thief (Book 5)

Crime & Passion Series
Mysterious Lover (Book 1)
Letters to a Lover (Book 2)
Dangerous Lover (Book 3)
Lost Lover (Book 4)
Merry Lover (Novella)
Ghostly Lover (Novella)

The Husband Dilemma Series
How to Fool a Duke (Book 1)

Season of Scandal Series
Pursued by the Rake (Book 1)
Abandoned to the Prodigal (Book 2)
Married to the Rogue (Book 3)
Unmasked by her Lover (Book 4)
Her Star from the East (Novella)

Imperial Season Series
Vienna Waltz (Book 1)
Vienna Woods (Book 2)
Vienna Dawn (Book 3)

Blackhaven Brides Series
The Wicked Baron (Book 1)
The Wicked Lady (Book 2)
The Wicked Rebel (Book 3)

The Wicked Husband (Book 4)
The Wicked Marquis (Book 5)
The Wicked Governess (Book 6)
The Wicked Spy (Book 7)
The Wicked Gypsy (Book 8)
The Wicked Wife (Book 9)
Wicked Christmas (Book 10)
The Wicked Waif (Book 11)
The Wicked Heir (Book 12)
The Wicked Captain (Book 13)
The Wicked Sister (Book 14)

Unmarriageable Series
The Deserted Heart (Book 1)
The Sinister Heart (Book 2)
The Vulgar Heart (Book 3)
The Broken Heart (Book 4)
The Weary Heart (Book 5)
The Secret Heart (Book 6)
Christmas Heart (Novella)

The Lyon's Den Series
Fed to the Lyon

De Wolfe Pack: The Series
The Wicked Wolfe
Vienna Wolfe

Also from Mary Lancaster
Madeleine (Novella)
The Others of Ochil (Novella)

CHAPTER ONE

A S THE CURTAIN came down on Signor Verdi's newest opera, Constance clung very tightly to Solomon's hand. The music had been sublime, the subject of *La Traviata* perhaps a little too close to home, dealing as it did with a tragic courtesan. Not that Constance considered herself remotely tragic. On the contrary, her life seemed to have turned into something magical and wondrous, and the opera music heightened everything into pure emotion.

The Venetian opera lovers clearly had their doubts about the performance, for there were catcalls amongst the applause. Constance glanced at Solomon, lifting her eyebrows.

"Well, some of the singing *was* a little weak," he said. "And it does require quite a feat of imagination to believe that particular lady to be dying young of consumption."

"You didn't enjoy it?"

He rose, drawing her with him. "Of course I did." His eyes were warm and intimate, and she marveled all over again that she should have this amazing man to share her life with. Her husband, Solomon Grey, the true source of all her emotion.

She smiled and led the way from the box to join the throngs in the passage. The crowd was loud and lively, but she did not mind. The Italian language was curiously musical, even when hordes of people talked at once.

It was just as they stepped out of the theatre and into the street that she saw the Englishman again.

She had noticed him before, just after the first act, in a box close to theirs, gazing at her quite fixedly. Constance, used to men's stares for all sorts of reasons, had thought nothing of it beyond the fact that he appeared somehow very British in his severe evening dress. Now her wide skirts almost brushed against him, and again he was looking right at her.

He must have been in his early fifties, tall and fit, wearing an expensive opera cloak and a silk hat on his iron-gray head. When she caught him staring, he merely smiled and touched the brim of his hat. It was a civil smile, neither threatening nor lascivious, but there was no embarrassment either, let alone apology for his obvious interest.

Constance ignored him and turned back to Solomon.

Venice at night was enchanting, full of grand squares lit by lamplight and dark, narrow passages. Waterways glinted in the moonlight, scattered with lanterns on the myriad boats that acted like the much more mundane hackney cabs of London.

"Did you see that Englishman?" she asked as they walked in the opposite direction of the crowd toward the Rio di San Luca, where their boat awaited them. "Do you know him?"

"Which Englishman?"

"The one we passed just at the theatre door. He looked at me. He was watching me at the last interval too."

"Men are always watching you. It is something I must grow used to. I thought you already were."

He was right. She had worked hard to inspire men's notice and there was no real reason to be outraged by that particular gentleman's unthreatening attention. "I wondered if you knew him and that was why he looked."

He covered her hand with his, drawing it further into the crook of his arm. "He stares because you are beautiful and look especially lovely tonight. You forget to hide your emotions when you watch the stage. You are breathtaking."

It was her own breath that vanished at his words. In the fortnight since their marriage, he had made her several such unexpected compliments, which meant all the more to her because he was not a man to give them easily. Quiet and self-disciplined, he never showed his passion to the world. But he showed it to her, and that was the greatest compliment of them all.

She laid her cheek against his arm. "I do love you, Solomon."

The world was perfect. At her side, this wonderful, complicated man, and surrounding them, this stunning city of unbelievable beauty and serenity. More immediately, people walked past them in various directions, and when they reached the water, some descended the steps to where their private boats awaited. The boatmen called to each other, guiding their distinctive craft with great dexterity. Constance and Solomon strolled on along the side of the Rio di San Luca. She was in no hurry, and they had asked their boatman to wait some distance from the Teatro la Fenice. They liked to walk.

Every few yards there were steps down to the water, and the further they walked, the fewer waiting boats they saw. It was a fine night, and the moonlight reflected off the water, along with the boatmen's lights. They approached their own boat at last. Alvise, their oarsman, or *gondoliere*, waved, still worried they would not be able to find him. Solomon lifted a hand in return.

"What is going on there?" he said suddenly.

She followed his gaze beyond their boat to the next stairs, where a group of men appeared to enjoying a spirited altercation. "No doubt a quarrel over politics or some finer point of philosophy. Or trade." They had observed many such arguments, most of which were good-natured if loud. But this one seemed to have turned ugly.

The men had surrounded one of their number. Punches were thrown. Constance was sure a blade glinted as the victim went down under the combined assault.

Solomon swore under his breath. "Wait here." He sprinted down the walkway, calling out in the hope of frightening off the attackers.

Alvise groaned and leapt up the steps from his boat. Constance gathered up her skirts and flew after Solomon. She wished she had filled her reticule with stones—an old trick she had used to defend herself in the past—for she had no other weapon to hand.

Ahead, the victim seemed to be back on his feet but still under attack, though two of the men had turned to face Solomon. Constance tried to run faster, but her arm was suddenly grasped from behind, pulling her up with a bump. A torrent of Italian told her it was Alvise.

"We need to help him!" she raged, trying to tug herself free.

But Alvise's usual friendly submission had vanished. He would not obey. "No, signora. You stay, or I cannot go." His voice was hard, impatient, forcing her to accept that he would be more use to Solomon than she would. And if he had to stay here protecting her, then Solomon would be alone.

"Go," she whispered.

Nodding curtly, he released her and loped toward the fight, drawing something from the belt of his trousers that glinted in the moonlight.

When she was sure Alvise would not look back, she began to move after him, forcing herself to walk sedately while trying to make sense of the melee ahead.

The two men came out of nowhere, grasped an arm each, and started dragging her toward the dark passageway on their right. She opened her mouth to call out, and a rough hand clapped over her face.

SOLOMON'S JOINING THE fight appeared to merely irritate the practiced thugs setting about their outnumbered victim. When he charged into the melee, hoping to scare them off, they tried to swat him away as though he were an annoying mosquito.

Interesting, he thought, as he forced his way to the victim's side. This young man, breathing rapidly, was already bloodied and winded, but seemed game enough, even flashing Solomon a very brief and weary smile of gratitude before a fist swung viciously for the side of his head.

It was Solomon who blocked the punch, grasping the attacker's arm and swinging him into his comrades, who were trying to surround their victim again, separating him from Solomon. They staggered into each other, allowing the defenders a moment of respite.

Solomon charged, head down, felling one man before swinging around, both fists flying to connect with another. The original victim, apparently heartened by this success, got in a few blows of his own.

Solomon's main worry was the blade glinting in the light of a passing boat. Its wielder was not so much stabbing as slashing, and it was only a matter of time before he injured or even killed someone. Solomon brought him down with a well-aimed kick to the knees, and stood on the man's wrist before swooping down to retrieve the knife from his nerveless fingers.

And then Alvise joined the fight, which changed the numbers to four against three. The attackers clearly did not like these odds, for they melted suddenly into the darkness, hurling only insults and threats as they backed off away from the canal to a narrow passage. Beyond them, back where Solomon had left Constance, two men were dragging a woman into darkness.

Constance.

He might have made some animal noise of fear, or it might just have been in his head. He didn't care which. He was already pounding down the street toward where he had last seen her, no conscious thought in his head except that he could not lose sight of her. All other concerns, recriminations, and regrets had to wait before the one vital necessity of keeping her in sight until…

Someone caught his arm. "Signor, there is no point!"

The passageway was empty. The victim of the attack and

Alvise stood on either side of him. He shook them off, but the man he had helped clung determinedly to his arm.

"No, signor. I don't believe they will hurt her. And I know where they are taking her."

Solomon stared at him, torn. Every second he wasted talking, Constance got further away from him. "This is part of your quarrel?"

"You helped me. They think she is connected to me, that this will hurt me."

"Where?" Solomon barked. "Where have they taken her?" Could he even believe this bloodied stranger?

"Palazzo Savelli."

Solomon flicked his gaze at Alvise. "Do you know it?"

Alvise nodded once. He exchanged some rapid words with the other Venetian. Solomon paid no attention. He was already striding back toward his boat.

"Send the police," he threw over his shoulder at the victim.

"Oh, no, the police will do nothing. They are mostly in Savelli's pocket. I come with you." The man kept pace with Solomon, although he limped somewhat. "We shall steal her back. At the very least, Savelli will release her in exchange for me."

Solomon did not waste breath on further speech until the three of them were in the boat and Alvise was rowing them up the Rio di Luca, turning into the Rio della Vesti. By the boat's light, he could more clearly see the face of his ally, wiping the blood off his cheek and chin. The sleeve of his coat was slashed, and there was blood around the torn knee of his trousers.

"Who are you and who has taken my wife?" Solomon demanded. He was hanging on to his intellect by a thread as the nightmare threatened to engulf him in sheer panic. It all felt too eerily familiar—disappearance, loss, fear—and yet it had sprung out of a moment of pure happiness, of the kind she had once wished for him, back when they first met…

Focus, fool—this will not help her.

His rather battered ally was speaking. "I am Ludovico Giusti, a gentleman of Venice. I believe your wife was taken by the men of Angelo Savelli, like those who attacked me. We are…enemies."

"Who is this Savelli?"

Giusti's lip curled. "A rather wealthy so-called gentleman of Venice. As he has clearly demonstrated this night that he has no honor. He is a traitor, collaborating with the Austrians, with whom he always sides, even when we had the chance of freedom."

Along with most of the rest of Europe, Venice had erupted in revolution in 1848, only five years ago, and thrown their Austrian overlords out of the city. The newly proclaimed republic had enjoyed only a brief moment of victory and liberal self-government, however, for just like all the others of that year, the Venetian revolution had been swept aside, and the city reconquered—by the forces of foreign oppression, according to the defeated, or by the legitimate government, according to the winners.

"We are British, and not involved in your political quarrels," Solomon said, with less sympathy than he might have acknowledged had Constance been by his side.

"Oh, our quarrels are more than political," Giusti said with a grimace. "They go back many years and involve jewels and faithless women and betrayals of all kinds. He has the woman. I have a jewel or too. It seems he wants everything. This little attack was meant to scare me, to force me to give him what he wants. Now he thinks your wife is his trump card." Giusti flashed a smile that was oddly attractive, even with his fattened lip. "He is right, for I am in your debt."

"But what has my wife to do with any of this?"

Giusti shrugged. "Nothing, of course. You ran to my aid, as though we are friends. She was with you. No doubt the fools imagined you are her bodyguard, her servant whom she sent to protect me."

Perhaps it would have been funny, without the violence, without the desperation. "This enemy of yours made the decision that you are my wife's lover on the basis that we just happened to see your being attacked on our way home from the opera?"

Giusti's darting gaze returned to Solomon, his eyebrows raised. For a moment Solomon thought he was about to ask which opera they had seen, but instead Giusti said, "Savelli himself was not there. He is not so stupid. His men are mere…" He struggled for the English word and gave up. "*Guardie del corpo mercenarie, condottiere,* hired as guards to do his dirty work so that his hands remain clean."

Contempt seemed to drip from his lips, which did nothing to allay Solomon's anguish. The thought of Constance in the hands of such people was unbearable, even knowing she had her own ways of dealing with them. Here she was, in a foreign country, able to speak very little of the language and with no knowledge of the local customs, and according to Giusti, they regarded her as the enemy.

"How much further?" Solomon asked between his teeth.

Giusti threw some instructions over his shoulder at Alvise, who nodded acknowledgment.

Giusti grinned at Solomon as though they were upon some grand adventure. His eyes were almost dancing with excitement. The overall effect, on a face beginning to bruise and swell, with traces of blood smeared across it, was almost grotesque, and made Solomon wish very hard that he had gone straight to the city authorities. Why had he relied on this stranger who quite clearly had his own agenda of quarrels and spite?

"We go in the back way," Giusti explained. "Take him by surprise. No one will expect us so soon…"

IT WAS A long time since Constance had been so frightened. When they had forced the gag in her mouth and yanked the wide hood of her opera cloak fully over her face like an impenetrable cowl through which she could see nothing but shadows, she had known this was more than a random street robbery. She was being abducted, kidnapped, for reasons she could only guess at. All of them terrified her.

Her whole body shook, because she was powerless as they dragged her through streets. She knew they passed other people, and yet she could not beg for help, could not break free. She trembled with shame at that helplessness, as well as with fury. They held her so tightly between them, walking so fast that her feet barely touched the ground. She probably looked like an errant wife being returned to her family.

When she tried to shake her head free of the hood, one of them held it closed. Fear had cut off her ability to think, even her *wish* to think beyond her silent screams of *Solomon!*

And more abjectly, *Help me!*

Somewhere she was aware that her abduction must be related to the attack on the stranger. And she didn't even know if Solomon was alive. How had their happiness broken so suddenly into this...? Whatever this was.

She was half carried down some steps and then recognized that she was in a boat on the water. She heard the splash of oars and came to the decision that she would throw herself over the side to escape. Her skirts would quickly hamper her, of course, but with her arms free, surely she could at least attract help...

She was never given the opportunity, for her captors never released her for a moment. She had tried alternately going limp in their hold and struggling ferociously, but at least one of them always held on, and their grip only tightened. Her arms would be black and blue from the cruel grasp of their fingers, designed to intimidate as well as to hurt. At least they had not struck her—not beyond an early buffet to her hooded head, which she had taken as a warning shot and ignored.

Their voices were rough when they spoke together in rapid

Italian. She barely understood a word of it, and none of it gave her any clues as to what was happening to her. She began to think she was safe as long as they were on the water, and dreaded their arrival. The filthy rag in her mouth had been tied in place now and dried her throat unbearably. All part of the nightmare, and yet she would gladly suffer it all if only Solomon lived…

Abruptly, she was moving again, hauled off the wobbling boat and dragged up a couple of steps. She was indoors, and her fear sharpened.

Oh God, why can I not even think?

There were more stairs, and the vague smell of damp faded. Although she could not see where she was, she knew there was light, and whatever building they were in was substantial, for she and her captors walked side by side without difficulty.

She heard a door open and was dragged inside another well-lit room. Still her captors did not release her, and most terrifying of all, rapid footsteps approached, and she felt her captors tense.

She wished she could stop shaking. She needed to be aware enough, swift enough to grasp the first opportunity to escape… Only how, when she could neither see nor speak?

Despair swamped even the fear, and then another presence entered the room, snapping questions at her captors, one of whom released a torrent of words.

Without warning, her bruised arms were released, and yet there was no point in throwing herself toward where she knew the door to be, because the newcomer stood right in front of her, blocking some of the light. Her hood was pulled back, away from her face, and she screwed up her eyes against the sudden glare. She heard the intake of the newcomer's breath, and then a blast of furious Italian. Her gag was untied by the newcomer, and she spat and dragged the disgusting rag from her mouth.

The man in front of her spoke again. *"Mi scusi, signora."*

That, at least, she could understand. She stared at him. He was no thug in appearance, but a well-dressed gentleman with a neat beard and turbulent eyes, though she had the impression his anger was not directed at her but at his minions, whom he banished from the room with an angry snap.

"No," Constance said, all the more furious because her words came out hoarse and faint. "I do not excuse you, and—" She broke off, coughing, and her captor, muttering under his breath, strode to a jug on a pretty inlaid table and poured a glass of water, which he brought to her.

She would have loved to dash it in his face, but she needed the drink, and she needed answers to the questions clamoring to form in her shaken mind. She drank. And looked about her. The room had grand proportions and had once probably been handsome, although now it bore signs of neglect, such as chipped, faded paint, and smelled somehow unused. There were no pictures on the wall, no carpets on the floor. It was sparsely furnished with two chairs and the small table. Was this to be her prison?

"You are English?" her captor said.

It spoke volumes for her weakened state that she was actually grateful he spoke her language. "I am. And suddenly I think very ill of Venetian hospitality."

"I am not surprised. I can only apologize once more for your rough treatment. Please, sit."

Again, she wanted to remain standing, but she needed to recover her physical strength more than retain her pride. At least he did not touch her, merely indicated the ornate chair closest to where she stood. She sank into it and took another sip of water. He remained standing.

A new possibility occurred to her. "Are you the *police?*"

His eyebrows flew up. "No, I am a private citizen."

"In my country, you would be charged with kidnapping and hanged."

"I should not go unpunished in mine, either. My fools misunderstood their orders and acted on their own initiative. Never a happy event. However, they associate you with one Ludovico Giusti, whom I think you know?"

The apology had faded from his eyes, leaving them hard and watchful.

"I do not," said Constance. "I have been in the city a matter of days."

"And yet you sent your men to the aid of Giusti."

She tilted her chin. "*My husband* sent himself to the aid of a man being attacked in the street by at least four others. If these were your men…"

"Giusti has something of mine. Of my wife's. I need it returned."

Constance stared at him. "So you send your thugs to beat him in the street? Is there no law in this city?"

To her surprise, a hint of color seeped into his cheeks. He seemed to be a serious, rather stiff man, and yet he was not old, surely not much over thirty.

"There is, of course," he said awkwardly. "But some things go beyond law. To honor."

"What honor is there is four men beating another to steal from him? In abducting a woman alone because her husband and servant had gone to the aid of the poor victim?"

"Giusti is no victim," he snapped. "And *he* is the thief, not I. My question is, what were you and your husband even doing there, since you claim not to know Giusti?"

She raised her eyebrows. "Returning from the opera."

He blinked, as though that were the last answer he had expected. "Which theatre?" he barked at last.

She arched her eyebrows. "La Fenice."

"What did you hear?"

"Verdi's new work, *La Traviata.* And what business is this of yours?"

The man dragged his fingers through his hair. "None," he said bitterly. His shoulders slumped. "Clearly none. Allow me to escort you to wherever you are staying."

For a stunned moment, she was speechless. Her jaw probably dropped. "I would not allow you to escort me from the room.

Where is my husband?"

He actually looked flustered. "I do not know. My men ran off, frightened of being identified when your boatman joined the fray. They mistook your husband for your servant."

Then he was alive, surely he was alive... Emotion burst into words. "He is no one's servant. Your men must be imbeciles. You may hire me a boatman entirely unconnected to you."

"Madam, if I am seen hiring another boatman for a lady..." he began, clearly startled. "Consider my wife—"

"Did *you* consider her when you abducted me? How is *that* compatible with respect while fetching me a safe means of transport is not? I owe you *no* consideration, and neither does my husband—who, if he lives, must be searching frantically for me!"

His eye twitched. But he said only, "Everything I do is for my wife. I have apologized for my mistake. Let me send you in my own boat—with a maidservant for your comfort and respectability. She and the boatman will stay with you until you are returned to your husband. I can only apologize once more for the rough treatment of my men, who are indeed imbeciles."

It was the best offer she was likely to get. And considering what she had feared during her journey here, she should thank God fasting he was letting her go at all.

Part of her wanted to refuse and rail and threaten him with the police and the British consul and the full prosecution of the law. But she had no cards to play here except his apparent goodwill, which was bizarre in the circumstances and could easily change.

Sense prevailed. She said, "Then lend me your boat and your servants."

CHAPTER TWO

ALTHOUGH SOLOMON'S OVERRIDING concern was his wife's safety, he rather relished Giusti's plan of fighting their way into her abductor's palazzo, tossing any guards into the canal. A rare, savage part of him wanted to punch and punish for what had been done to Constance, even though his thinking self knew it would not compensate her for her fear, for whatever pain had been inflicted...

He could not bear that he had left her unprotected. And the red mists of shame and fury would not save her.

Never had it been so hard to summon his much-vaunted self-discipline.

"That is the back door to the Palazzo Savelli," Giusti murmured in his ear. They were gliding unlit, close in to the side of the waterway. "The wide one there. Wait, it is opening!"

Alvise stilled the boat. The palazzo door opened almost directly onto the canal, and from the sudden lights emanating from it, Solomon could make out hooks in the wall used as moorings. Two boats were already tied up there. The man who emerged stepped nonchalantly into one of them.

Solomon's fists clenched. "Savelli?" he whispered.

Giusti shook his head. "One of his boatmen."

A woman emerged, and Solomon's heart leapt.

Giusti drew a sharp breath. "Is that her?"

"No." She was not Constance shaped. She did not move like Constance, even an injured Constance, and the boatman handed her into the vessel much too familiarly.

"Maidservant," Giusti pronounced as Alvise pushed them onward, gently, casually nearer. "Perhaps Signora Savelli is going out secretly."

The canal was not a particularly wide one, but even so, Alvise guided their boat down the middle in an unthreatening manner that clearly did not disturb the Savelli boatman. He slowed, allowing them to peer through the wide-open door.

"Stop," Solomon said, for it was Constance who stood framed in the doorway, her head held high, her posture rigid. Her bright hair glowed like burned gold in the blaze of lights. Behind her, a man hovered.

Solomon gripped the side of the boat. Alvise swung sharply toward the first of the mooring rings, and Constance turned her head from the other boat to his. Her lips parted.

The man moved out from behind her.

"Savelli," breathed Giusti.

Savelli gestured toward the vessel containing the maid and his own boatman. Constance did not even look at him. Her gaze was locked on Solomon's face. She lifted her arms, curiously like a child, and his heart threatened to break. He reached up for her and she stepped into his hold.

"Go," Solomon told Alvise.

Giusti seemed about to object, but Alvise obeyed. Solomon held his wife to his heart, absorbing her fear, her relief, and his own. Over her shoulder, he met the gaze of the man responsible.

"He let me go," Constance mumbled, almost reluctantly.

He took you in the first place. This is not over.

But it was for now. She was safe in his arms as their boat sped down the canal, past Savelli and his vessel, and through the magic of Venice by night. As if nothing had happened to disturb the city's serenity.

"He was sending me home," Constance said, clutching the fabric of Solomon's coat. "How did you find me?"

"Signor Giusti here knew where you would be."

Giusti grinned. "We came to mount a rescue, signora, but you appear to have rescued yourself."

"She does that," Solomon said with pride, though he was afraid his voice cracked. He pushed her gently onto the cushioned bench and sat beside her, holding both her hands and searching her face for signs of fear or injury. "What happened?"

"It was so quick, I had no chance. Almost as soon as Alvise left me to go to your aid, two men seized me and dragged me down the narrow passage between the buildings. People must have seen, Solomon, but no one helped."

"The city is afraid," Giusti said sadly. "And suspicious. We pretend—perhaps your captors are police, so we don't wish to be involved. Or you are an errant wife who deserves a husband's discipline. I am ashamed. And I am so sorry for my part in your experience."

Constance, though she held very tightly to Solomon's hands, seemed already to be recovering her usual spirits. "You appear to have come off worse than I, signor. My captor was also responsible for the attack on you. He said you have something of his."

Giusti's cut lips twisted. "He has something of mine."

"He thought I was your lover."

Rather to Solomon's surprise, Giusti actually blushed. "That is his shame, and mine, most certainly not yours. Forgive us. At least he is not so lost to honor that he tried to keep you." He switched his gaze to Solomon. "My home is nearby. Allow your boatman to set me down at the next steps. But perhaps I may call upon you tomorrow to express my thanks?"

"There is no need," Solomon said. "But we will be happy to receive you. We are at the Palazzo Zulian—do you know it?"

"In Cannaregio? Yes, a good place, quiet and yet close to everything you need."

Warily, Solomon scanned the side of the canal while Alvise held the boat steady.

Constance said, "Is there someone at home to care for your wounds, Signor Giusti? Are you safe?"

Giusti laughed. "Tonight, I have never been safer. It is Savelli who is now awaiting my reply. Forgive us for mixing you up in our quarrels. Goodnight."

He sprang up the steps with an airy wave and vanished into the night.

Beside Solomon, Constance relaxed and leaned into him. They glided on through the city in silence, save for the gentle lapping of the water and the splash of Alvise's oar.

"IT TOOK ME by surprise," Constance admitted when they were finally alone in her bedchamber, and she had been bathed and dressed in a soft nightgown. Solomon had seen the bruises on her arms, but though his lips tightened, he made no comment. He was waiting for her to tell him, and for that, she was grateful.

"It felt like a nightmare," she said, sitting on the bed while he watched her from the shuttered window, "coming from nowhere out of our perfect idyll. And now it is already faded, a nightmare I haven't forgotten but one I know has not harmed me. *Cannot* harm me. The bruises are just from the men's hold—they had to be harsh because I struggled so much. But beyond that, they did not hurt me. My host was furious with them—and not just for taking the wrong woman. He was appalled that they had gagged me."

"What did he expect?" Solomon said, trying to keep the savagery from his voice. "If he abducts a lady from the street—"

"To be fair, I don't believe he instructed them to do so. They acted on their own initiative because they thought I had sent you and Alvise to help Signor Giusti. Don't look like that, Sol. I can't deny I was frightened, but he was perfectly civil. The worst part was not even knowing if you were alive."

"I was afraid I had lost you," Solomon said hoarsely. "Forever."

Like her, he had been a lonely but self-sufficient person before they met. This connection between them, this love that had bound them so inextricably, had taken them both by surprise, and since their wedding, they had grasped the happiness with both hands in the foolish assumption that nothing could threaten it now. Well, there *were* threats. But nothing could break the bond.

She rose and went to him, taking his hand and kissing it. "You and I know better than that. Come to bed, Solomon."

They lay together in a loose, gentle embrace. Perhaps it was sheer relief at their safety, but with their bruises salved and the comfort of his presence, she felt curiously at peace.

"Do you want to leave?" he asked, just when she thought he was falling asleep.

She shook her head, taking his face between her hands in the darkness. "No. Not unless you do. It was just another adventure. I love this city, but it would not be natural if it didn't have a darker side. This Savelli is not a cruel man. He loves his wife, and in his own way, he is as intriguing as your Giusti. I think we have a task for Silver and Grey. To find a way to end their feud."

"I have always loved your optimism."

She smiled, her lips against his skin. "There will be no fee, of course, so if we fail, we lose nothing."

"And no one in England needs to know."

She knew from his voice that he was finally smiling, too. She had found, she thought, the perfect way to get over the ugliness of their fright. They would use it to do some good and enjoy the new adventure.

At least, that was the plan.

THE EVENTS OF the evening had appalled and shamed Angelo Savelli. If anything could have pulled him up short, shown him how out of proportion this feud had grown in his head and his heart, it was this unforgivable abduction of another man's frightened wife. A wife who loved her husband—they had been on their damned wedding journey!

Closing his eyes, he rested his forehead against the connecting door to his wife's room. Never had he yearned so badly to be with her. Or known so completely that he was unworthy.

What had been thinking to go after Giusti like that? To hire those damned mercenaries in the first place? Villains and thugs, all of them, especially Ugo and Pellini, who had brought the Englishwoman. What sort of a man had he become that they should even imagine he would tolerate such behavior, let alone applaud it, make use of it? Even if she *had* been Giusti's woman, there would have been no excuse for it. As it was...

He had brought this upon himself, losing his perspective over Giusti and Elena. He had hired Pellini and the others largely to protect his wife from Giusti's machinations and had gone on the offensive first. A warning that he had to obey, to hand over the jewels.

Or had he just wanted someone to punch Giusti, if he could not do it himself? Stupid. He knew Giusti. Threats like that would only make him dig his heels in harder.

God, it was like a madness, this fear of losing Elena to Giusti, whom she had once promised to marry. It was making him behave in a way guaranteed to disgust his wife, not win her over. And if word ever got back to her...

It would. Venice was a small city. Everyone would know by noon. He knew what he had to do for everyone's good, for his own self-respect—what was left of it. He tapped on the door and went in to the dressing room. Walking through it, he knocked gently again and found himself in her bedchamber.

She was not in bed but sitting by the window looking out.

She turned to face him.

God, she was lovely. She was everything.

"Angelo." Her voice was husky and welcoming and he went to her at once, took her hands, and held them firmly between his own.

He blurted it all out at once. "I want you to know I have behaved like a lunatic. I have been a little mad and I am ashamed. I will pay the bodyguard off in the morning."

"Why?" she asked. She did not seem very interested.

"Because it is too easy to make use of them. And they are too stupid to be trusted. They abducted a foreign lady because they assumed she was Giusti's mistress."

Her expression never changed. "Was she?"

"No, but they brought her here as some kind of bargaining tool. I tried to send her home again, but Giusti had already led her husband to the back door. I will find him tomorrow and apologize."

"I suspect he might find you first."

"That works too. He will be quite within his rights to go to the authorities. I will smooth everything over, of course, but I don't want this to hurt you."

For an instant, irritation flashed in her eyes. She gave a small tug as though to pull her hands free, then changed her mind and gripped his fingers more strongly. "This…*vengeance* of yours hurts me," she said. "I don't even know what you are avenging. Let this be a warning, Angelo. Leave it, for both our sakes."

"You are right," he said. "I don't know how I let it go so far… But it will be different now, I promise. I will be a better man, a better husband." He raised her hands to his lips, one after the other, and released them.

As he walked away, she said, "Are you not staying?"

He walked steadily on, blindly, for he had closed his eyes again. "Not tonight." For he did not deserve her, not yet.

He returned to his own dressing room. He had paced there for some time before it struck him that, just possibly, he was punishing her for his own shame. Where had all his mad joy in winning her gone? Warped into a determination to win *everything*, into this stupid war of vengeance on Giusti for loving her first. For Elena loving him first.

This was no way to live, in a stupid feud with someone who

had once been his friend. They had gone different ways, but the last thing he wanted was to alienate Elena, whom he loved with all the more passion because she was *all* he loved.

The war had made everything worse, of course. It bred hatred. But he should never have allowed that hatred to become so demeaning.

With a new spring in his step, he went back downstairs to his study, where he spent the next couple of hours pottering amongst the glass cases where he kept his collection of antique arms.

As usual, he paid particular attention to the Savelli dagger, a beautiful fifteenth-century weapon with a jeweled hilt and a razor-sharp blade. It was the centerpiece of his collection, beautiful and deadly, a symbol of his family's wealth and power stretching back through the centuries. Dusting and polishing it returned him to a sense of peace and proportion. He laid it carefully back in its case, conscious of an exciting sense of renewal. As he locked the case and returned the key to his safe, he felt, finally, that he was leaving the past behind and facing the future with hope.

It was late but still dark when he finally returned, exhausted, to his dressing room. As soon as he relit the candle there, a stone thudded against the window, startling him.

THE LAST FRINGES of her fright had vanished altogether by the time Constance left the Palazzo Zulian the following morning. After all, she was no delicate flower, by birth or experience, and there were other delicious attractions, namely making love with Solomon and reveling in his tender care.

And then there was Venice herself. Whether bright or cloudy or teeming with rain, there seemed to be some special quality to the light that enchanted.

Although it had rained a little earlier in the morning, by the time they left the palazzo in search of their favorite coffeehouse, the sun was out. They walked arm in arm toward the nearest bridge, where they paused to watch some of the distinctively shaped Venetian boats go by. Pointed at one end and built for maneuverability around the canals and the lagoon, they were known as gondolas to some. A few belonging to the wealthy were very ornate, brightly painted and scattered with comfortable seats and cushions—like the one about to pass beneath the bridge now. It held only one occupant, a prosperous, very correctly dressed Englishman whom she was sure she had seen at the opera the night before.

"There he is again," Constance said, nudging Solomon. The man tipped his hat, meeting her gaze quite openly, as though he remembered her.

"Savelli?" Solomon said at once.

"No! The man who was at the opera. He does seem to be everywhere."

The man and his boat vanished beneath the bridge and Solomon and Constance moved on.

"He bothers you," Solomon remarked. "Do you think he was connected with what happened last night? Did you see him when the thugs seized you?"

"Oh, no. I think last night was a purely Venetian affair."

"Unless he too has some tenuous connection to Giusti."

"It's more likely to be connection to my establishment," Constance said dryly, referring to the very expensive and discreet house of ill repute that she ran in Mayfair. "He certainly looks rich enough to afford it. Though I don't recall ever seeing him there."

Of course, since meeting Solomon and beginning their inquiry business, Silver and Grey, she was at the establishment less often. But she still cared about it. She had never wanted respectability—in fact, scandalous impropriety had worked very much in her favor—until she met Solomon, and even now it was for his sake that she sought a kind of rehabilitation. His wife should not be a whore, a brothel madam.

And yet she would not give it up. Too many people relied on her. Besides, there was no point. Her reputation would only follow her. It was Solomon, seeing her torn between his world and her own, who had begun a kind of reformation for her reputation, reinventing the establishment as a charity in the minds of some rich and powerful people.

In fact, it had always been half charity. She took a few—a pitifully few—endangered girls off the streets and gave them a choice of a safe place to ply their trade or help to enter a new one. But Solomon had brought a handful of well-chosen friends to one of her nightly "parties," inviting them to donate to her charity. So now, the philanthropic and respectable gentlemen rubbed shoulders with those who came for the girls. And if Constance would never be invited for tea with their wives, well, she *did* receive the odd distant nod of acknowledgment for her good works. Plus, the establishment had considerably more money to contribute to the education and training of the women who wanted out of the old life.

Solomon still deserved better, of course. But he had chosen Constance, as she had so irrevocably chosen him. It still stunned her that she was his wife as well as his partner. Somehow, she was even his love, and God knew he was hers...

She caressed his sleeve as they walked on, and he covered her hand with his. This unique man, this unique city... Who cared about last night's little fright? She breathed a sigh of utter contentment and knew from his posture, from his very silence, that he felt it too.

They drank coffee and breakfasted, seated at a table in the morning sunshine beside the water, talking idly and watching the world glide by, listening to the sounds of the birds and the gentle lapping of the water mingling with nearby laughter and the shouted conversation between a woman at an upper window and someone in a boat below. She loved the musical sound of the language, though she recognized few words. The Venetians had their own dialect, of course…

When they had eaten and drunk enough, they strolled back to the palazzo. Constance opened the French doors of the drawing room and stepped onto the little balcony. It had already become a particular pleasure to absorb the sights and sounds and smells of the city from here, while writing letters or reading. When it rained, she simply moved into the doorway.

Solomon came out to join her, but did not sit down in the other chair. "I have a little business to attend to. I shall not be long."

Her stomach tightened with a return of last night's nerves. For while it was quite likely that Solomon had spotted some business opportunity in Venice, she knew it was not that kind of business he meant.

She reached behind her, catching his coat. "Sol—"

He detached her hand and kissed it. When she opened her mouth to remonstrate him, he bent and kissed her lips.

He said, "I have to speak to Savelli if we are to reconcile him with Giusti. And just at first, it has to be me alone."

He was right, of course. She had to trust him not to pick a fight, but, remembering his barely contained fear and fury last night, that was not easy.

Her heart in her mouth, she watched him emerge into the street below and climb into the boat via the steps opposite their front door. He looked up, smiling, and lifted his hat. She waved back, as though all was well. But it was not. She knew it was not.

SOLOMON WAS NOT going to pick a fight with Savelli. But he absolutely *would* speak to him and leave the man in no uncertainty as to his opinions. Nor had he ruled out involving the Venetian police or the British consul, but exactly what he would do depended very much on Savelli himself.

He should have known Constance would not buy his "business" excuse. He had not meant to leave her with such anxiety, but it had to be done.

This time, Alvise tied the boat up at the front of the Palazzo Savelli, on the Grand Canal itself. And Solomon, almost with the ease of the native, stepped straight off and ran lightly up to the front door, where he rapped the large, ornate knocker loudly.

Even so, there was a short delay before the door flew open suddenly and a man stared at him. Not a gentleman, but then, he hardly expected the owner of the palace to open his own front door. Still, the slightly untidy specimen before him did not seem much like a servant either.

Solomon stretched out one hand with his card between two fingers. "Signor Savelli, *per favore*," he said, and walked straight past the man into the large, tiled foyer.

His footsteps echoed. So did the closing of the front door. The manservant, or whoever he was, indicated a wooden settle with cushions and asked him to wait. At least, Solomon gave him the benefit of the doubt, but in truth it sounded more like an order. Solomon was prepared to wait, just not for very long. He sat.

He was not given long to examine the ceiling moldings and the frescoes that brightened the impersonal hall. It was not, he thought, a place where honored guests were left kicking their heels.

The servant had ambled up the staircase in a leisurely manner, but it was quite another man who came down only a minute later—a younger man of energy and determination who clearly felt no need to prove his authority to anyone, he descended at the run and strode across the hall, his hand held out.

Savelli? Solomon had no desire to shake Savelli's hand.

"Mr. Grey," the newcomer said briskly. Not particularly tall, he had brown hair and bright blue eyes that met his without a hint of subservience. "My name is Foscolo."

Solomon deigned to accept the proffered hand, though briefly. "How do you do? My business is with Signor Savelli."

"And what business, precisely, is that?" Foscolo asked.

"Signor Savelli is well aware."

Foscolo's steady eyes grew piercing. "Actually," he said, "Signor Savelli is aware of nothing. He is dead."

CHAPTER THREE

"**D**EAD?" SOLOMON STARED at the man, suspecting some kind of subterfuge to avoid an angry husband, a mere foreigner of no account. But there was no jest, no slyness in Foscolo's sharp face, only profound interest in Solomon's reaction. It was how Solomon himself—and a couple of policemen of his acquaintance—often looked at people, which gave him his first, uneasy clue.

"Dead," Foscolo repeated.

"He was very much alive last night," Solomon said slowly.

"When exactly did you see him last night?"

Solomon raised his eyebrows. "I am afraid if you wish me to answer your questions, Signor Foscolo, I require rather more than your name."

"Of course you do. I am a policeman—perhaps you would call me an inspector?—of the city of Venice. Would you care to join me upstairs, where my…superior is also eager to meet you?"

There was only the slightest pause before the word *superior*, but it was enough to remind Solomon of the uneasy government of the city. It was only five years since Venice had rebelled against its Austrian masters, who had only retaken control with some difficulty and much ill feeling. And many lost lives.

Solomon inclined his head and accompanied Foscolo toward the staircase. Although the Venetian had dashed down to him with the brisk steps of a busy, active man, he now set a slow, ambling pace, like someone enjoying a private conversation during a stroll.

"So, at what time last night did you see Signor Savelli?" he asked with deceptive mildness. Clearly, he was not a man to be distracted.

"I did not see him at all," Solomon replied. "Except as a shadow in the back doorway. About eleven of the clock, or perhaps a little after. Before midnight, at any rate. I was in my boat at the time. I came to confront him today because he abducted my wife."

Foscolo blinked rapidly, his only sign of startlement. "Are you sure?"

Solomon met his gaze and a smile flickered on the policeman's face and vanished. He was not without humor.

"You are sure," Foscolo said. "Where and how did this happen?"

Solomon told the tale of the abduction briefly and without embellishment or obvious emotion. Even so, he could almost feel the policeman's skepticism. Or perhaps it was just surprise.

"This is not usual behavior for Signor Savelli," Foscolo remarked. "Are you sure he was responsible for such wickedness?"

"Yes," Solomon said dryly. "I found her at the back door of this building. Apparently, Savelli was sending her home, but you will understand I chose to take her myself."

"You must have been very angry."

"I still am." There was no point in pretending otherwise. "According to my wife, his ruffians acted beyond their orders, and on a complete misunderstanding of the situation. Savelli released her immediately with apologies, but you will understand I could not let the matter rest there. How did Signor Savelli die?"

If the police were involved, Solomon doubted the cause was natural, though it may simply have been a mark of respect to a prominent gentleman of the city. His mind flitted to Savelli's sworn enemy, and he wondered uneasily if Giusti had merely gone home to bind his wounds and then returned to the Palazzo Savelli to continue the fight in person.

"We will come to that. How well did you know him?"

"Not at all. We never met. I have been in Venice only a few days."

"And what brought you here, sir?"

"Pleasure. My wife and I are making a wedding journey."

Foscolo's eyes softened. "The honeymoon," he said. "Your marriage is recent?"

"Indeed. I compliment you on your English."

"Thank you. This way."

Foscolo led him into a large, airy room containing two desks with chairs on either side, as well as more comfortable armchairs. Leather-bound books, some of which looked old and valuable, lined the walls, and several glass cases stood on cabinets at the far end, presumably containing other valuables.

The man who had admitted Solomon to the house stood to attention by a small table. Another fair and well-dressed man rose from the large walnut desk slanted across one corner of the room. Although probably about the same age as Foscolo—surely not many more than Solomon's thirty years—he had an air of authority that seemed to be natural.

Foscolo made the introductions in English. "My superior, Signor von Lampl. Signor, Mr. Grey, from England."

Solomon was not blind to the undercurrents. Apart from the word *signor*, which he seemed to emphasize, Foscolo continued to speak in English, no doubt in the hope that his superior—clearly an Austrian—would not understand.

But Lampl, looking weary, merely offered one smooth, elegantly aristocratic hand, saying, "How do you do, Mr. Grey?" Having indicated a chair for Solomon, he turned back to Foscolo and a quick barrage of Italian was exchanged.

Over the years, Solomon had picked up bits and pieces of many languages. In this rapid fire, he caught that Foscolo was repeating what Solomon had told him.

"But this is outrageous, Mr. Grey," Lampl said, swinging on him quite suddenly. "Complete strangers pluck your wife from the street, from under your very nose, and yet you knew exactly where to go to get her back from said strangers?"

Solomon owed Giusti a debt of gratitude for that, but there was no way he could tell his story honestly without betraying his name. "It was not exactly under my nose. I was distracted at the time, by four men setting on a fifth. I went to help, leaving my boatman with my wife."

"That was brave of you, sir," Lampl said, his face expressing only politeness, "especially in a strange city and where your aid was unlikely to alter the outcome, since it still left four to two. Did you know the man being attacked?"

"No. I could not even see his face until I was in the thick of the fight," Solomon replied. "It turned out to be a gentleman by the name of Giusti."

Foscolo and Lampl exchanged glances, an instinct that appeared to embarrass them both.

"Ludovico Giusti?" Foscolo asked. "Had you or your wife met him before?"

"No. But it was while we fought off his attackers that two other men abducted my wife. I saw them drag her away down a side street."

"But you remained to fight Signor Giusti's battle?" Lampl asked.

"The battle was over by then," Solomon said. "We had scared them off."

"Two against four," Foscolo said without emphasis.

"Actually, it was three against four by then, since my wife had sent our boatman to help us. Which left her unprotected."

"So, you went after her? Alone?"

"No, Signor Giusti returned my help by accompanying me and my boatman to the Palazzo Savelli. He claimed to recognize those attacking him as Savelli's men, recently hired bodyguards, and was convinced my wife would be brought here."

A frown of irritation tugged at Lampl's brow. "With what possible purpose when you and your wife are strangers to him?

To all of Venice, in fact! Did Giusti tell you some tale of Signor Savelli's villainy?"

"He told me about a feud, over a lady and some jewels. Giusti believed Savelli's men acted under the mistaken idea that my wife was connected to Giusti, and I was merely her bodyguard."

"Because you went to Giusti's rescue," Lampl said slowly. "That *almost* makes sense. So, on Giusti's advice, you came directly here? Did you see Signor Savelli?"

"I think so, though only for a moment. He stood in the back doorway, watching as his servants prepared to take her home in his boat. Only, when she saw me waiting, she obviously came with us instead. Neither Savelli nor his servants objected."

"And Giusti," Foscolo said, "did he leave you at the Palazzo Savelli?"

"No, he came with us. My boatman took him to his own house on the way to her own."

"And where is it you are staying, Mr. Grey?" Foscolo asked.

"The Palazzo Zulian. We have rented it from the owner for six weeks."

Foscolo's eyebrows lifted. "In Cannaregio?"

Solomon inclined his head.

"And how is your wife after her ordeal?" Foscolo asked. "She must have been terrified."

Solomon stared at him, clenching his fists involuntarily. "Being forced away from me by strangers? Being gagged and blindfolded by her own hood? The men held her so roughly that she has huge bruises on both arms. Of course she was terrified."

"And that is why you came this morning to visit Signor Savelli?"

"Yes."

Both men regarded him. He could almost see them wondering why so angry a husband had not confronted the villain last night. Or, indeed, if he actually had.

Controlling his fresh spurt of temper, Solomon said coldly, "My wife explained that Savelli apologized to her and offered her no further insult. He was angry with his own men, even before he discovered she had no idea who Giusti was. On the other hand, I could not let such an act simply pass."

"What did you intend to do here this morning?" Foscolo asked.

"Speak to him before I determined whether or not to involve authorities such as yourselves and the British consul."

"Very proper," Lampl said.

Impossible to tell if he was mocking or approving or simply understanding.

"I hope you have not changed your mind about Venice," Foscolo said. "Your unpleasant experience should not encourage you to leave the city."

"It hasn't," Solomon said, understanding the warning. "Or, at least, not yet."

Foscolo held out his hand in clear if civil dismissal. "Thank you for your cooperation. We know where to find you."

For the first time, Lampl looked irritated, as if he had more questions, or at least preferred to be the one doing the dismissing. "I'm afraid we will also have to speak to your wife and servants. I hope that will not further upset her."

"My wife is a most resilient lady," Solomon said, releasing Foscolo's hand and turning his gaze on the Austrian. "I shall not allow her to be upset. Although we are both happy to assist with your inquiries. May I know how Signor Savelli died?"

There was no exchange of glances between the policemen this time. Although Lampl answered, both men watched Solomon without blinking.

"He was found at the back doorstep of this house, his body half in the canal. He had been stabbed to death."

Solomon caught his breath. "When was this? When did he die?"

"He was found early this morning, around six of the clock. We are not yet sure exactly when he died." Foscolo did not smile. "You might well have been one of the last people to see him alive."

CONSTANCE WAS GIVEN little time to worry about Solomon's meeting with Savelli, for less than half an hour after he left her, she had a visitor.

Duly announced by the well-trained servant who had been hired with the house, Ludovico Giusti walked into her drawing room with a quick, urgent step. Despite his bruised face and worried aspect, he managed to smile and bow with a flourish.

"Signora! Forgive my intrusion. I was looking for your husband, but they tell me he has gone out."

"He has, but he claimed he would not be long. Might I help you instead?"

Giusti blinked in surprise, and then, as she resumed her seat, he sat down quite suddenly opposite her and leaned forward. There was a particularly colorful bruise around his eye. "Perhaps you can. I suppose you do not know?"

"Know what?"

"About Savelli."

"Only what I learned last night and what you told my husband."

Giusti waved that away as if it were of no account. "No, no, I mean today. Savelli is dead. Murdered."

Her lips parted in shock. At least there was no triumph or rejoicing in Giusti's eyes. In fact, just for an instant, between the cuts and bruises, she was almost sure she saw grief.

"Solomon has gone to see him," she said slowly.

"I was afraid of it. I came to warn him not to, because the palazzo will be full of policemen. Hopefully, they will send him away as a foreigner of no account."

"Why do you hope that?" Constance asked, bewildered and distracted. Savelli had been a strange man, and she had been furiously angry with him, but somewhat to her own surprise, she had not disliked him. And now he was dead, his life wiped out by…

By his sworn enemy?

Giusti seemed unaware of her sudden suspicion. "I told the police about my...disturbance last night, but I did not mention you or your husband. I merely said Savelli's men were frightened off when other people threatened to join in."

"Why?"

Giusti sighed. "I thought I was doing both of you a good turn. I did not want you drawn into whatever...circus is made of this murder. You know, of course, that I am their prime suspect?"

"Being Signor Savelli's sworn enemy?"

"I am not the only one. His support of the Austrian government is not popular in certain circles. But, especially with the fight last night, I do seem to have an added motive for violence."

The knowledge seeped in slowly. "And so does Solomon, because of me. That was why you did not mention us to the police."

"It would have been poor recompense for his good deed."

"Except that Solomon will tell them the truth. He is not the kind of man to be brushed away as of no account."

Giusti sighed. "I was afraid of that. I am sorry to bring this upon you."

Constance regarded him. There was something—a great deal, no doubt—that he was not telling her. She guessed him to be a man of quick passions and not entirely averse to violence. "How did Signor Savelli die?"

"Stabbed through the chest and left to die on the steps at his palazzo's back door."

Exactly where she had stood when she saw Solomon had come for her.

"I did not kill him," Giusti said, almost conversationally. "When you stepped into our boat and I saw his shadow behind you, I found I was no longer angry. I felt this foolishness had to stop."

"Solomon and I thought that, too. We even talked about trying to reconcile you."

"And now it will never be." His voice was bleak. "We were friends once, you know. I am sorry he is dead."

She thought he was. More than that, she believed he had not killed Savelli. Or perhaps she just hoped. There was something instantly likeable about him. "Who were his other enemies?"

Giusti sat straighter, blinking in clear surprise.

"At home," Constance said, "Solomon and I have a business of private inquiries. We have been quite successful."

"That is what you do?" Giusti asked incredulously.

"It is a small but important part of what we do. If neither you nor Solomon nor I killed Signor Savelli, perhaps it behoves us to find out who did. How competent are your police?"

"In matters such as this…I have no idea," Giusti said frankly.

"And yet Savelli felt free to attack you in the street, to steal from you? Was he so confident that the police would not intervene?"

"Our…disagreement is well known. Neither of us would have complained to the police. But this is different. They will not ignore this, especially not since Savelli was a supporter of the Austrian government."

"Could his politics be the reason for his murder?"

"I would be surprised," Giusti said. "The revolution is over. There is ill feeling, of course, but no one wants to go back to those days of violence. If he was not assassinated in '49, why now? Why kill him at all?"

Again, she was sure she glimpsed genuine grief, or perhaps just anger, in his expression. He threw his arm out as he spoke, as though gesturing to where the murder had happened.

"He associated with some unpleasant men," Constance pointed out. "Like those who attacked you and abducted me. Could one or more of them have turned on him?"

Giusti shrugged. "Unlikely. Some of those men may have been servants, not hired bravos. Servants rarely attack their masters. As for the others—why bite the hand that feeds them?"

"Then a random attempt at robbery? Or a planned one?"

Giusti sighed. "I suppose that is what the police will investigate. But…why was he at the back door? He has servants to take deliveries."

"Perhaps he was meeting someone who did not want to be seen? Or—" She broke off as another thought struck her. "*When* did he die? He was at the back door when you and I last saw him."

THE SAME MAN who had let Solomon into the Palazzo Savelli was delegated to show him out. As the door of the room was closed behind him, the silence of the rest of the house felt oppressive. As though even the sound of walking was disrespectful to the dead. In London, sometimes, houses of mourning put sawdust down in the street to deaden the noise of horses' hooves and wheeled vehicles. Here, he could almost imagine there was no one else in the house.

Until a lady swept across the landing to the stairs and paused as she caught sight of their approach. She was young and pale and dressed all in black. Her hat was covered by a heavy-looking veil that had not been drawn down over her face. She was not conventionally beautiful. She did not dazzle as Constance did. But there was something about her that caught and held the attention, without any effort on her part.

"How odd," she said in Italian. "I have no idea anymore who is in my house. Are you another policeman or a friend of my late husband's?"

Solomon bowed. "I can claim to be neither. My name is Grey. I merely called to see your husband and was interviewed by policemen instead. I offer you sincere condolences, signora."

"You are English?" she asked in that language. A spark of interest showed in her otherwise glazed eyes. He wondered how much she knew about Constance's abduction.

He inclined his head. "I am."

Her chin tilted slightly. "About what did you wish to see my husband?" she asked with conscious boldness.

"Nothing that is relevant anymore."

"Many things no longer matter," she said, an odd catch in her voice. She began to descend the stairs, and Solomon walked beside her. "A house of death always *feels* wrong. As if it is no longer real. Like a bad dream."

"Are you going to stay with family?" Solomon asked.

"Oh no. I shall stay here, of course." She drew the veil over her face. "Once I have walked. Goodbye, Mr. Grey."

At the foot of the stairs, she increased her speed, all but striding across the foyer to the front door, where a manservant stood to open it for her. He continued to hold it for Solomon, who watched the widow's straight, tragic figure vanish to the left. By the time he climbed into his waiting boat, he could no longer see her.

ON REACHING THE Palazzo Zulian, Solomon heard that Constance was entertaining. Although glad she had company, he was somehow not best pleased to discover that her visitor was Ludovico Giusti.

The sight of him sitting in a chair close to Constance, a glass of wine in his bruised hand, deep in serious conversation, made Solomon pause in the drawing room doorway. Whether the reaction was due to jealousy or distrust, he hid it, as both pairs of eyes turned eagerly toward him. And both jumped to their feet.

Constance hurried toward him. "Oh, Solomon, you're back! Did you go to the Savelli house? Signor Giusti says he has been murdered!"

Her eyes were anxious, relieved, excited, all at once, and her hand slipping through his arm comforted whatever misgivings the sight of Giusti had caused.

"That is what the police told me when I called," he said calmly.

"I came to warn you not to go there," Giusti said, "but clearly, I was too late. In my defense, the police kept me back with questions, so I came as soon as I could. I am so sorry to have brought this trouble to you."

Constance flitted away to pour another glass of wine, which she brought to Solomon before all but pulling him down onto the elegant sofa beside her. "What happened? What did they ask you? What did you learn?"

Quite suddenly, the situation became familiar, almost comfortable. Silver and Grey exchanging facts and ideas of a crime. They had done this so many times before. He just hadn't really expected to be doing it on their honeymoon.

A half-smile tugged at his lips. "I was invited into the palazzo and interviewed by a Venetian called Foscolo and an Austrian by the name of Lampl, who seems to be his superior in some way."

Giusti snorted. "Foscolo does the work and Lampl carries it to his government. As if they cared. It is unnecessary oversight."

Solomon inclined his head politely. "Savelli seems to have been killed during the night or very early this morning. But whenever it happened, it seems that we three were among the last to see him alive. And we all have considerable motive."

"I should go," Giusti said uneasily. "We do not want to be accused of conspiracy. Foscolo is suspicious enough."

"They will want to interview you, too," Solomon said to Constance. "And the servants."

"Signor Giusti did not tell them about your part in the fight or my abduction," Constance said. "I presume you did?"

"I saw no point in trying to keep it quiet. It was bound to come out. They did not appear to be terribly surprised about the fight, although your abduction did seem to throw them. They asked after you, so they might believe me. Just to be clear, Giusti, what did you do when you left us last night?"

Giusti did not take obvious offense. "I had a bath and went to bed, where I slept like the dead until I was wakened at some ungodly hour by policemen battering at my front door. What did you do?"

"Much the same," Solomon replied. "With a gentler awakening. Then you were not tempted to go out again and remonstrate with Savelli? Did you not feel that your little feud had got out of hand?"

His deliberate disparagement of the quarrel as "a little feud" did not appear to provoke Giusti.

"Of course I feel that. But it was not something I could resolve that night, with anger and no doubt shame running so high."

"What exactly was your quarrel with Savelli?" Constance asked.

"I told Mr. Grey. Jewels and women and politics."

Solomon kept his gaze on the Venetian's bruised face. "I spoke to Signora Savelli."

Giusti tore his gaze free. Some sort of internal struggle clearly went on. In the end, the words seemed to be dragged out of him as though he couldn't help them. "How is she?"

So, Savelli's wife was the woman in question, not some mistress or actress as Solomon had half suspected.

"Dazed, I think. Definitely shocked. She went out alone. Does she have no family to be with her?"

"They disowned her when she married Savelli."

"So now she is entirely alone," Constance said quietly.

Giusti's gaze flew to her face, then fell back to his wine glass. He took a drink, almost blindly. "Yes. I think so."

"How long have they been married?" Solomon asked.

"For four years." Abruptly, Giusti set the glass on the table beside him and rose. "I will go. I'm sorry. This mess is poor recompense for being the Good Samaritan you were to me. We must hope the police solve the murder quickly and to everyone's satisfaction. Signora." He bowed. "Goodbye!"

CHAPTER FOUR

AFTER WALKING WITH Giusti to the door, Solomon returned to the drawing room to find Constance by the window, watching his departure.

"What is she like?" Constance asked. "The wife?"

"I don't know. Dazed but not broken. Or not yet."

"Is she beautiful?"

To his surprise, Solomon had to think about that. "I don't know," he said again. "But she is the sort of woman one remembers."

"Giusti remembers," Constance said. "She is the true cause of their quarrel, isn't she?"

"I would not be surprised."

"Do you think he did it?"

"Murdered Savelli? Why now? Why not before or just after Savelli married her?"

"You don't want it to be Giusti?"

Solomon slipped his arm around her waist, and she rested her head on his shoulder. "No, I suppose I don't. I like him."

"I actually liked Savelli, in an odd sort of a way," she admitted. "I felt almost sorry for him somehow. Alone with his thugs and a woman they had wronged in his name. He loved his wife. I wonder if she loved him?"

"More than she loved Giusti, I imagine," Solomon said wryly.

"Women marry for all sorts of reasons," Constance said. "Especially, I suspect, in the midst of revolution and war."

He looked down at her. "They married in 1849," he said, "when the Austrians were taking back power. Savelli backed the Austrians. I wonder what Giusti was doing?"

"Fighting the Austrians," Constance said. "By accident or design, she chose the winning side. I wonder where the jewels come into it?"

Perhaps it was inevitable, but still he felt the familiar stirring of excitement. "Are we investigating this crime, then?"

"We do seem to be," she replied. "No honeymoon holiday for us."

"Oh, I don't know," Solomon murmured into her ear, which his lips suddenly found quite fascinating. "I'm sure we can fit both into our busy lives."

The catch in her breath fed his own arousal, and he found her mouth, sensual and eager. That this amazing woman was his still astonished him. That her desire matched his own felt like a blessing, or even a miracle, both a relief and a wonder.

They were married and they were in Italy. There was nothing to stop them retreating to the bedroom in the middle of the afternoon. So they did.

It was after five o'clock before Foscolo called upon them. Constance, lethargic after her afternoon of love, tried to refocus her mind on murder and policemen, but only the realization that Solomon was likely to be the prime suspect—with or without Giusti—forced her back to reality with a bump.

Foscolo appeared to be an experienced man, though not yet forty years old, she guessed. Like other policemen she had met, there was a certain cynicism, even weariness about his eyes, but they were steady and perceptive and not without humor, and she doubted many people could lie to him successfully. Nor was he afraid to let admiration show in his face as Solomon introduced them. However, she doubted such appreciation made a blind bit of difference to his conclusions.

"Your husband told me of your ordeal at the hands of Signor Savelli's servants," he said, as the three of them sat down in the drawing room. It was still sunny and the doors to the balcony were open. "I must apologize for such lawlessness in my city. I only hope you came to no lasting harm."

"None that will not heal."

"I commend your bravery, signora. Perhaps you would tell me in your own words exactly what happened to you?"

Before she could speak, the drawing room door opened again. A servant said, *"Scusi!"* in a frightened voice and another man strode in.

Constance, something of an expert in judging men, found him a completely different specimen from Foscolo. A year or so younger, maybe, and considerably wealthier, he was definitely of the aristocracy. His eyes were neither cynical nor weary. On the contrary, they were bright and determined. A driven man. He also appeared to be irritated.

Foscolo and Solomon had both risen to their feet. It struck Constance that Foscolo was no less irritated than the newcomer. Just for an instant, it tightened his mouth and almost spat out of his dark eyes, and then his face smoothed into blandness.

"My superior, Signor von Lampl," he said to Constance. "Signor, Mrs. Grey."

Lampl snapped a bow, not without grace. "Mrs. Grey. Mr. Grey." He turned to his underling and released a torrent of Italian that Constance could not follow. Nevertheless, she got the gist that Foscolo should not have come here without him, while Foscolo himself clearly saw no reason for his superior's presence.

However, the Venetian inclined his head to the Austrian in apparent acceptance and returned to English. "Because of your status as an important visitor to our city, Signor von Lampl believes his presence is an important sign of respect to our British allies."

And no one wanted Foscolo, a policeman rather than a diplomat, upsetting the wealthy Mr. Grey, let alone the British consul?

"Naturally, Mr. von Lampl is welcome," Solomon said mildly. "My wife and I are happy to answer the questions of the police, whoever asks them."

Foscolo inclined his head with, perhaps, a hint of irony. "I had just asked Mrs. Grey," he told his superior, "to describe her ordeal at the hands of Savelli's servants."

Lampl nodded curtly and sat. Constance told her tale calmly from the moment they had seen the attack on Giusti, until she had stepped out of the back door of the Palazzo Savelli and into the boat with Solomon and Giusti.

When she had finished, Foscolo sat forward as though to ask a question, but it was Lampl who spoke first.

"You are quite admirably calm about the whole experience, madam. You must be extremely brave."

"The servants were mere thugs," Constance said, "But Signor Savelli neither threatened nor frightened me." It was true, of course, and throughout her life Constance had faced down considerably scarier people. But she realized quite suddenly that she could not tell the policemen this. Her past was an insult to Solomon. Nothing could change that.

"My wife *is* a brave lady," Solomon said shortly. "And if you do not believe in the roughness of her handling, perhaps you would like to see her bruising?"

This time, Foscolo spoke before his superior. "If you please, madam, and if it does not discommode you."

Constance drew back her wide sleeves to reveal the bruises on her forearms and then tugged them back further to show the larger, angrier marks above the elbows. Lampl's breath hissed.

Foscolo said, "They look very painful. I am sorry such a thing occurred at all, let alone here."

"Signor Savelli was angry with his men, not with me."

"Then he believed you," Foscolo said, "when you explained

you had nothing to do with Ludovico Giusti?"

"Of course he did. I have been in the city a matter of mere days."

"And yet," Foscolo said, "I believe Signor Giusti visited here today. While Mr. Grey was at the Palazzo Savelli."

It almost took Constance's breath away, but only the truth would serve—especially since, beside her, Solomon had stiffened alarmingly. Lampl was glaring at Foscolo, apparently speechless.

"He did," Constance said. "He was looking for Solomon, to tell him about Signor Savelli's death. I believe Giusti had already spoken to you and had not mentioned our involvement in the fight last night. He wished to be gentlemanly and keep us out of it, but obviously that could not happen. As we both told him."

"Foscolo will revisit Giusti," Lampl said. He met Solomon's gaze. "Do you wish to make charges against Signor Savelli's men?"

Solomon turned to Constance. They had talked about it already, but he left it to her to answer.

"I would not add to his widow's pain over what was clearly a misunderstanding, however lawless. But we would like to talk to the men at some stage."

"*Talk* to them?" Lampl repeated, startled.

Foscolo was frowning, gazing in bafflement from her to Solomon.

"I imagine you regard us as suspects," Solomon said mildly. "We would like to help discover the true culprit. Or culprits."

"That is unwise and could well be dangerous," Foscolo said. "It is *our* duty to investigate, but you should know that your boatman and your other servants have already confirmed what you told us about your movements on the night in question. So there is no need for you to—"

"To help us in our investigations," Lampl interpolated hastily, as if afraid Foscolo would have said *interfere*.

"Do you know more precisely when he died?" Solomon asked.

"We think between three and five o'clock this morning," Lampl replied.

"And the weapon?" Solomon asked. "Do you have any idea what it was?"

"Every idea," Lampl said coldly. "It was left in his body and it belonged to Signor Savelli himself."

"Can you be certain of that?" Constance asked.

Lampl blinked at her as though uncertain whether to be disgusted by her interest.

"Yes," said Foscolo. "It was one of only two ever made."

"And the only one extant," Lampl said stiffly. "I have seen it in his home many times." He rose rather heavily to his feet and bowed. "We thank you for your cooperation and apologize once more for your unpleasant experience of Venice. Come, Foscolo."

Foscolo's expression gave little away, though he did appear to take his time gathering up his notebook and pencil, placing them back in his pocket and getting to his feet. He too bowed before following his superior from the room.

Constance looked at Solomon. "What an odd pair. They neither like nor trust each other."

"Like Omand and Napier," Solomon remarked, naming two London detectives with whom they had had dealings in the past.

"At least these two here dislike each other more than they dislike *us*. I wonder if it's personal or political?"

"Both, I imagine. In these times, they will be difficult to separate. We need to learn more about Savelli. I think we should call on the widow."

"Will she receive us?" Constance asked. "What if she has heard that her husband kidnapped me?"

"Then I'm sure she would like the matter cleared up. And yes, I think she will. It could be that she is floundering in this tragedy to the point of desperation, and any company will be better than none."

"Could she have done it?"

Solomon considered. "I think she *could*. I would say there is great strength beneath the frail surface. But I have no idea what feelings lurk there. I don't even know if she is grieving, though she is certainly shocked."

"Giusti cares for her. He doesn't want to, but he does. It was in his face, his voice, when he asked you about her, as though the words were dragged out of him without permission."

Solomon grimaced. "One way or another, it doesn't look good for Giusti. And yet I still find myself hoping he didn't do it."

LUDOVICO GIUSTI, LUDO to his many friends, was reckless by nature. Since the crushing of the revolution to which he had given his heart and soul, he seemed to have forgotten that. He remembered it again during his second interview with the policeman Foscolo, when he had the urge to physically kick him out of his house.

Once, he would probably have done it. But Foscolo was a good man who had fought beside him against the Austrians and was only doing his duty. So Giusti kept his worn-out boots on the floor and explained about Grey's part in the fight with Savelli's men, and their mission to rescue Grey's wife.

"I wanted to keep them out of it," he said.

"Murder is more serious than that."

Giusti almost laughed. They had both seen more than enough men killed in their time.

"When did you last see Signora Savelli?" Foscolo asked.

That was when Giusti's feet were in most danger of kicking. But he shrugged. "How do I know? Venice is a small city. I noticed her in San Marco some time in the last month. In a particularly dazzling shade of gold."

"I mean, to speak to."

"That is easier. 1849."

Foscolo had pressed him no further on that score, but that

was when the recklessness took hold in more than fantasy.

So, when it was dark, Ludo took his own boat and traveled the familiar waterways to the Palazzo Savelli. He knew where to wait and watch and blend in with the stone so that no other passing boat would endanger him, nor anyone make him out from nearby windows.

Savelli's house was in darkness, at least from the back. It was all locked up and there would be no comings and goings even among the servants, on the night after their master's death.

Using his oar, Ludo glided silently nearer. He didn't go as far as the Savelli steps, but even so, he had to wait, lying flat on the bottom of his boat, until another had passed and gone on its way. Then he simply climbed out and up.

He was quick and agile and old enough to know better. But there were many hand- and footholds in the old stone and the ornate carvings. His hope was that in a house rattled by sudden death and police investigation, the servants would be careless about locking windows. And he was right—although he had to try three, and almost lost his footing entirely on the third ledge, before he managed to push a window open and wriggle through.

He had brought his own candle and tinder box, so once he had picked himself off the floor, he lit it and found his way out of the room—some minor reception room he couldn't recall ever being in before—and on into the dark passage beyond. He found the staircase without difficulty and climbed. A few of the steps creaked, but not enough to disturb anyone's sleep.

Though he knew she wouldn't be asleep.

He also knew where her private rooms were. Roughly. Though it was difficult in the dark with one tiny candle, and he had never counted windows and doors.

It was the palest glow that gave her away in the end. More like a lighter shade of blackness beneath the ornate door. He went in as quietly as he could. Another dark room—a sitting room, he thought, from the brief waving of his candle. Its chief interest to him was the fact that a more definite light shone beneath another connecting door.

He caught his suddenly ragged breath. But he had come this far.

He walked carefully toward the light, and when he came to the door, he halted and listened for a long time. He knew instinctively she would not have a maid in the room. She would be alone. And he would terrify her.

Recklessness got one into all sorts of difficulties. Perhaps last night's fight had dealt him one too many blows to the head.

It was time to leave.

And yet he didn't. He turned the handle and opened the door.

And blinked in the sudden brightness.

She stood barely a foot from him, a tall, carved branch of candles in her hand. She wore a velvet silk dressing gown that covered her from neck to toe, but her raven hair was loose and she looked magnificent. Brave and angry and unafraid, she stared at him, no doubt taking in his disreputable cuts and bruises and the tears in his clothing from the climb.

Elena. Dizzyingly close after all these years.

"What are you doing here?" The faint tremble in her voice almost undid him.

"A call of condolence," he said, and of course it came out wrong. It sounded brash, mocking, when all he really wanted was to be sure she was…what? Fine? Well? Coping?

"You were always an idiot," she said contemptuously. "Get out of my house before we are both crucified for this."

She was right, of course. This was beyond reckless, unforgivably so because it was Elena's reputation he was risking. He turned away to obey, but her voice stayed him, husky and yet harsh.

"Ludovico."

He waited, though he could not bring himself to turn back to her.

"Did you kill him?"

He shook his head. "Did you?"

There was silence. And then, flat and emotionless, "Then you didn't come for absolution?"

He breathed again. And yet he wanted to throw things, even his candle, set the house and the whole world on fire.

"You are undoubtedly correct that I am an idiot," he said between his teeth. "And perhaps there was a time I would have killed him for you. But after four years? When I can never have you anyway? Even I am not that big an idiot."

He heard the catch in her breath, and abruptly, her manner changed.

"I *saw* you, Ludo."

Slowly, he turned back to face her. He did not ask, but she answered anyway.

"Last night. In the little boat your servants used to use."

"No, last night I was in an Englishman's fine gondola. We came to rescue the poor woman your husband had abducted."

"She went home before midnight," came the calm response, so clearly this was not news to her. "You were there at three o'clock in the morning, at the back of the house. I saw you."

He lifted one side of his mouth. "Then you were also up at three in the morning."

"Shall we tell on each other and see whom the police arrest?"

"Oh, I don't think you will need to do that to see me arrested. It is between me and the Englishman. Although," he added inconsequentially, "he looks a little African to me."

"I think I met him." She blinked in the candlelight, as though surprised to be conversing with him. "Can you get out the way you got in?"

He nodded.

She said, "Don't do it again." And quietly closed the door on him.

The light beneath it went out. Very gently, he laid his forehead against the wood. He wanted to weep.

Instead, he straightened and trailed back the way he had come, forcing himself to concentrate on not falling into the canal or otherwise giving himself away.

CHAPTER FIVE

T HE MAGIC THAT was Venice burst upon Constance afresh as Alvise guided their boat into the Grand Canal in the spring sunshine. It seemed impossible to mix this beauty of light and color and sheer, bustling life with the ugliness of murder.

Just for a moment, she longed for the uncomplicated peace of their first days in the city with only wonder to disturb her, and the pleasure of enjoying it all with Solomon. But they had never been able to walk away from a mystery.

Alvise—who had also been interviewed by the police—eased the boat into the steps before the magnificence of the Palazzo Savelli. It was hardly the most splendid of the city's palaces, but it was certainly larger and more ostentatious than the modest beauty of their own borrowed house.

Solomon climbed out and handed Constance up. They walked together across to the front steps of the palazzo. She was glad to see no obvious police guard there. Solomon knocked on the door, and it was opened by a smartly dressed manservant in livery. Though Constance looked at him closely, she did not recognize him as one of her abductors. Not that she had seen them for long, only while Savelli had been telling them off and they had shuffled from the room like naughty schoolboys. And she had tried to recover her courage.

Solomon presented their joint card to the servant—not the Silver and Grey business card, but the new visiting card: *Mr. and Mrs. Solomon Grey*, with their new London address.

"If Signora Savelli is able to receive us," Solomon said in creditable Italian.

The servant admitted them to a large, echoing hall with a tiled floor, painted walls, and a massively high ceiling. A magnificent staircase swept upward. The servant indicated a wooden settle with cushions, then made his stately way up the staircase. Only then did Constance notice the other liveried servant by the front door.

Visitors were not left alone. The household guarded its lady, much like in Constance's far-less-reputable establishment. She wondered if they would be sent away, and if so, how much they could learn from the servants between here and the front door.

But when the servant returned, he invited them to follow him upstairs. He led them along another magnificent hall to a drawing room filled with light. Like most of the city's interiors that Constance had seen, the windows provided as much art as the walls. But the room was furnished with taste and elegance, without the overblown splendor apparent in many.

Intriguingly, an easel covered with a dust sheet stood in one corner.

A lady in black rose from a brocade sofa, at once commanding Constance's attention.

Elena Savelli was probably not beautiful, but no one would ever notice that. A little taller than Constance, with luxuriant jet-black hair beneath a wisp of black lace, she had pale skin and dramatic black eyebrows. All her features were strong, from the high, intelligent forehead, to the slightly too-long nose, firm mouth, and determinedly pointing chin.

Solomon had described her as dazed yesterday. Perhaps she still was, for Constance saw no signs of unendurable grief. Shadows beneath her eyes spoke of sleeplessness, perhaps, but her eyes themselves were clear and brilliant.

"Mr. Grey," the widow said in charmingly accented English. "Somehow I did not expect to see you again so soon."

"I hope we are not intruding," Solomon said, bowing. "If so, you must forgive our ignorance of local customs."

Signora Savelli waved that aside as though such customs did not apply to her.

"May I present my wife, Constance," Solomon murmured.

Constance curtseyed. "My condolences, signora. I am so sorry."

For the first time, she had the widow's full attention and felt a prickle of awareness. Elena Savelli's gaze was sharp, perceptive, and veiled. A woman used to keeping secrets. Constance could not hold that against her.

"You are kind," Elena said. "Especially when, I understand, you sustained injury at my husband's hands. For that, I add my apologies to his."

"It was a misunderstanding," Constance said, wondering if she had heard of the incident from her husband or from the police. Or even from Giusti.

"Then you are not acquainted with Ludovico Giusti?"

"We are now," Constance said.

Two maidservants appeared with wine and the ubiquitous small savories known as *cicchetti*, and Elena invited them to sit. When they were served and the maids had withdrawn, their hostess regarded them with frank curiosity.

"While you are very welcome in my home," she said at last, "I am surprised either of you can bear to be here. And my husband is beyond any retribution you may seek."

"We have not come for retribution," Constance said, waving that aside. "We were merely in the wrong place at the wrong time. In fact, our purpose in calling is to try to help."

Elena's lips quirked into a faint smile of pure scorn. "You are a fashionable medium? You speak to the dead? Or revive them, perhaps?"

"If you truly thought that," Solomon said quietly, "you would already have sent us about our business. We offer our help to you in discovering the truth of your husband's death." Fishing in his pocket, he produced another visiting card and stood up to take it to her.

"*Silver and Grey*," she read aloud. "*Inquiries.*" Her eyebrows flew up. "What kind of inquiries?"

"Into all kinds of mysteries and puzzles," Constance said. "From missing possessions to murders." She smiled faintly. "I am Silver. I only recently married Mr. Grey."

"So this is your partnership? Your business?" Elena sounded more intrigued than offended. "But in London—forgive my ignorance—do you not have the police?"

"We do," Solomon said. "Though it is still a novelty in some circles, and their inquiries are frequently regarded as unwarrantable intrusion."

"And yours are not?" Elena asked politely.

"Oh yes, of course they are," Constance said. "But no one likes suspicion held over them—which is how our partnership began, in fact. And now we find ourselves once more under suspicion."

"For my husband's murder," Elena said.

Solomon inclined his head.

"I think Ludovico Giusti beats you in that race. He and my husband have been feuding for years."

"Over you," Solomon said, and sipped his wine.

Elena shrugged. "At one time. Mostly over revolution and jewels."

"What *is* the story about the jewels?" Constance asked.

Elena's head tilted slightly to one side as she regarded her. Then she said, "My parents died shortly before the revolution of 1848. You may know that I was betrothed to Ludovico Giusti. I gave him my father's favorite ring, some other jewels. Some I know he used to pay for weapons, and to feed his men—with my blessing, you understand. But...nothing went as planned. The revolution did not succeed, and I did not marry Ludovico. I married Angelo Savelli, and my husband wanted my jewels returned."

Constance took one of the savory bites without looking at it.

"Signor Savelli did? Or you did?"

Elena swirled the wine in her glass. "I accounted them lost along with Ludovico."

"You thought Ludovico was dead?" Constance said cautiously.

"I did, for a little. So I betrothed myself to Angelo. And then Ludo came back and I had to choose." Her fingers tightened on the stem of the delicate glass, twisting it. She set it down carefully beside her. "It was a choice that cut me off from the remainder of my family and my old friends. I have been accused of betraying Venice, of dishonoring the sacrifice of patriots by choosing wealth over love."

"Did you?" Constance asked.

The other woman blinked as though surprised to be asked. "I chose survival, Venice's as much as my own. We tried and failed to win our cause, and must live with the consequences. Savelli is as Venetian at Giusti. He just chose a different path and one that would bring the city much-needed peace and stability. He has— had—influence and interests that have helped Venice, but there are those who refuse to see that."

"Like Giusti?" Solomon said.

"Well, he has ulterior motives. As did my husband when he demanded my jewels. It wasn't that he wanted them for me, or himself, let alone for Venice. He wanted them because I gave them to Ludovico. And Ludovico would not return them for the same reason. They were poking at each other like schoolchildren, increasingly vicious and determined. To be fair, Ludovico did send some back—a necklace of my mother's and one of my own that he had not sold. He sent the messenger to me, of course, without informing my husband. It was not enough. My husband really wanted my father's antique ring—it was wrought gold with lapis lazuli—probably because Ludovico flaunted it under his nose at some meeting."

She stopped talking, picked up her glass, and took a drink. "Perhaps I will leave Venice. Do you find traveling beneficial, signora?"

"Yes, but I will go home again," Constance said. She sat forward. "Signora, was it for this ring that your husband sent men to attack Ludovico the other night?"

"He did not tell me so. He didn't tell me anything at all until the incident was over, but yes, I suspect that was the reason. He knew Ludovico was returning from some formal party, so he probably expected him to be wearing it. You see the level of idiocy their quarrel had reached? I wish I had kept the wretched thing myself. Or thrown it in the canal."

"I don't blame you," Constance said frankly. "Was this the first time they had resorted to physical violence?"

"Oh no." For an instant, fresh anger tightened Elena's lips. She sighed. "But it was probably the first time they had involved others. It was a measure of contempt that Angelo sent his men to beat Ludovico and take the ring by force. He hired some of them as bodyguards, you know, without considering the nature of the men concerned. They could have killed Ludovico." Her gaze refocused on Constance. "And they certainly overstepped by taking you. Rumor must have reached them of some new mistress of Ludovico. And they must have thought you, Mr. Grey, were of their own type, some hired bravo. Imbeciles."

"Would you mind if we spoke to them?" Solomon asked. "And to your other servants?"

Elena raised her eyebrows. "Please do, but I would advise you to watch your back. And be quick, because I will certainly turn most of them off."

"Is that wise?" Constance asked quickly. "Until we know what happened to your husband, should you not keep all the protection you can?"

The widow's eyes widened infinitesimally, as if the thought had never entered her head. Because she knew who had killed her husband and why? Her eyelashes swept down, masking whatever lay behind them. Constance thought suddenly that she was very alone and had probably been so long before the death of her husband.

In marrying Savelli, she had alienated her family and friends and made an enemy of Giusti. The quarrel between the two men was clearly well known in the city, certainly to the police.

"You must know Giusti very well," Solomon said. "Do you think he is capable of murder?"

"Of course he is," Elena said impatiently. "He killed in the war. Angelo fought for the Austrians. Do I think he *did* kill my husband? No. Angelo told me he left in the same boat as you did."

"Perhaps he came back," Solomon said.

"Perhaps *you* did," Elena countered. "After all, my husband was responsible for kidnapping your wife and no doubt terrifying her. That is not easy to forgive."

"No, it isn't," Solomon said. "Which was why I tried to call on him yesterday. Signora, when did you last see your husband alive?"

"When he told me about Giusti and Signora Grey. About one in the morning, perhaps a little later."

"Did he go to bed?" Constance asked.

"Not with me," Elena said, holding her gaze. "But he has his own rooms, of course."

"May we see them?"

Again, the widow's eyes widened. "You want to see my husband's rooms?"

"And speak to his valet, if he has one," Constance said, getting everything in at once.

Elena stared at her, then at Solomon, as if unsure whether to be angry. She gave a graceful shrug. "Very well, why not? What else do you want to know?"

"Who hated him? Who bore a grudge and a temper violent enough to kill him? Giusti implied he had business rivals."

"Doesn't everyone?"

"Oh yes," Constance said. Some of her own would have cut her throat in passing. Once upon a time. Now, she had no real rivals, since her business was unique, though that didn't mean everyone loved her. "Who were your husband's?"

Elena drummed her fingers on the arm of her chair for a moment, then said, "Nicolo Premarin was trying replace him in some government contract. He was boasting about it, claimed the contract was signed. Only it wasn't, and Angelo kept it. I heard Premarin was angry. But then, I don't care for the man, so I would say that. Don't you think you should be looking further down the"—she paused, struggling for right word in English—"the ranks of our population? An opportunistic thief or someone of that nature?"

"Was anything stolen from your husband?"

"Not that I know of," she said reluctantly. She swallowed some wine, set down the glass, and pushed it across the table. "There was coin in his pocket and he still wore his ring and his cuff links. But…" She jumped to her feet in sudden excitement. "He *did* witness a robbery in San Marco last week. Someone snatched a lady's purse and Angelo caught the fellow, handed him over to the authorities after returning the purse to the lady. The thief was loud in his cursing and promise of retribution."

"Ah." Solomon had risen with her. "Did you tell the police about this yesterday?"

"No, for I had forgotten until now. They should know already, since they took charge of the culprit. But I will remind them. Come. I'll show you Angelo's room if you really want to see it."

Frustratingly, the dead man's bedchamber gave away little of his character. It was comfortable but not luxurious, containing everything a gentleman should have and all in the finest quality. But there was nothing extravagant in his taste, no clue as to his interest in books or art or pastimes. His dressing room, which looked onto the back of the house, was much the same: functional, tidy, and tasteful.

"He was a very private man, your husband?" Constance said. She made it a question, and Elena merely nodded.

"Yes. But then, he only slept here. He conducted correspondence and business from his study or the dockside offices."

Constance glanced at Solomon.

"Would it be too much of an intrusion," he asked, "to see his study? His correspondence?"

It was a question that risked their being thrown out of the house, and Constance more than half expected it. Certainly, Elena's bold eyebrows rose very high.

Unexpectedly, she laughed. "You are looking for evidence of his secret life? The dancing girls and the mistresses? The vices that a mere wife is never shown? Come, then, but you are wasting your time."

"I believe you," Solomon said. "But there may be other things to see—acrimonious correspondence with some enemy none of us knows of, or even with Giusti. Or some cause for having left the house by the back door in the early hours of the morning."

Elena paused at the door and glanced back over her shoulder. "You think he went outside to meet someone there? Why would he do that without protection? Especially if it was Giusti, whom he had just had beaten. Or you, Mr. Grey, whose beautiful wife had just been taken and frightened by strangers."

"That is a good point," Solomon agreed. "Especially when he had hired bodyguards. Why did he do that, by the way? Was it normal? Or did he fear some particular threat?"

"He did not say so. He said it was for me. But I am irritated by followers and prefer my own company."

She led them down the grand staircase again and threw open a door beyond the drawing room. From his expression, Solomon recognized it.

"This is his private study," Elena said, "where he could bring friends when he chose to. He has offices downstairs, too."

It was another lovely room, flooded with light and lined with books and furnished in beautiful walnut wood. Elena wandered toward the glass cabinets at the far end.

"My husband collected antiquities," she said with odd bitterness, waving one hand over the first cabinet without looking at it.

"Weapons, largely, as you see."

She was right, Constance saw with one cursory glance. If the man collected antiquarian jewelry like Elena's father's ring, it was not obvious.

Nor did he keep correspondence here. No papers littered his desk. Only blank paper, pens, and inks were kept in the drawers. As if, even here, his personality was suppressed.

Wordlessly, Elena led them out and down a less-grand staircase to the ground floor, where a suite of rooms were clearly used as offices. The largest and most comfortable was clearly the master's.

Here at last was a busy room, full of bookcases and desks, ledgers and papers. Everything seemed to be tidy and ordered.

Elena stood by quite rigidly as Constance and Solomon poked around his desk, rifling through a few business letters. Because it was different, Constance picked up an invoice.

"Who is Signor Rossi?" she asked.

"Domenico? He is—was—painting our portrait."

Constance laid it down again.

"My husband was a good man," Elena said with sudden sadness. "And a good husband. No one had a reason to kill him."

"There is always a reason," Solomon said. "Even if it isn't one the rest of the world understands."

"You are being very cooperative and very patient with us," Constance said. "Does that mean you believe us to be innocent of the murder?"

"I don't think you would be—ah…inquiring into the crime if you had committed it. You would invoke the protection of the British consul and flee. Or at least keep quiet. Are you protecting Giusti?"

She may have been speaking to both of them, but it was Constance she looked at, and just for an instant there was deep feeling in her secretive eyes. Constance could not read it. And then it vanished.

"He is easy to like," Elena said, just a little too carelessly to be natural.

Is that jealousy? In a dog-in-the-manger kind of way. She chose Savelli, but no one else should have Giusti either?

Elena moved toward the door. "Come. I'll take you to the servants."

They followed her, though Solomon cast a last look over his shoulder, as though still trying to learn something that the room was determined to hide.

"How was your husband in the last few days?" Constance asked her. "Did he seem anxious about anything or anyone?"

"No. But then, my husband was not a talkative man. He would not…upset me with his concerns."

Constance heard the tiny pause before the word *upset* and suspected the dead man's reticence had hurt his wife. She could understand that, for Solomon had once been similarly inclined. That he had unbent and trusted her, that their relationship had grown into this partnership, this companionship, was a matter of happiness and pride to her.

Did you try? Did you love your husband? Impossible to ask right now.

As was, *Did you kill him?*

"Then he behaved as usual?" Solomon asked.

"Well, no, he did not usually abduct respectable women off the street, not even by accident."

Solomon ignored the sarcasm. "But it was normal to send his men after Giusti?"

She threw back her head in a gesture that might have signified frustration or anger. "Their quarrel was getting out of hand," she said. "I thought it would fade with time, but it got worse… Ludovico ignored both of us unless he was poked. But Angelo seemed unable to leave the matter alone. He thought Ludovico wore my father's ring to insult him or rile him, and maybe he did. But Angelo used the missing jewels as an excuse, as though the property was his only concern."

"That must have hurt," Constance said.

Elena caught her breath and stopped, her eyes guarded as she flung a quick glance at each of them. "It angered me." She walked on more swiftly, her whole posture discouraging further questions.

CHAPTER SIX

DELICIOUS, TANTALIZING SMELLS of cooking grew stronger as the lady of the house led them into the servants' domain.

The servants displayed none of the horror of many large English households at being invaded from "upstairs." There had been a hum of subdued chatter as they went about their tasks, and that broke off as they acknowledged their mistress's presence. Constance gathered that they were used to her frequent appearances, although a few curious, even suspicious glances were thrown at the strangers behind her.

Elena addressed them in rapid Italian that Constance had no hope of following. A couple of people began to detach themselves from the crowd, and someone else was summoned from another room. Elena turned to her visitors.

"How much Italian do you speak?" she asked in English.

"Very little," said Constance honestly, "though Solomon understands more."

"Perhaps not in Venetian, which can be quite different. I will translate for you."

They murmured their thanks as several male servants began to crowd around them. There was a middle-aged, well-dressed man, surely a valet, another younger man in sober clothes, and a boatman in white shirt and black breeches and waistcoat. Among those trying to skulk behind, Constance spotted a black eye and a cut cheek. Those who had attacked Giusti, perhaps?

"This is Ricci, my husband's valet," Elena said, drawing Constance's attention back to the first man. "What would you like to know?"

Solomon said, "First, please pass on our sympathy for the loss of their master."

Elena spoke quickly, and several of them nodded. "I have also told them you are friends who wish to help find and punish the killer, and that they should cooperate with you."

"Thank you. Would you ask Ricci about Signor Savelli's mood in the days leading up to his death? Was there anything unusual in his manner or his behavior?"

Another exchange of Italian and Elena replied, "He behaved as normal, but seemed preoccupied the night before."

"Did Signor Savelli confide his problem to him?"

Elena spoke, but the negative was clear enough without her translation.

Constance said, "How long has he worked for Signor Savelli?"

"Ten years," the answer came back.

"Was he a good master, then? Did you like working for him?" Of course, with Elena and the other servants standing by, Ricci was unlikely to say anything but *yes*. Still, Constance hoped to learn something from his expression.

She didn't, although she caught some sly grins among the less-reputable men behind. Her stomach tightened as she wondered if those were the men who had seized her in the street.

"When did you last see your master alive?" Solomon asked.

"About one in the morning," Ricci replied, via Elena.

"Did you help prepare him for bed?"

"I set out his nightclothes and he sent me away. He often did. He would stay up later and work."

"Is that what he did that night?" Solomon asked.

"I don't know. I went to bed and I never saw him alive again."

"What was he wearing when he died?" Constance asked.

Elena blinked at her in surprise but still asked the question.

"I mean," Constance clarified, "did he wear the same clothes as on the night before? Was he fully dressed? Or in his night attire?"

"The same clothes except for the coat," Ricci replied. "He wore no coat."

"No coat?" Solomon pounced. "But it was surely cold at that time of the morning... Did you not say he took his purse with him?"

"It was in the pocket of his trousers," Elena said, without referring to the valet.

"Who found the body?" Solomon asked.

The boatman stepped forward.

"He did," Elena replied after a brief exchange. "When he went to make sure the gondola was in good order."

"When did he last use the boat?" Solomon asked.

"The previous afternoon, when he came home from the lagoon."

"Remind them, if you please, that I am not a policeman," Solomon said, "but I want to speak to the men who attacked Signor Giusti."

Four men shuffled forward, including the bruised ones Constance had noticed earlier.

"How did you travel to find Signor Giusti?" Solomon asked.

"By foot. We knew where to look, and it was not far."

Solomon nodded and suddenly stepped forward, causing some of the men to leap aside and reveal the two slyly grinning men Constance had also seen before. "And yet those who abducted my wife brought her by dark alleyways and by boat. From more or less the same place. Why was that?"

The two men did not appear remotely intimidated. One spoke and looked directly at Constance as he did so. She had met his type often before. He liked to intimidate with his eyes and his words.

"Pellini," Elena snapped at him, and he subsided. She did not translate, but then, she didn't need to, for the man had spoken with deliberate clarity so that even Constance could understand. *"She liked the company."*

"And you like to hurt women?" Solomon said softly, surprising everyone. Constance held her breath. "What a big, proud man you must be."

Color suffused the man's face. He tried to outstare Solomon, who smiled at him so encouragingly that he might as well have said the words, *Please, try to hit me, just give me a reason.*

Elena snapped again, and the man dropped his eyes. Here was one woman he did not choose to frighten. Which was interesting.

"Did you use Signor Savelli's gondola?" Constance asked them.

Pellini and the man next to him did not look at her, but at Elena as she translated and brought back the answer. "No, they used one of the smaller boats that the servants use for supplies."

"Were you looking for a particular woman?" Constance asked. "Or did you just grasp what you thought was an opportunity?"

Elena spoke without expression and returned the slightly sheepish answer of the thugs. "They took the opportunity because Pellini had heard that Giusti had a mistress. They misunderstood, thinking you were with him. My husband was angry with them."

To Constance's relief, Solomon turned to another subject. "Did anyone see or hear Signor Savelli go outside during the night he died?"

There was a lot of shuffling and head shaking. The younger of the upper servants said, "After the lady left before midnight, everyone came back inside, including Signor Savelli, and I locked the back door. When Stefano, the boatman, went out, he found the door unlocked."

"Why would Signor Savelli have gone out at that time, in the dark?" Constance asked. "Had he done such things before?"

"Not without his coat," Stefano the boatman said, and the valet nodded.

"Had his bed been slept in?" Solomon asked the valet suddenly.

The man shrugged and Elena translated his torrent of speech. "He might have lain on it. The bedding was disturbed, but he did not appear to have changed into his nightclothes or slept between the sheets."

Elena turned away. Impossible to tell if it was because she was bored or upset or hiding something she knew to be important.

"WELL?" ELENA ASKED as she led them out of the maze of kitchens toward the big entrance hall. "Did you learn anything of use?"

Solomon was wondering the same thing. "I believe we learned much." Though its use to their inquiry was another matter. "Thank you for your help. It can't have been easy for you."

"Easier than sitting alone and waiting for the police to return my husband's body."

A surge of sympathy took him by surprise. Did she really have no friends, no family she could turn to in her hour of need? Perhaps she was too proud to ask, but a true friend, a sister, a cousin, would surely come anyway. Savelli's death could not be a secret in the city or beyond. Had she burned her boats so badly by marrying Savelli? Without making new friends? If so, her life must have been lonely enough before her husband's horrific death.

Was that enough of a reason to do away with him?

"Did we ask the same questions as the police?" Constance said.

"Some." Elena shrugged. "Foscolo is no fool. He will do his duty, whatever the cost."

"You know Foscolo?" Solomon said in surprise.

"Of course. He comes from an old family, if not a particularly distinguished branch of it. He was a nationalist, in the revolution. Like me, he has made his peace with reality."

"Do you know Lampl as well?" Constance asked.

"Yes, ever since he came to Venice three years ago. Angelo knew him before. He liked him. He is not…" She paused, clearly looking for the words. "He is not a policeman. He is an administrator. An official of government with responsibilities that cover police inquiries of a particular kind."

"The kind that involves important people?" Solomon suggested. "When he came to interview us, we gathered his presence irritated Foscolo."

"Foscolo is an irritable man." She turned, giving her hand to Constance. "You will feel free to call again? I will help all I can."

"Thank you," Solomon said, bowing over her proffered hand in turn. "It is much appreciated."

Alvise was in shouted conversation with another boatman close by, though he quickly broke off to help Constance into the gondola. It struck Solomon suddenly that they had not made full use of the man's knowledge.

"Do you know the Savelli gondolier, Stefano?" he asked him.

"Of course. We are both members of the guild."

"Is he a friend of yours?"

"He is older than me. Not a friend. I respect him."

"Would he have approved, do you think, of his master employing his so-called bodyguards who attacked Signor Giusti and abducted my wife?"

"No."

A man of few words, Alvise.

"Why would Savelli have hired such men?" Constance pressed. "Is it normal?"

"Not usual, no." Alvise shrugged. "He must have felt threatened. His position on the council, his friendship with the Austrians… Feelings still run high."

"Then it wasn't a personal threat that inspired this…protection? For example, Signor Giusti?"

"Perhaps both. I don't know. Perhaps Giusti is part of the same problem."

"Being a nationalist," Solomon murmured. He frowned. "How loyal would these bravos be to Savelli's family?"

"Very. As long as they are paid."

Then they did not expect Elena Savelli to stop paying them as she had threatened during her first conversation with Solomon. They still obeyed her without question, despite her clear disdain. Interesting. Possibly…

Like him, Constance seemed unwilling to discuss too much in front of Alvise, whose grasp of English was increasing daily. Back at the Palazzo Zulian, Solomon dismissed the boatman, and Constance almost flew into the house and up the stairs to their favorite drawing room.

By the time he closed the door behind them, she had already found paper and a pen and was seated at the charming little bureau between the two central windows. He knew she would be writing down everything they knew about the case and those involved with it—not in case she forgot, for actually she remembered everything that was said to her and everything she read, almost verbatim. But it helped her—helped both of them—to see connections and different points of view.

Constance said, "I don't want her to have done it either. But she could have. She is hiding *something*. Something besides discontent and loneliness."

"It need not be anything incriminating. After all, she is happy for us to question her servants, even to keep coming back."

"Is she?" Constance looked up, her pen stilling. "Can you be sure she translated all our questions accurately? Let alone the answers?"

"No," he admitted. "Not completely sure. But I didn't catch any obfuscation."

Constance sighed. "Do you think she regretted marrying him?"

"I think it left her without family and friends. Whether that is enough…"

"Is it enough for you?" Constance said suddenly.

"I had very few friends in the first place and, to my knowledge, no one rejects you. Or me. We may be an odd couple, but our marriage hurts no one. I think Elena's did."

"Giusti, for one."

"And possibly Elena herself. In which case, if Savelli knew it, he would also have been hurt."

Constance began to write again, furiously. "There are too many oddities here. What was Savelli afraid of to have hired such men? It seems incongruous. He was not a brawling man. He was much too refined and self-disciplined. And yet he sent them after Giusti. And made them feel it was permissible to abduct Giusti's mistress—me, apparently."

"Something was bothering Savelli, at least on the night he died, but possibly for much longer. If he didn't sleep well, he might not have been thinking very clearly. He might have made several bad decisions."

"Like hiring these men in the first place," Constance said. "Like assaulting Giusti. Like going out unarmed and half dressed in the middle in the night, his bed not properly slept in." She stopped writing again and stared at him, her eyes gleaming. "He was waiting for someone!"

"Perhaps," Solomon allowed. "His dressing room overlooks the back of the house. He could have seen someone arrive by boat and dashed out to meet them."

"A lover?" Constance suggested. "That would certainly explain Elena's unhappiness. And her secretiveness. She would hide it, pretend she neither knew nor cared…" She frowned and shook her head. "Except I could swear he loved his wife. He was more concerned for what she might think about my departure from the house than about anything else. He did not want her hurt or humiliated, and not just because it might earn him an earful of abuse. He cared for her."

"And she chose him over Giusti. We keep coming back to Ludovico. Somehow, he is involved in this story."

"He had another woman," Constance recalled. "And I don't

think Elena liked that. She definitely disliked the idea of Giusti and me knowing each other."

"Well, you can't help being a threat to any woman's amorous ambitions."

Constance stuck out her tongue at him. "She is not indifferent to Giusti. But it might just be a dog-in-the-manger-ish possessiveness. I don't know her well enough to say."

"Shall we go and see Giusti this afternoon? I want to know why he was so determined to hold on to those jewels, including Elena's father's ring. That does not seem very…gentlemanly."

"We could and should see Giusti," she replied, a sparkle in her brilliant eyes. "But first, we could discover the portrait painter's view of the Savellis."

Solomon raised his eyebrows. "Do you have his name?"

"I read his invoice," Constance said with relish. "I have his address."

A maid came into the room with a letter, which she presented to Solomon with a curtsey. It was a large, official-looking envelope emblazoned with a familiar coat of arms.

"It's from the consulate," Solomon said in surprise.

"Telling us to keep out of Venetian business?" Constance asked, intrigued enough to leave her desk and come to lean over his shoulder. He could not resist leaning his head back so that their cheeks touched. She moved hers, caressing him like a cat, which made him smile.

"It's an invitation to a reception tomorrow afternoon," he said thoughtfully. "I wonder whom we will meet there?"

Although the invitation was printed, a note had been inscribed by hand on the back by a secretary, apologizing for the short notice, which was only because the consul had not realized until today that such a distinguished British visitor was in Venice.

"He must mean you," Solomon said.

"He can't *know* about me," Constance said wryly, thinking of her past. "We are both invited."

"Which is as it should be. Perhaps they heard of our involvement in the Savelli murder. Either way, it will certainly be interesting to learn what the British here think of Savelli. Official government sympathy is generally with the nationalist cause."

He rose and put the card on the large marble mantelpiece. "But that is for tomorrow. Perhaps you would like your portrait painted while you are in Venice?"

She smiled. "I would like yours. If he's good. What a pity Signora Savelli didn't show us hers. That must have been what was on the covered easel in the corner of her drawing room."

After a cup of coffee—they had more or less given up on finding decent tea in Italy—they duly summoned Alvise and set off in search of the painter, Domenic Rossi. It had clouded over and there was a fine mizzle of rain. Unlike rain at home, this did not detract from Venice's charm, merely changed it subtly to one of brooding moodiness. No wonder artists were drawn here. Or born here.

In fact, Domenico Rossi lived pretty close by. According to Alvise, there was a tradition of painters living in this quarter of the city, including the great Canaletto. They could easily have walked the short distance, but the novelty of traveling everywhere by boat had not yet worn off. After tying up the craft, Alvise pointed them down a narrow passageway and they set off to find the painter's house.

Thoughtfully, he had nailed a sign to his door, consisting of a small, square view of the Cannaregio Canal with his name inscribed below it. Solomon raised the knocker, which was loose, and rapped on the door. After several moments, he rapped again. A male voice shouted within, easily heard through the open window on the floor above. Footsteps clomped nearer and the door opened to reveal a young, ill-dressed woman with a tangled mass of black hair, a curvy figure, and a face of exquisite beauty.

"Signor Rossi, *per favore?*" Solomon said politely.

"He's not in," the girl replied with blatant untruth.

Solomon raised one eyebrow. "Then that was not his voice I heard?"

"No."

"Then we shall wait."

The girl moved forward to block him when he would have brushed past her. "There is no point. Come back tomorrow. Early. The earlier the better."

She would have shut the door, only Solomon, suspicions aroused, placed his hand on it and pushed back. The girl stared at him with more hopelessness than aggression.

"Are you his wife?" Constance asked gently in her careful Italian.

"God, no," the girl said fervently. She raised her voice. "I have not yet sunk so low!"

Whatever the man above said, it sounded like a curse. He clattered downstairs and the girl made one last effort to close the door.

"Useless girl," the man roared behind her. "Don't send my bread and butter away!"

The girl threw up her hands, releasing the door. "Please yourself. Come in if you want," she added to the visitors. "It won't do you any good, because he's drunk as an English lord."

"Ha!" said the man, striding somewhat unevenly into view. "Even drunk, I paint better than anyone else in the city. Come in, and welcome!" He bowed elaborately, only just keeping his balance. He smelled like old socks and new wine.

Straightening, he regarded them from beneath thick, bushy brows. There was something leonine about him with his wild mane of reddish-brown hair and oddly noble features—apart from bloodshot, unfocused eyes.

It went against the grain to take Constance into such inebriated company. But it was she who sailed first through the door, taking the matter out of Solomon's hands.

"*Buon Giorno*," she said briskly. "Do you speak English, Signor Rossi?"

Rossi concentrated hard on his finger and thumb to show about an inch of space. "Little," he said, and lumbered back to the stairs. "Come, come."

Solomon followed Constance inside, and the girl closed the door behind him. "I'll bring coffee," she said resignedly.

Surprisingly, the house was clean but appallingly untidy, especially in the main room, where clearly the artist worked. Rossi waded through fallen sketches and easels, lifted a pile of canvases off a chair for Constance, and looked around for somewhere to put them. Finding no available surface, he dropped them on the floor, gestured for Constance to sit, and swept a pile of brightly colored paint rags off another chair for Solomon.

Then he half sat, half fell onto a three-legged stool and grinned at them. "Soon, I am sober. What can I do for you?"

"I thought," Solomon said, "you might paint my wife." *If you can see her.*

However, Rossi's gaze was suddenly perfectly focused as he stared at Constance. A gleam entered his bloodshot eyes. He began to smile more naturally and turned his gaze on Solomon. Then he reared back as though trying to take in both of them at once. Solomon exchanged quick glances with Constance and knew she was about to laugh. Which would have set him off, so he looked hastily back to Rossi.

The painter caught his breath. "Damn, I will paint you both. Together. I never see a couple like you before. I have not the words in English. I paint."

"Not now," Solomon said hastily, and Rossi laughed uproariously.

The girl came in with a large tray containing coffee and wine, cups and glasses, and a little plate of cicchetti. Rossi did not move, so Solomon rose to take the tray from her. She revealed a table by the painter's own simple expedient of sweeping everything on it onto the floor, and Solomon set the tray down.

In an understandable breach of etiquette, the girl served their host first, shoving a full cup of coffee into his hands. "Drink. Now." Then she poured wine for Constance and Solomon and offered them the plate. They each took a savory with murmured thanks, and she placed the rest under Rossi's nose. Then she swiped up the jug of wine and retreated.

The artist smiled after her. "Isn't she wonderful? I don't know why she puts up with me."

Neither did Solomon, until his eyes finally fell on the canvas nearest him. It showed the Cannaregio Canal in the rain, and Solomon could almost feel the pattering on his face. The water of the canal seemed to move, slopping over the road above. The painter had caught several figures in flight, too, rushing for cover and slopping through the puddles.

Oh yes, Domenico Rossi was good. Unable to stop himself, Solomon rose and examined the picture more closely. One figure, dancing through puddles with all the fun of a child, bore the unmistakable features of the swerving girl.

Almost afraid, he moved it to look at the picture behind—a portrait. At first glance, it appeared to be just another middle-aged worthy, but this particular worthy's character quickly seized and held his attention. Surely this was a handsome man of strength, intelligence, and nobility, yet with some subtle, tragic weakness about his eyes and the set of his mouth. It was a face of hope and hopelessness at the same time.

"I know him, don't I?" Constance said behind him.

"Daniel Manin," Rossi said. "Our glorious leader in '48."

"I've never seen him quite like that before."

It was as if Rossi had painted the doom of Venice into the face of its erstwhile leader, now in exile.

"Waste of a man," Rossi growled. "But a lot of men were wasted then."

Solomon dragged his gaze from the portrait. "We plan to be in Venice for the next five weeks or so. Could you paint our portrait in that time?"

Rossi smiled. "I insist upon it, signor. How did you find me?"

Solomon had hoped he would ask that, but he let Constance answer.

"Signora Savelli said you were painting her and her husband."

A frown darkened Rossi's face. "I was. Not now."

"Then you heard of Signor Savelli's sad demise?"

"Of course. I could still have finished the portrait. It would have been good, and she would have liked to have it."

"You mean you could finish it without Signor Savelli's being there?" Constance asked.

"Of course I could."

"She won't let you?" Solomon said. "Or you are too delicate to ask?"

Rossi threw back his head and roared with laughter. "Delicate? Me? No, Savelli himself dismissed me, paid for my time as though I am a house painter or a layer of bricks, and dismissed me."

"Didn't he like your painting?" Constance asked, with just the right shade of incredulity.

"Of course he liked it," Rossi scoffed. "Who wouldn't? Already it was a great portrait. It was *me* he didn't like." He sighed. "That too is understandable. I drink too much; I speak my mind. And suddenly I am persona non grata."

"What particular part of your mind did you speak?" Solomon asked.

Rossi sighed. "The part should remain quiet. I gave him advice on the conduct of his marriage. He should have listened. But there, which of us listens to advice about women?"

Constance kept her gaze carefully on the artist. "What did you say?"

"I told him she didn't want jewels—she wanted love, attention. A woman wants your soul, not your house and your money. Although," he added judiciously, "house and money can't hurt, eh?"

"I always insist upon them myself," Constance said. "So you don't think their marriage was a happy one?"

"She should have taken Giusti. There's a fun boy for you. Savelli, not so much. But there, I must have hurt his feelings."

Constance seemed to be waiting for more, but when it didn't

come, she said, "You don't actually care about his feelings, because he hurt yours by dismissing you."

Rossi tried to laugh, but he couldn't quite hide the surge of fury in his eyes before he covered his face behind the large coffee cup and both hands. He drank it all down in one go, and when he set down the cup, Constance moved to refill it while he absently reached for another savory.

He pretended to have forgotten Constance's accusations, turning instead to Solomon. "Where I paint you? Here? Where you stay? Hotel?"

"In the Palazzo Zulian."

He perked up. "By the canal! Perfect. You want the view behind you, and yet it will be you two who dominate even that beauty. When can I begin?"

Stuffing the rest of the bread into his mouth, he scrambled around for paper and charcoal and began to draw on the back of some other sketch, his fingers flying, his eyes darting between Constance and Solomon and very occasionally the paper.

"Tomorrow morning?" Constance suggested. "I believe early is best."

Rossi emitted a crack of laughter. "So it is. Damn her. Don't worry, I'll be good."

It was only as they rose to leave that Solomon said, "What happened to your Savelli painting? Is it here?"

"No." The artist's eyes kindled again. "He kept it so I could not even finish it."

"Just as a matter of interest," Solomon said, "when did he dismiss you?"

Rossi drew in his breath. "The day before he died."

CHAPTER SEVEN

"**T**HAT *HAS* TO be significant," Constance said eagerly as they walked up the passage toward Alvise and the boat. The rain had gone off, so there was no need to rush. "Rossi blunders drunkenly into insulting Savelli's marriage and blabbing about jewels, and suddenly Savelli sends his men after Giusti to steal his wife's jewels back. And yet I don't see him as a man of such temper."

"The *dismissal* is the direct result of Rossi's verbal blunders," Solomon said. "But the attack? That makes little sense to me however I look at it. Except as jealousy. You are sure Savelli loved his wife, even in some repressed, excessively formal way. But that did not kill him. On the other hand, Rossi might have."

"Because he was dismissed with only half the portrait painted?" Constance said doubtfully. "He even got paid—some of his fee, at least. It doesn't seem much of a motive for murder."

"It might when you're drunk enough."

Constance thought about that. Drunkenness and violence went together all too often, as she had cause to know. Although there was something rather appealing about Domenico Rossi, even drunk as a wheelbarrow. She would need much more information before she would let him near her girls—always a useful guide. And once she accepted that...

"Savelli knew him," she said slowly. "If he was awake that night and saw Rossi arrive at his back door, he might well have nipped down to speak to him—to ask him what the devil he was doing, or even ask him to finish the painting after all. Only Rossi was too drunk and angry and stabbed him. Probably with more luck than science."

"Artists tend to know the human body very well. I wonder if he has a boat?"

"We can ask him tomorrow morning," Constance said. "If he turns up."

"The girl will make him. Though actually, I don't think she'll need to. He seemed quite keen. And he's good, isn't he?"

Constance nodded. "I hope it isn't him," she said as they emerged from the passage. "But then, I haven't met anyone yet I *want* it to be. Except Savelli's own thugs. That Pellini..."

"Well, they're worth looking into, if we can find someone to talk about them."

"Elena herself might. She doesn't like them."

Solomon handed her down into the boat, then climbed after her.

"Where to?" Alvise asked.

Constance glanced up at the sky, where the sun was beginning to peek through the clouds. There was even a patch or two of blue. She looked at Solomon. "Giusti?"

He nodded.

"Palazzo Giusti," Alvise said, and picked up his oar. As the sun came out, he lifted his voice and began to sing, and Constance was beguiled all over again. She took Solomon's hand and let Venice enfold her.

CLEARLY, THE PALAZZO Giusti had once been an impressive structure. It was old, probably older than the Zulian, and at a distance, still a gracious, beautiful building. Only as they drew closer could Constance see that some of the stonework was crumbling, and the whole house had an air of neglect.

The door was opened quite casually by an ill-dressed young man who blinked in surprise when he saw them on the doorstep. Solomon asked for Giusti, and the servant held open the door and waved them inside with a gesture somehow more resigned than mocking.

The theme of neglect continued inside. Although clean enough, the paint was faded, and some tiles were broken. The entrance hall, which should have been as impressive as Savelli's, was empty of furniture and hangings and caused their footsteps to echo loudly.

The servant strode along, and they hurried to keep up as he led them upstairs and along another faded, empty passage to a set of open double doors. He called inside, saying something about a lady and gentleman, and stood back.

Giusti himself appeared at the door, clearly surprised and curious, though his face broke into a grin when he saw them. His bruises looked less angry but more colorful.

"My friends! Welcome to my abode, crumbling as it is. Luigi, if we have wine, bring it."

The room retained an ancient, faded beauty. A once-lovely carpet that the moths had found had lost most of its color. There were patches of brightness on the faded walls where pictures had been removed. Again, the furniture was sparse, but there was enough to be comfortable, though the upholstery was threadbare and had probably also suffered from moths at one time. But the old, exposed beams of the ceiling had been recently varnished, and the windows had been thrown open to the sunshine, flooding the room with light and the kind of view one never tired of.

"You are admiring the faded glory, signora?" Giusti said with a crooked smile.

"It is a beautiful room," Constance replied honestly, taking the seat he indicated on the sofa. Solomon sat beside her.

"It is still home. To be frank, I have no money to keep it as it should be kept, and none to go anywhere else—not without selling it, and I can't quite bring myself to do that."

"You gave all your money to the revolutionary cause?" Solomon said.

"It seemed a good idea at the time. It was to herald a new age of prosperity for all the people of Venice, only it didn't quite."

Although Giusti spoke lightly, deprecatingly, Constance glimpsed a deeper pain in his eyes. The revolution had mattered to him. Whatever he pretended, he cared. It was possible—even probable—that when he accompanied Solomon to rescue Constance from Savelli, he had done it as much from kindness and gratitude as from a desire to hurt Savelli in any way he could.

"Have you no means of business?" Solomon asked.

Giusti shrugged. "Little enough before the revolution, less now. Austria takes what it can and crushes native entrepreneurial efforts. Venice loses business to other ports."

"It shouldn't," Solomon said thoughtfully.

Constance could see there were ideas forming and percolating in his mind. From Giusti's steady gaze, he knew it too.

With a hint of hope, he said, "What is your business, Mr. Grey?"

"Largely shipping. I like Venice."

Giusti's eyes flared for a moment, but he seemed too polite to press further. "That is good for us. Ah, rejoice! There is wine. And even cicchetti."

Luigi poured the wine and offered the plate of cicchetti before leaving the jug and the plate on the table and striding off.

"Is he your only servant?" Constance asked.

"Practically, yes. He and his father, who is really too old. Most of the servants died during the siege. Cholera was our enemy within."

"You have much tragedy in your life," she said. "Much to resent."

"And I do, of course. But I cannot change the past, not by blaming myself or others. And I am alive. Was there a particular reason you chose to visit me this afternoon?"

"We have set about proving our joint innocence," Constance

said lightly. "And we need your knowledge."

"Of what in particular?"

"Of the people and the motives," Solomon said. "We need to know about the jewels, which were such a bone of contention between you and Savelli. Signora Savelli told us she gave them to you, implying they were for the revolutionary cause, but that you did not sell them all."

"I couldn't," he said simply. "I thought she might need them. I chose to beggar myself. I could not do the same to her."

"And yet you did not give them back to her."

"I gave her back what was left of the jewels we had agreed I should sell. The others were a gift."

"*Did* you sell them?" Solomon asked.

"I am not a thief. I can show you them if you like." He gave an open, careless smile, and Constance understood.

"You kept them because they were hers," she said.

A flush came to Giusti's face. "Her father's ring was a personal gift."

"Which you wore to annoy Savelli."

He looked at his hands twisting together and forced them to stillness. "It was the only fun I could find for a while."

"And the other pieces?" Solomon asked.

"I had seen her wearing them." Giusti drew a breath and looked up to meet Solomon's gaze. "And perhaps I hoped she would come and ask for them. I would have returned them then. Even her father's ring."

"But it was Savelli who asked."

Giusti's lips twisted. "*Commanded.* And then tried to steal. I'm only surprised he didn't try to break in here."

"Why was he so determined?" Constance asked. "He did not need the money. He could have bought her other jewels, his own gifts, untainted by you."

Giusti shrugged. "Greed. Maybe." His eyes fell again. "I don't think he wanted me to have anything of hers. He feared he was second best. But he wasn't, was he? She chose him. And she never came near me."

"You still love her," Constance said softly.

He leapt up and swung to the window, as though her words were unbearable. "What can I say?" he flung over his shoulder. "My nature is damnably loyal."

To a cause. To a woman he would always love. And yet… "There is a rumor you have a mistress," Constance said. "That is why I was abducted."

"I know." There was self-deprecation as well as defiance in his voice. "But believe me, in recent years, none of my brief passages with women could justify the title of mistress."

"Giusti," Solomon said, "did you ever go there? To Savelli's house?"

Giusti shook his head, but he did not turn back. Constance and Solomon exchanged glances. Was it Giusti who had drawn the wakeful Savelli from his house the night of his death? Was the idiocy of love responsible for this tragedy from which none of them could return?

Constance changed the subject. "Are you acquainted with Domenico Rossi?"

Giusti turned in clear surprise. "The painter? I've come across him once or twice. Quite the character. Larger than life, you might say, but too fond of the drink. He churns out souvenir paintings by the dozen, but in among them are gems. He has talent."

"We've asked him to paint a portrait of us," Solomon said. "Apparently, he half finished one of Signor and Signora Savelli."

"Then let us hope history does not repeat itself," Giusti said flippantly. Then he frowned. "Wait. Do you suspect Rossi of the murder? Why should he kill his customer?"

"Savelli dismissed him the day before he died."

"Did he?" Giusti's frown deepened. "Seems to me Savelli was behaving very oddly."

"Apparently, Rossi had made some remark about women— Signora Savelli in particular—preferring love to jewels."

"Jewels again."

"Was Savelli unbalanced?" Solomon asked. "You were his friend at one time—what do you think?"

Giusti came back and sat down. He reached distractedly for his wine glass. "He was always…obsessive. Which was good for his business. And his studies. But never to the point of madness when I knew him." He took a sip of wine, then said in a rush, "He was loyal to the government, to Austria, if you like, but only because he believed it was best for Venice at this time. He wanted the unity of Italy too but thought—rightly, as it turned out—that it could not yet be achieved. So he was loyal in his way, to Venice. And to Elena. He always loved her, even when she was betrothed to me. I knew that and thought I had nothing to fear from him. I was wrong. But then later, he feared me because I was first. Maybe. I would never have killed him, you know. I would not do that to her, let alone to him."

Giusti's gaze refocused on Constance. "If he was mad, Elena would know. Though she might not tell you. To preserve his reputation. He was always the sanest man I knew."

As though unaware of the contradictions falling out of his mouth, he took a savory from the plate and ate it in two bites.

"Is Elena capable of murder?" Solomon asked, timing it nicely so that Giusti took a breath and choked on some crumbs.

"No," he gasped. Which told Constance nothing except that he would defend Elena.

"What about their household? Would someone else kill for Elena? Would those hired thugs of Savelli's have turned on him?"

"Only if he refused to pay them, I imagine." Giusti looked thoughtful. "Which I suppose he might have done after they abducted you, signora. But I know little of such men. They are probably not even Venetian."

"Might we ask your manservant if he has heard any rumors?" Solomon asked.

Giusti glanced at him, an oddly shrewd look in his eye, as if he knew that was not the only question the servant Luigi would be asked. But he said only, "Of course."

Constance sipped her wine. "Why would Signor Savelli leave the house in the early hours without his coat?"

Giusti laughed with a trace of bitterness. "An assignation? Wouldn't that turn everything on its head! I almost wish it were true. Only, I can't see it."

"Neither can I. But he must have gone to meet someone, and someone was definitely there."

"Someone he did not fear," Giusti said, "since he went out alone."

"Or someone he did not respect, since he went without his coat," Solomon said.

Giusti smiled. "Like me?"

"Oh, I think he respected you. He sent four men against you, with another two in reserve who came by boat."

"They were not very good men, since they were seen off by you and me and your gondolier. And the other two picked on a gentle lady."

"I am not so gentle as you might think," Constance said, and he gazed at her with frank curiosity.

"We thought," Solomon said, setting down his glass, "that we might call on Signor Premarin tomorrow. You said he was a rival of Savelli's."

"He is. But perhaps I should have said *friendly* rival."

"They were friends?"

"Oh yes, Premarin is impossible to dislike. He is a good man and everyone knows it, so he stays friends with everyone."

"Austrian and Venetian?" Constance asked.

Giusti nodded. "He supported the revolution and made peace when we had to. He bears no grudges, and nor does anyone else against him."

"And his business thrives?"

"Pretty well." Giusti cocked his head to one side. "You are wondering if he killed Savelli to take his business more easily. I would find that unlikely."

"Unless he too has a *tendre* for Signora Savelli," Constance said.

"He probably does. She is that kind of woman." His eyes gleamed at her. "Like you."

"Oh, I doubt that," Constance murmured. "Was Elena faithful to her husband?"

The smile died in his eyes. "How would I know? I am the last man she would turn to." He straightened, as though conscious he had given too much away. "But in my opinion—for all that is worth—if she chose a lover, it would not be Premarin."

"Why not?"

"He is a clever man, an entertaining man, and a wealthy one. But he is old."

And now Elena did not like him. Was that significant?

WHEN THEY ROSE to leave, the light was fading, and Giusti yelled for Luigi to show them out, the act of a man who had nothing to fear from whatever his servant might say to them.

Solomon lengthened his stride and caught up with the manservant. "Signor Giusti suggested I ask you if you knew anything against Signor Savelli's servants."

"I meet some of them sometimes. They are mostly decent men."

"What of the new men he hired as bodyguards?"

Luigi shrugged. "I wouldn't accuse them lightly of cheating at cards. But I've known worse."

"Did you ever hear why he might have hired such men?"

"Protection for the signora."

"Is that why they attacked your master?"

Luigi curled his lip. The contempt was not for his master. "He is no danger to her. Only to himself."

"What do you mean by that?" Solomon asked.

"Nothing. Is there anything else?"

"Yes," Solomon said, ignoring the insolence. "The night your master was attacked, what time did he come home?"

"Not long after midnight. As I already told the police."

"I am not the police. I have no authority at all. But I need the truth to prove Signor Giusti's innocence."

"And your own, from what I hear."

"You hear correctly. Did you tend his wounds that night?"

"Yes."

"What time did you leave him?"

"About one, or a little after."

"Did you see him into bed?"

"Mostly. He is not a baby and can look after himself."

"Did *you* go straight to bed?"

"Yes. It was half past one and my father wakes me early in the morning."

"It is a big house," Solomon said, "with hardly anyone living here. Would you hear if anyone came in or out?"

"Of course. My father and I sleep near the kitchens, on the ground floor, at the back of the house. I hear both the front and the back doors. They are heavy and the hinges need oiling."

"Did you hear him go out again that night?"

"No." Luigi looked him in the eye, and Solomon knew he was lying. "No one went out or came in."

AN HOUR LATER, they sat on the floor by the window of their drawing room, various pieces of paper covered in Constance's neat handwriting strewn around them. The candles were lit and the windows closed, but they could still make out the shifting water of the canal and the lights of the boats still passing up and down.

"Why do people lie to us when they need our help?" Constance demanded. "And I'm sure they are all lying about something."

"They don't trust us," Solomon said. "Why should they? We don't trust them. And unless they know differently, we are more likely to have murdered Savelli than they are. We are the strangers, and I have the best motive of all."

"And the best alibi," she reminded him. "The servants here know that neither of us went out again that night. But I think Giusti did. And Rossi. I even think Elena might have. If we don't know where they went, then it could easily have been the back of the Palazzo Savelli. I wonder if the police know more than us."

"They can't know less. I wonder if we can fit in a visit to Signor Foscolo tomorrow."

"He might well be calling on us."

Solomon reached out and caressed her hair, the curve of her bent neck. "Shall we go to bed?"

Her eyes softened as she looked up at him. He imagined they glowed, for him. She moved, resting her cheek on his shoulder, her hand comfortable on his thigh.

"Yes," she said. "Let's go to bed."

CHAPTER EIGHT

DOMENICO ROSSI WAS full of hope and excitement as he walked across the bridges and footpaths that led to the Palazzo Zulian.

His artistic senses tingled at the memory of the English couple's beauty, but more than that by the pleasing nature of the light and dark side by side. So close that they were almost one, and yet so different. Two sides of the same coin, perhaps, with different aspects of character and strength. Unique experience and pain gazed out of those two young faces, along with irrepressible curiosity and desire for life. He felt drawn them more than to any subject in years.

It was a miracle they were letting him paint them. Such a pity he had been quite so drunk. Perhaps Adriana had been right to try to keep them out and make them come back later, for while he could remember perfectly what they looked like and how he wanted to paint them, he couldn't remember what they had talked about and what, if anything, they had agreed upon. And the sketches he had made of their heads were terrible. He was ashamed.

This was not good.

Drinking was fun, necessary even, when he had nothing to paint and no desire to look. Melancholy was a curse but he'd begun to think that wine was not the answer. Not when he forgot things.

Something niggled at the edges of his mind. To do with forgetting, and the English couple, and the Savelli portrait. Was there a connection there? Savelli had died, stabbed through the heart, they said. Which Domenico didn't like to think about. Not after his furious, drunken dream when he had…

He refused to think about the dream. And he certainly wasn't about to tell anyone about waking up on his studio floor the following morning, with his clothes wet and dirty as if he'd swum in the canal and rolled about the street like a dog.

Adriana knew, of course. She'd washed his clothes and called him a drunken pig. But there was nothing to imply the drunken nightmare was more than there. There had been no blood on his clothes—or at least only from his own grazes.

Well, it was a warning, a sign from God, maybe. If He had not given up on him. Rossi would stop drinking, and he would paint the most exquisite portrait of the English couple that would become famous throughout Europe. He might even marry Adriana…

He approached the Palazzo Zulian, the most distinguished building on the canal. Straightening his back, he lifted the knocker.

IT WAS AFTER noon before they were able to leave the palazzo. Rossi, full of inconsequential chatter and great roars of infectious laughter, was, nevertheless, quite a martinet in his own way. Prone to barking out orders as though they were dogs or private soldiers under his command, he could be impatient and fussy one moment, and the next lapse into some funny story to make them laugh.

But his eyes were clear and keen, his hand steady as he sketched and sketched again. He was nowhere near ready for paint, he said. He needed to watch the light on the water for a bit, and make sure his subjects were posed for maximum impact.

"When it is right," he said. "Then, I go fast."

By tacit agreement, they did not ask him anything further about Savelli or the unfinished portrait. There would be other days, when he was more comfortable. And they might know more of the right questions to ask.

When he finally left, he announced that he would come back tomorrow afternoon. And as hostages, he left his paints and easel and two canvases.

"Early is best," Constance murmured. "I wonder what state he'll be in when he does come?"

Solomon had no answer to that, so they changed into more formal attire, summoned Alvise, and set off to call on Signor Premarin.

As it happened, they met the entire family almost in the doorway of their palazzo. It was a pleasantly chaotic scene, with children playing and laughing and asking questions while their elders, dressed to go out, tried to make themselves heard, giving instructions to servants and to one of the older children. The boy, however, was clearly more interested in the games of his siblings at whom he was grinning while he kept repeating, "*Si. Si.*"

Oddly, it was the inattentive boy who saw Constance and Solomon first. The liveried servant who opened the door to them was trying to explain in harassed tones that Signor Premarin was busy when the boy's sweeping gaze lit on them as, no doubt, a useful distraction. He interrupted his parents with a torrent of words, and suddenly the master of the house was gently pushing the servant aside.

"*Buongiorno,*" he murmured, whipping the visiting card from the servant's hands. He was a small, round man, his balding head thrown back in a proud posture that should have been laughable and yet was not. Perhaps because his black eyes gleamed with interest and good nature. Although he did not appear even to glance at the card he had appropriated, he greeted them by name, then added, "Forgive me. We were about to go out, to pay our last respects to the late Angelo Savelli."

Solomon had not even known that the police had released the body. It added to his growing sense of working in the dark in an alien if beautiful place.

"I apologize for the poor timing," he said carefully. "Perhaps we could make an appointment to call…"

"Of course, of course," Premarin said genially. "To be frank, I have been looking for an excuse to call on you, Mr. Grey. Your reputation is well known to me. Would you care to walk to San Marco with us? Oh, allow me to present my wife." He beamed proudly, and Solomon bowed to the much younger lady who came obediently to her husband's side.

Signora Premarin was the opposite of her husband in some ways—quite tall, slender, and shy, blushing as she greeted them in a small, almost mousey voice. Solomon presumed she was Premarin's second wife, for she could not have been much more than twenty, too young to be the mother of the oldest boy in the foyer. Her eyes widened with hopeless admiration when Solomon introduced Constance.

Premarin's eyes gleamed brighter as he reverently kissed Constance's hand. There was nothing hopeless about his clear appreciation. He was a man who noticed women.

Somehow, the door was closed on the noise within the house and the friendly Premarin strolled at Solomon's side, leaving the women to follow. They conversed in a mixture of Italian and English that felt oddly comfortable, perhaps because it was something they were both used to doing in their business worlds.

"Were you acquainted with Angelo Savelli, Mr. Grey?" Premarin asked.

"We never met," Solomon replied.

"He was a great friend of mine," Premarin said. "So tragic to lose him, and in such a way. So difficult for his lovely wife. My heart goes out to her."

"Indeed. I didn't know he was being buried today."

"After the service in the basilica. Do you join us?"

"I think it would be an unwelcome intrusion."

Premarin looked at him with apparent surprise. "How so?"

"I daresay you have heard something. Through certain…misunderstandings, I had a grievance against Signor Savelli. As it happened, I had no chance to quarrel with him, but I know the police still suspect me."

"Scandalous," Premarin said, shaking his head. "A man of your importance! I shall use all my influence with the authorities to remove any such suspicion. Lampl is a reasonable man. Excellent old family, most influential."

"We haven't come to ask for your intervention," Solomon said quickly. "In fact, we are trying to resolve the matter by finding out the truth."

Premarin spread his arms in an expressive shrug. "But where does one begin?"

"You knew Savelli well. You were his friend as well as his rival in business."

"We did compete sometimes, in the friendliest of ways. Sometimes, I win the lucrative contracts. Sometimes he does."

"Who won the last one?" Solomon asked lightly.

"He did," Premarin said without obvious resentment. "It was a good one, too—government business always is."

"Austrian government?"

Premarin grimaced. "Is there any other kind? Odd sops thrown our way when it is something the Austrians themselves cannot or will not do for themselves. The cleverest of us work around the system and make the most of it. Savelli and I could do that."

"But Giusti could not?"

Premarin sighed gustily. "Giusti had nothing after the war. If it had not been for his friends, he would be in exile like poor Manin. Or worse."

"Friends like you?" Solomon asked.

Premarin smiled. "I am quite the diplomat."

"Yet I understand you too were on the losing side of the quarrel with Austria."

"The cleverest of us leave all doors open," Premarin said vaguely. "And rightly so. No one is always one hundred per cent correct. I understand Savelli's position. I understand Giusti and the young men of noble ideals. One must deal with reality. In which I like to think I have been successful. As was poor Savelli."

"He and Giusti were enemies, I understand."

"Foolish young men…"

"You don't think their quarrel was serious enough to lead to murder? Even in self-defense? An argument, a fight, even, that got out of hand?"

"The police found no evidence of a fight," Premarin said. "Only unprovoked murder. That is not Giusti's way."

Solomon's instincts were much the same, though there were unplumbed depths of emotion in Giusti. "Who would resort to such a way? Who would have a motive strong enough to commit murder? Or to send an assassin to do so?"

"No one," Premarin said. "There has been enough death in Venice. And Savelli was good for the city."

"And yet he is dead," Solomon said deliberately. "Do you know why he hired his bodyguards?"

"To protect his wife."

"From what?"

Premarin smiled, almost indulgently. "From his imaginary fears."

"Have we come back to Giusti?"

"No," Premarin said. "To Savelli himself. Elena is as virtuous as she is beautiful. Everyone knows that."

"But Savelli didn't trust her?"

"He didn't trust himself. He never forgot that she was once betrothed to another. Even though Giusti never went near her."

"These men that he hired, do you know anything about them?"

"No, but the police do. Unsavory types. And then there was the thief Savelli apprehended, who escaped. My firm belief is that one of those low creatures committed this crime."

"Isn't that a little too comfortable?"

"It does not comfort me," Premarin said with dignity. "Nor Signora Savelli, I daresay, who lives under the same roof as these men."

Solomon suddenly remembered Elena ordering about the men who had tried to intimidate Constance. They had obeyed her immediately, and she had clearly expected them to. She was a strong woman, of course, and used to commanding her household, but what if...

What if one of those bravos had turned on Savelli *on Elena's orders*?

Shoving that possibility aside for future consideration, Solomon tried to concentrate on Premarin while he had the man's attention. They were in St. Mark's Square now, and the magnificence, the beauty, struck him all over again. The Basilica of San Marco, with its domes and spires, rose in unique, unequaled splendor. He could almost imagine himself among the ghosts of men who had walked here hundreds of years ago.

"When did you last see Signor Savelli?" he asked.

"The day before he died. When we heard about the government contract. He was quite gracious about it."

He could afford to be, since he had won it. "Did you mind?"

"It hardly ruined me."

"How was he that day? Did he seem well? Worried or distracted?"

Premarin seemed about to wave away such concerns, but his hand fell back to his side as he considered. "Actually, he was a little...unlike himself. He did not appear to be particularly elated—not as I would have been—to win the contract. He *was* distracted, as though something else entirely was on his mind."

"Did he tell you what that was? Give you any clue?"

"He was not a confiding sort of a man. And to my shame, I did not inquire. I was thinking of my own disappointment."

They were drawing nearer to the basilica now. Lots of somberly dressed people were walking in. The service would be well attended. Solomon wondered if this would be any comfort to the widow.

Premarin halted and turned to face him. "Mr. Grey," he said seriously, "I would advise you to leave the matter in the safe hands of the police. Foscolo is a good man. And no one wants the truth more than Herr von Lampl, who is ambitious and quite obsessive. You are quite safe from prosecution. You are recently married, yes? Enjoy Venice with your wife." He beamed and offered his hand. Leaning closer, he whispered, "And in a day or so, perhaps you and I might talk business."

CONSTANCE, AWARE OF the constant conversation in front, found her own companion harder work. For one thing, Signora Premarin spoke no English, and Constance had very little faith in her own poor Italian. Also, the younger woman's wide-eyed stare was quite disconcerting. Constance had to make all the effort.

"It is a tragic day for Signora Savelli," she said in Italian. Or, at least, she hoped that was what she said. "Are you a close friend?"

The girl shook her head with surprising firmness and issued a sudden blast of words, which Constance eventually untangled enough to understand that Signora Savelli was her husband's friend and much too clever for poor Bianca Premarin. Signor Savelli, however, was the kindest man in the world.

"Kind?" Constance repeated, to be sure she had understood the word. No one had mentioned Savelli's kindness before.

"To me," the girl said with a blushing, proud, yet secretive smile.

Constance tried again. "Did the couple visit you?"

"Yes. Sometimes." A pause. "We visit them also. We dine together."

"When did you last dine together?" Constance asked hopefully.

"Last week."

"Ah. Um… Were they a happy couple?"

"Beautiful," said Signora Premarin reverently, but again with the secretive smile.

"How long have you been married, signora?"

"For two years."

"Then you have a lively stepfamily."

The girl shuddered, though it may have been due to a sudden gust of chilly wind as they entered St. Mark's Square.

"Did you see Signor Savelli again? After the last time you dined together?"

This time, color flooded the young woman's face and she increased her pace, muttering, "My husband…"

By the time they caught up, the men were already shaking hands to part and there was much bowing and curtseying before the Premarins turned toward the great doors of the church, and Constance and Solomon stood gazing up at the stunning stonework and glass.

She had already seen the wondrous inside of the church, but she doubted one would ever get used to the beauty, either of the inside or out.

They turned reluctantly, retracing their steps to return to their boat. Constance dragged her mind back to order.

"That girl," she said, "was infatuated with Savelli."

Solomon looked startled. "Really? Were they having an affair?"

"That would rather turn everything we think we know on its head, wouldn't it? But honestly, I don't see it. I think it's all in her mind, like a fantasy. A young woman married—no doubt by her family—to an older man who must present quite an unheroic figure to a romantic girl. And then there is Savelli, young and handsome and equally successful, apparently kind to her."

"Not more than kind?"

She shrugged. "There is no accounting for taste, but if I were married to Elena, I would not look twice at that girl. I'm not sure

Premarin does."

"But from Savelli's point of view… He is married to that strong woman whose feelings he suspects of ambivalence at the least. Would the doe-eyed devotion of a starry-eyed young woman not be appealing?"

"No one has suggested either Savelli was unfaithful. Her infatuation might have been balm to his troubled soul, but I doubt he acted upon it. She is not exactly grieving, from what I observed. It's just a story to her. Did you learn anything from Premarin himself?"

Solomon shrugged. "Just that Savelli won a lucrative government contract they both wanted and didn't seem to appreciate his good fortune enough. This was the day before he died, and Premarin found him a little distracted. He admitted he resented not being granted this contract—though he might get it now that Savelli is dead, I suppose. I don't know what happens to the business."

Contance blinked. "It would be quite cold to murder someone just to win a bit of business."

"Especially when they seem to have been friends of a sort. Besides, Premarin might be quick, clever, even ruthless, but he is hardly stupid enough to take such a risk as to murder a man at his own back door."

"Not for business. But then, no one would murder for such a reason, would they? There has to be something deeper involved."

Solomon cocked an eyebrow. "Like Premarin's wife?"

"Many men do regard their wives, however neglected, as possessions, and they certainly don't like other men to touch." She sighed. "Though on the face of it, she is unlikely to inspire a crime of passion."

"What if it isn't?" Solomon said, his face suddenly intense. "Think about it. One blow straight through the heart—can that be luck? Or is it the skilled attack of an assassin? And there were plenty of those, surely in his own house."

"Because he didn't pay them?" she said doubtfully. "Dismissed them for abducting me? Then why would they stay? They are still at the Palazzo Savelli."

"Because they acted for Elena."

Her breath caught. "Could she do that? *Would* she? If she wanted to be with Giusti, why did she choose Savelli?"

"Because he is rich. Giusti has nothing. This way, she has the chance of Giusti and, presumably, Savelli's fortune."

Constance did not like it. She could tell Solomon didn't either, yet they had to consider it. And it made a horrible kind of sense. "She was so helpful to us when I expected her to throw us out."

"Perhaps she could afford to be. At worst, she can cast the blame on whichever bravo committed the murder. Her hands are clean, and it is her word against his."

She shook her head. "But why was Savelli outside in the dark without his coat? Dealing with some perceived crisis made up by his murderer? It's possible, isn't it? But there's no proof, and I don't like it."

"Premarin wants us to leave it all to the authorities. He seems to admire Foscolo. And Lampl. In fact, he thinks we should just relax and enjoy our honeymoon."

"It's a valid point of view, but I would rather know the truth before they haul you off to prison."

"I'm sure it will be a great comfort."

INSIDE THE BASILICO di San Marco, Bianca Premarin fixed her gaze upon the beautiful face of the *Madonna Nicopeia*, the icon that had been Venice's pride and joy for centuries. Signor Savelli had told her once that it had been stolen from the Christians of Byzantium, which was probably why it meant so much to her. Not because it was stolen or came from a country that no longer existed, but because he had talked to her about it.

The smell of incense, and the droning voices of priests and mourners, spilled suddenly into her consciousness and she realized he would never talk to her again. She would never see him again. He was dead.

Grief flooded into her eyes, along with sheer hopelessness. What did she have now, except her rich old husband and his maddening children?

No wonder the Madonna looked disappointed in her, pointing to her own child. In sudden terror, Bianca recognized her terrible sins, sins she could never confess, let alone be absolved of. She was doomed to hell for love. For murder.

Paralyzed, silently weeping, she could not even see the Madonna now except as a blue-and-gold blur. But she could not hide from God or her sin. And she would never have Angelo to lend her strength.

Lost. I am lost. What have I done…?

CHAPTER NINE

IN THE PAST, when Constance had insinuated herself into respectable Society, she had done so in the spirit of flimflam and a brash, devil-may-care attitude. It had even amused her to think of her companions' horror if only they knew she was the bastard daughter of a drunken whore and fence of stolen goods, and a genuine brothel madam in her own right.

That was before Solomon. She was no longer pretending to be his wife, though sometimes she still felt as if she were acting a part on the stage. Like now. Entering the consulate reception on his arm, she had to stop her nervous hands smoothing her gown and fluttering about her hair. She felt stiff, her smile like wax. She would never admit nervousness, even to Solomon, but in truth she would have died rather than let him down.

She tried to imagine she was in her own establishment, greeting guests at the civilized evening parties that were the tasteful prelude to expensive transactions. And that helped. At least she could relax her grip on Solomon's sleeve to that of a mere vise.

Only the first person she saw was *him*.

The gray-bearded Englishman she had first noticed at the opera and then on the gondola sailing beneath the nearest bridge to their house. She had forgotten all about him in the recent excitement, but now the odd nature of his stare came back with a vengeance, for he glanced over his companion's shoulder and saw her.

For an instant, he looked stunned—he most certainly recognized her—but this time it was he who looked away.

Solomon winced, and she realized she had dug her fingers into his flesh rather than his coat sleeve. She loosened them at once. "Sorry. He's here, that Englishman we keep seeing."

"Well, it is the British consulate," Solomon pointed out.

She was lost then in a maze of introductions as they were formally welcomed and a young man called Mr. Simons attached himself to them.

"I'm so glad you could come," he gushed. "We had no idea you were in Venice until Mr. Kellar told us."

"Mr. Kellar?" Solomon said, accepting a glass of wine that Mr. Simons ferried to them from a waiter's tray.

"Mr. Sebastian Kellar," Simons clarified, nodding toward the mysterious Englishman, who, in fact, was chuckling away with another unexpected figure—Ludovico Giusti.

For some reason, this gave Constance a fresh jolt. Was this Kellar somehow involved in Savelli's murder? Or at least in her abduction by Savelli's thugs? He *had* been watching her...

"Are you here in Venice for business or pleasure, Mr. Grey?" Simons asked.

"Oh, definitely the latter," Solomon replied. "This is our wedding trip."

"Oh! Congratulations, sir! I wish you both very happy indeed! Are you acquainted with Mrs. Hargreaves?"

It was, Constance realized, a familiar kind of party, designed to gather gossip and provide opportunity for British people to do themselves and each other favors in the way of trade and diplomacy. Naturally, much of this involved fellow foreigners as well as Venetian natives, and Constance soon found herself in conversation with a British diplomat's wife, two Italians, an American, and a German. She had nothing to offer any of them, but they seemed flatteringly enchanted with her anyway. Perhaps they were looking for an introduction to Solomon.

But it was clearly not the thing to chat too long to one group of people. Everyone mingled, flitting from group to group like bees collecting pollen. To Constance, the party was suddenly easy to navigate—it really *was* like evenings at the establishment. She was only there to look pretty and make introductions. Men laughed and admired her, almost eating out of her hand. It even seemed her struggling Italian was improving.

She met up again with Mrs. Hargreaves and reminded herself why she had wanted to come. "Tell me, ma'am," she said confidentially, "were you acquainted with Angelo Savelli, who died so tragically a few days ago?"

"Of course. I believe he would have been here tonight. So shocking! I have always found Venice such a delightful, friendly city."

"Indeed, that is my experience. But someone murdered Signor Savelli. Can you imagine why anyone would possibly do such a thing?"

Mrs. Hargreaves shuddered. "That is for the police, my dear. They have to do something other than read people's letters and spy on their conversations. Talking of whom..." She glanced significantly across the room, and, following her gaze, Constance saw the Austrian policeman Lampl enter, along with Signor Premarin. They appeared to be deep in conversation.

"He is *that* sort of policeman?" Constance said.

"Is there any other here?" Mrs. Hargreaves said cynically, and flitted away.

Constance sipped her wine and wondered if there were any truth in the older woman's accusation. She knew Venice well, after all. But Constance had found Lampl genuinely interested in the case. She did wonder if he would be quite so interested in the murder of someone like Giusti, who was not Austria's friend, but he had seemed to be encouraging Foscolo and asking pertinent questions of his own.

Perhaps she should approach him here in this sociable environment... But before she could move toward them, someone else caught her eye—a maidservant in a slightly crooked cap and ill-tied apron, who was collecting abandoned glasses and plates onto the tray she carried. She looked familiar, yet it took Constance several moments to place her.

The surroundings were vastly different, and the girl's hair was considerably tidier. Also, her expression was less exasperated, less aggressive. But it was undoubtedly Adriana, the girl who appeared to live with the artist Domenico Rossi, though whether as maid, mistress, or model was not quite clear.

How odd to find her working here… Or perhaps not. No doubt the money was useful during Rossi's lean—and drunk—periods.

Constance watched her balance the tray or her hip, add another glass to the collection, and then vanish with her burden through the service door at the back. The Englishman, Kellar, strolled across her line of vision, drawing her eyes with him to the elegant buffet table.

She cast a quick glance at Lampl and Premarin, who had been her original quarry. She still wished to speak to them.

But first, she thought, turning back to Kellar with a surge of determination, *you.*

She made no effort to disguise her goal, walking straight toward him, and as he turned from the buffet table, a small plate in one hand, he saw her coming. The hand reaching for whatever delicacy was on his plate fell back to his side. As their eyes clashed, he acknowledged her as before with a small inclination of his head and moved on.

It had never entered her head that he would try to avoid her after staring so often. *Interesting.* She changed her direction to match his and kept walking, like a warship on a course of interception.

And like the pursued ship, he paused, then turned to face the inevitable.

"Good evening," he said pleasantly, abandoning his untouched plate on the nearest table.

"Good evening," Constance replied. "Forgive me, but I seem to know your face so well that I'm sure we must have met before."

She held his gaze with conscious boldness but sensed no threat. There was wariness and curiosity in his intelligent gray eyes and a hint of tension in his posture.

"No, we have never met," he said. "But you do remind me of someone. I suppose this is where I should apologize if I offended you by staring. The similarity is really most marked. My name is Kellar. Sebastian Kellar. I am something of a roving diplomat in Italy, though I contrive to be in Venice as often as possible."

She offered her hand. "Constance Grey. I am visiting the city for the first time with my husband. It is our wedding trip."

There was no surprise in those amiable eyes. None of this was news to him. He had told the consulate staff who Solomon was.

"Allow me to wish you every happiness. Your husband is an interesting man. I had not realized he was so young."

Was it Solomon who interested him, then? Why? "He will get older in the normal way of things. So, you must know Venice and all these people"—she made a small hand gesture encompassing the reception room—"very well?"

"I am acquainted with most of them."

She held on to his gaze. "Perhaps you knew the man who died. Angelo Savelli?"

"I did. Another interesting man. And a tragic loss to Venice— also to Austria, I suspect."

"And to Britain?"

He smiled faintly and took a glass of wine from the tray being offered. "Her Majesty's government supports the notion of a united and independent Italy. *Risorgimento*. Savelli did not, but he was a man we could all work with."

"Was he?" Wild ideas were flying through her mind. *Had* the British been able to work with Savelli? Or had they found him so unbending and so capable that their secret forces—even this roving diplomat himself—had removed him?

Is Kellar an assassin?

The notion chilled her blood, even while her brain scoffed at such melodramatic imaginings. And yet those outwardly kind, affable gray eyes hid something. Why had he noticed her? Was his notice the real reason Savelli had abducted her? Had the Venetian's outrage at her abduction been manufactured that night? She had not thought so at the time, but…

She threw off the welter of speculation before it drowned her.

"Oh yes," Kellar was saying, "I believe so. He was a good man in many ways. But I have heard your experience might be…different."

She raised her eyebrows, refusing to hide or be ashamed. She had plenty of practice in that. "You heard about my abduction?"

His brow twitched very slightly. Surprise? Distaste? "Then it is true?"

"It was apparently a misunderstanding by his servants. He released me almost immediately. By which time, my husband was already at his door."

"Mr. Grey must have been extraordinarily angry."

Oh, no, you will not pin your own crimes or anyone else's on Solomon. "He was more concerned with my safety. By the time he called on Savelli to demand explanation, the man was already dead."

"I was not accusing your husband," Kellar said mildly. "On the contrary, Her Majesty's government would take a very dim view of any such suspicion."

Constance remembered her wine with sudden gratitude and sipped it, giving herself a moment to think. "Is that meant to comfort me?"

"I hope so. The local police regard it as a local matter. You really do remind me of someone most strongly. Might I know your maiden name?"

Fresh alarm bells rang in her mind. Had he attended her establishment in the past? She remembered most faces that had passed through over the years, for safety reasons as well as business ones. Guests liked to be remembered and greeted as old friends on return visits. No, she was almost certain he had never been there. He could still know her name, but then, there had never been any point in keeping that secret. She and Solomon had married openly.

She tilted her chin. "Silver," she said, without dropping her gaze.

His wine rippled in its glass. Around his beard, his face seemed to whiten. Then he laughed softly, as though he couldn't help it.

"Of course it is. I knew your mother."

As THEY HAD agreed, Solomon was using the reception to learn what he could from the privileged and the knowledgeable. Savelli's name was certainly mentioned several times in hushed tones, by both Venetians and foreigners, though few brought the subject up directly in conversation.

One who did was Mrs. Collins, the wife of a British wine merchant. "I suppose you will have heard of this shocking murder," she said almost as soon as they had been introduced. She didn't trouble to lower her voice. "One of their most prominent citizens, apparently. And to think someone assured me that Northern Italians were so much more civilized that their southern brethren! I told Mr. Collins that I simply refuse to go to Naples."

Solomon blinked. His instinct was to give a biting rejoinder on the nature of British crime, prejudice, and rudeness. But he doubted either of them would learn anything from such a lecture.

"Were you acquainted with Signor Savelli?"

"He was pointed out to me once." Her nostrils flared. "By his wife. Oh, we are not friends, of course. I doubt she has many of those, for she is a most proud and disagreeable person. Only the men cluster around her. One can only speculate as to why."

Startled, Solomon missed his moment to defend the widow, for Mrs. Collins barely paused to draw breath.

"Oh, she is beautiful, I grant you, if you care for that heavy, dramatic look, but I could tell at once she was not the sort of female one ought to know. If you ask me, she did away with her own husband."

Solomon fixed his gaze to the self-satisfied yet outraged woman beside him. "What makes you think so?"

"She ignored her husband, spent all her time talking to other men."

Solomon had rarely found the business of investigation so distasteful. But he managed—he hoped—to keep all expression from his face, save polite interest. "Which other men?"

She flapped one dismissive hand, her gaze darting around the room. "*Him*, for a start." She indicated the small, bustling figure of Premarin, who had just entered the room with Lampl. "Both of them, in fact. Though they say she had been conducting an affair for years with someone called Justin or something, *and* with some common portrait painter."

"Giusti?" Solomon murmured. "And Rossi? Really? One wonders where she found the time to fit those other gentlemen in."

She blinked at him several times, as though she suspected him of mockery but could not find the proof. "Foreigners," she pronounced finally, as though that sealed some argument.

"One finds them everywhere," Solomon murmured. "Especially abroad." From the corner of his eye, he saw Constance, talking to the Englishman who kept crossing their path. Kellar. He hoped she was learning something.

"Are *you* English?" Mrs. Collins asked suddenly.

Solomon brought his gaze back to find her peering at him quite closely. "On my father's side."

She sniffed, as though that were better than nothing. "Mark my words. The wife did it."

"I KNEW YOUR mother."

The words seemed to crash over Constance with all the force of a wave at high tide. Abruptly, Kellar's hand closed around hers on her wine glass, and she realized she had been about to drop it. She grasped it more firmly, keeping her eyes on his face, and after a moment, he released her hand.

"I startled you," he said.

That was an understatement. No one admitted to knowing Juliet. Well, no one with any claims to respectability.

"It was many years ago," he added, with a hint of anxiety. "I hope she is well?"

He was afraid she was dead… "Actually, she is very well, better than she has been for years." Having given up whoring in favor of fencing stolen goods, Juliet had now given up both, and, with Solomon's help, was running a rather charming shop of antiquities and curiosities in Covent Garden. She had even—almost—given up the gin. Did Kellar know all this?

"Might I ask you a personal question?" he asked.

"Why not?" she said, just a little wildly.

"How old are you?"

This time, her fingers tightened on the glass. They were shaking as she raised it to her lips. "I am twenty-seven years old."

Something changed in his face. She could not tell if it was relief or disappointment, but it was profound.

"It has been thirty years since I last saw your mother," he said, his voice casual, although his eyes were not.

His eyes told her it mattered, and she knew why. Ever since she could remember, she had wondered who her father was. She had even tried to find out, tracing some of her mother's old clients of the right time and place. In fact, it was on one such foolish errand that she had got to know Solomon. But that was irrelevant here. She hadn't wanted her father to be some drunken ne'er-do-well, some vice-ridden brute who visited whores on a Saturday night and beat his wife on Sundays. She had fantasized that her father was a gentleman, and not even because she had wanted a share of his money—she hadn't. She had wanted to belong to something, someone, who was not squalid or sordid.

Foolish. Gentlemen visited whores too. And beat their wives. Vice and corruption were not the preserve of the lower orders.

Somewhere in the last year, she had lost that secret dream. She belonged to Solomon and he to her. And Juliet, she had finally recognized, had always done her best for her. She had taught her to read and write and to survive. The rest didn't matter. Everyone had frailties.

Yet now, when she didn't care, here was a man she might have liked to be her father. *Might*. He spoke of Juliet without contempt, remembered her name and, whatever else, had been prepared to acknowledge Constance as his daughter.

Only she could not be.

She laughed. "Is that what scared you? That I might have been thirty-one years old?"

"It scared me that I might have behaved so badly in youth and was not even aware of the consequences. Did your mother ever speak of me?"

She stared at him. "No. She never spoke of men to me, except in warning."

He closed his eyes, hiding.

And then someone touched her elbow. She did not have to look to know it was Solomon. Everything was suddenly bearable again.

"This is my husband, Solomon Grey. Solomon, meet Mr. Kellar, apparently a friend of my mother's."

If Solomon was surprised by the connection to Juliet—and he must have been—he gave no sign of it, merely shook hands with Kellar, who, apparently overcoming whatever emotion his past had aroused, was once more urbane and smiling.

"Mr. Grey. A pleasure to meet you at last. What do you think of Venice?"

They made small talk for a little, and then, as Constance had expected, Kellar excused himself.

Quite *unexpectedly*, however, he caught her gaze. "I believe you are staying at the Palazzo Zulian in Cannaregio. Perhaps I may call on you there?"

"We would be delighted," Constance said at once, although she wondered if it were true.

As Kellar smiled and moved away, she turned impulsively to Solomon, ready to pour everything out—whatever everything was. But Solomon had changed his position, and instead she almost bumped into Giusti, who appeared to be in something of a rush. He paused and smiled at them both, while Solomon rescued Constance's again precarious wine glass and placed it on the table beside Kellar's untouched plate.

"We meet again," Giusti said amiably. "How go your inquiries?"

"In circles," Solomon said. "Though everyone appears to have an opinion."

"How many people told you it was me?"

"A few."

Giusti sighed. "At least the British still invite me."

"What is your connection to the consulate?" Constance asked.

"None. Except they occasionally throw me a bone—a little business to keep the wolf from the door. Or the tiles on the roof." He lowered his voice and winked. "Everyone keeps in with the British, but they prefer my politics."

"And Premarin's?" Constance said lightly.

He sighed. "Mostly. He is here, too."

"I saw that. We met him earlier today. He was on his way to the funeral service. With his wife."

Giusti was silent for a moment. Then he said, "I thought about going, but decided in the end I should not be welcome. I thought of him. I'm sorry he is dead."

"Tell me," Constance said, looking casually about her to ensure she would not be overheard, "was there ever as much as a whisper about Savelli and Signora Premarin?"

Giusti blinked. "Not that I heard. But then, I avoid gossip." He considered it. "I would not be surprised at gossip, only the reality. As I said, ask Elena. If such a whisper existed, some kind friend will have made sure she heard it. Goodbye!"

He dodged around them, trying and failing to dart away before Lampl reached them.

"Signor," Giusti said, bowing elaborately to the Austrian before blowing a kiss to Constance and sauntering off with an impudent grin.

"I'm very glad to see you here," Solomon said to Lampl. "It will hopefully save our calling upon you in the morning."

"Is there something I can help you with?" Lampl said politely. "Or do you have information for me? Something you have remembered, perhaps?"

"No," Solomon said apologetically. "I merely wanted to ask what your medical examiner had to say about the body. I assume his examination is complete, since Signor Savelli was buried today."

Lampl regarded Solomon carefully, as though weighing whether or not it would hurt to answer him. "He is satisfied, of course."

"And what were his findings?"

Lampl frowned, casting a warning glance toward Constance.

"You may speak in front of my wife," Solomon said.

Lampl clearly did not approve. He said stiffly, "Very well, then. Savelli was stabbed through the heart with the long, thin blade we discovered still in his body. He died, probably immediately, of that wound. There was no water in his lungs, so he did not drown in the canal."

"And you believe this blade belonged to Savelli himself?" Solomon asked.

"We know it did. It is a weapon I have seen in his house

many times."

"I see," Solomon said.

One of the bodyguard? Elena? "Could they tell from the angle of the wound," Constance asked, "whether he was stabbed by a taller or a shorter person?"

Lampl looked scandalized by the very question. Or perhaps just the fact that a woman had asked it. "No," he said coldly. "The wound was precise."

"If the blade was Savelli's own," Solomon said, "that surely limits your suspects to his household."

"You would think so," said another voice between the table and Solomon. It was Foscolo, underdressed and out of place. "But, in fact, we believe Savelli himself carried the dagger with him, perhaps for protection. There were threads on it that could have come from his trousers, which were torn below the waist as though the knife had poked through or ripped the fabric when being drawn."

"What are you doing here?" Lampl asked with suppressed anger.

Solomon did not give Foscolo time to answer his superior. "So, the killer snatched the victim's own knife?"

"We believe so. Which certainly does not *preclude* members of his household." Foscolo turned to Lampl, but Solomon had more questions.

"Signora Savelli told us about a thief her husband apprehended in San Marco a couple of months ago. He made threats against Savelli."

Lampl gazed at him haughtily, as though he would not discuss the matter. Constance suspected he simply had no idea what Solomon was talking about.

Foscolo said, "He did, but he went to prison just the same."

"Is he still there?" Constance asked.

Foscolo's lips twitched. "Yes, signora, he is."

Constance met Solomon's gaze, with a resigned lift of one shoulder. A hopeful suspect eliminated.

"Do you have a moment, signor?" Foscolo said to Lampl.

Lampl moved, grasping his underling by the elbow.

Solomon stepped aside to give them privacy, murmuring, "Excuse me."

He did not move far, however. No doubt his ears, like hers, were straining to catch what was said. Constance, however, could not make heads nor tails of the rapid, almost whispered sounds, and from his frustrated frown, neither could Solomon.

"Excuse me," he said again, retrieving Constance's glass from the table beside the policemen, and returning it to her before offering his arm. "I still heard nothing," he murmured.

Constance grimaced, looking about her. "So, we are back to the suspects we like."

"Apparently so." He nodded across the room. "Premarin?" he suggested.

"Why not?" She took his arm as they walked between groups of people who chattered in similarly cultured tones, but in many different languages and sometimes in a mixture. "What else have you learned?"

"That I don't like the British abroad. How does Kellar know your mother?"

"I have absolutely no idea. I'm still staggered that he admitted to it without threat of violence. There he is."

Premarin appeared delighted to see them and introduced them to his companions.

"How was the funeral service?" Constance asked sympathetically.

"Moving," said Premarin with a sigh. "And so sad. We returned to the Palazzo Savelli to pay our respects to the signora, but I don't think she was in a fit state, so we did not stay. Poor Elena."

"Is Signora Premarin very upset too?"

Premarin blinked. "Of course. Oh, you mean that she does not accompany me to this reception? Between ourselves, she does not care for such events, and she feels hampered by speaking no

English."

It was just a little too much explanation. Covering, perhaps, for the fact that he had not asked her. Or thought of her, probably.

With an air of mischievous conspiracy, Premarin swiped an open bottle from the tray of a hurrying waiter and topped up Constance's glass, then Solomon's and his own. "The wine at these affairs is always excellent," he confided, his eyes twinkling. "Of course, I supply it…"

Constance noticed Foscolo leaving again. She wondered if he had come only to pass something on to his superior. Or if he had been invited and Lampl had jealously sent him away.

"I saw you talking to Mr. Kellar," Premarin said jovially. Adriana slipped past him, collecting more plates and glasses. "One meets him all over Italy. Do you know him well?"

"No, this was our first meeting," Solomon said. "He is a diplomat, I believe."

"At the very least. He has a finger in many pies. A little like yourself, Mr. Grey."

"I have never been a diplomat."

Premarin smiled. "There is still time. I wonder why Foscolo did not stay? Perhaps Lampl sent him off to follow Giusti."

"I suppose Giusti has to be their prime suspect," Solomon murmured.

Premarin made a dismissive gesture with one hand. "It is not in his nature. Not like that. My money is on Savelli's own servants. Which would really be the best outcome for everyone."

Except Savelli. Constance sipped her wine and shivered. She felt suddenly chilled, as though an ominous cloud was growing closer. It made her feel slightly dizzy.

CHAPTER TEN

HALF AN HOUR later, she was heartily relieved when Solomon suggested leaving. For the last few minutes, she had felt distinctly shaky and unwell, and besides, the guests were thinning out.

She was glad of Solomon's arm out in the fresh air, like an anchor in a suddenly unsteady world. Kellar had disturbed her more than he should, and she was anxious to discuss him with Solomon, the good and the bad suspicions.

But Solomon was talking, and it was oddly difficult to concentrate. "…divided between Giusti and the widow. Though one Englishwoman's opinion seemed to be based solely on the fact that they were all foreign. She accused Signora Savelli of multiple affairs, including with Giusti, Premarin, and even Domenico Rossi."

Constance frowned and peered at him. "Is Kellar a spy of some kind? An assassin? Am I tipsy?"

Solomon smiled. She loved his smile, but it died disappointingly quickly and now he was frowning. "Actually, you don't look well."

"I don't feel well," she admitted. "Where is Alvise?" *Don't let me be sick in the boat…*

But the movement of the water beneath proved too much for her roiling stomach and she was violently ill. The delight of traveling by traditional gondola vanished into misery, until she latched on to one incredible idea.

Some women were terribly ill during pregnancy, at least in the early stages.

Admittedly, it was generally in the morning, but not always. Until Solomon, she had never imagined she would ever have children, and even when they were married, the idea had been sweet, confusing, and unreal. Now, her skin clammy, her head swimming, and her stomach in torment, she hung on to the idea with fierce, desperate hope. She could bear anything for this reason…

But she was barely aware of anything else. She knew Solomon was carrying her off the boat and into the house, heard his urgent voice demanding a doctor in both Italian and English, but by then her main concern was not losing any more dignity, and she somehow staggered alone into the privy.

After that, awash with pain and sweat and shivering so violently that she couldn't speak, she knew very little.

IT WAS STILL early in the morning when Elena Savelli somewhat listlessly broke her fast with coffee and bread. She felt exhausted, but then, she had not been sleeping well since Angelo's death—or before, really. She seemed twisted up with guilt and grief as well as hopelessness. But she was so tired of those feelings, vaguely aware that they had been building within her for some months before he died.

Before he was murdered.

Yesterday, she had buried him. She had sat in the great, beautiful church, trying to pray for Angelo's soul. She had accepted the condolences of, it seemed, the entire city—certainly of all the most prominent citizens and their Austrian masters. Veiled and numb, she had accepted it all, had even hosted the gathering here at the palazzo, with generous amounts of food and wine. She had been going through the motions, giving Angelo the respect that was his due, but then, so had they, and most had not stayed long.

Her own family had stayed away.

It was done now. He was buried. And she had no idea what to do with herself. The lawyers had told her everything was hers. His houses, his businesses, all his possessions. Many people wanted to manage everything for her. But she could manage everything just as well, she thought, given time. She just couldn't summon the desire or the energy.

Soon. Soon, I will. Perhaps when Foscolo arrests someone—or gives up.

"Signora, Dr. Donati is here."

Elena blinked at her maidservant. "Why? Who is ill?"

"He has come to see you, signora."

In fact, the young doctor stepped around the maid, bowing. "Forgive the early hour, signora, but I was passing and your servants told me you were up."

"But I am not ill."

"You will be if you do not sleep."

Elena flicked one finger, dismissing the girl. She invited the doctor to sit and regarded him. "So will you. You look dreadful."

He smiled wearily. "I have been up all night with a patient. Which is why I call on you now, so that I can sleep with a clear conscience."

"You cannot doctor loss. Though I admit I would welcome something to help me sleep. I hope your night's work was successful."

"So do I," Donati said ruefully, reaching into his bag. "A young foreign lady, terribly ill from…food poisoning."

"Poor creature. Bad clams?"

"Not clams." The doctor took a large bottle from his bag and began to decant some of it into a smaller bottle. "Two drops of this at bedtime and you should sleep until morning. I will come back in a week if you don't send for me before. Are you eating properly?"

"Yes," she said, though in fact she wasn't sure. "What did the foreign lady eat?"

"Nothing, apparently."

She frowned at him, interested in spite of herself. His face was carefully expressionless. Clearly, he did not want to talk about it, but he was troubled, worried.

"Is what she did *not* eat something you should report to the police?" she asked.

Deliberately, he thrust the little bottle of sleeping draft across the table to her. He said nothing, yet some emotion flickering in his eyes caught at her breath.

In spite of herself, she leaned forward. "Who is this lady?"

"The Englishwoman. Signora Grey."

Her blood seemed to surge. Without intending it, she was on her feet. "No. I cannot allow it. Will she live?"

"I hope so."

"But she has no one to nurse her but servants. I will go to her."

"Signora, is that wise?" he blurted.

She stared at him. "Meaning if she dies, I will be under suspicion for two murders?"

He blushed painfully. "I know better. Besides, I see no reason for Signora Grey's illness to be connected to your husband's death."

Except by me. "I have to go. Thank you for the medicine. Go home and sleep."

She was already walking away. But at least her brain had cleared. She knew the risks to herself, to her reputation, but in truth, she did not care.

Half an hour later, she strode into the Palazzo Zulian, at her most imperious. She did not even wait, following the servant directly upstairs to the sick room.

"Signor, Signora Savelli—" the servant began.

Elena brushed past her. "How is she?"

Constance Grey was deathly pale, almost one with the pillow cases that surrounded her, apart from her bright red-gold hair.

Her eyes looked bruised, the lids like scribbled-on paper, and she lay so still that Elena was afraid she was already dead.

From the chair beside the bed, Solomon Grey stumbled to his feet. "She is asleep."

His appearance was almost as shocking as his wife's. The urbane, handsome man, whose personality had so easily commanded her drawing room, had shrunk. His golden-brown skin looked gray, his clear, melting brown eyes distraught with more than exhaustion. Much more. Even recognition seemed to take time to register.

"She was poisoned," he said harshly.

It might have been an accusation. "Where? When? Who was there? How could it have happened? The doctor told me she ate nothing."

He blinked. He was in no condition to consider causes and culprits. His whole being was concentrated on his wife's recovery. Elena's heart contracted and seemed to swell, breaking through the fog of her own misery, for right now, his was greater. She had never seen such fear in a man, even during the siege. That had been a different kind of fear. This, she had no name for.

But her words reached him. She saw them register. Yet still he stared at her. "Go home, signora."

His suspicion did not even hurt. She understood it perfectly. "I am the last person in the world to hurt her. If she dies while I am here, nothing can save me."

The woman on the bed stirred, as though their voices had disturbed her. Abruptly, Grey sat down on the edge of the bed and took his wife's hand. Her eyes fluttered open.

"Sol." It was little more than a sigh, a croak, but incredibly, the woman's beautiful mouth twitched into something approaching a smile. Even now, his mere presence made her happy.

Elena's heart ached. Not with resentment but with loss.

Constance's eyelids drooped again, then suddenly opened again. She was looking at Elena.

"Is she real?" she asked her husband.

"Yes."

"I came to help," Elena said, "if I can. You have no family here, after all."

"Neither do you."

From nowhere, tears crowded into Elena's throat.

The Englishwoman's eyes closed. "I am so tired. Look after Solomon..."

SOLOMON HAD NEVER spent such a night of fear and anguish. Not even in childhood when his brother David had vanished, for that had been a much more gradual understanding. This sudden, visceral knowledge that he was losing Constance, when he had only just found her, devastated him. He could only bathe her hands and face in the hope of comforting her fevered body. He would have given everything to take her pain himself.

Despite her suffering, she had wept only once, when the doctor first arrived and asked if she could be with child. It was Solomon who had told him it was possible, but Dr. Donati had quickly ruled out the possibility. He told Solomon it was food poisoning and went very quiet as Solomon explained that Constance had eaten nothing since midday.

Urgently mixing potions, the doctor had asked questions about where they had been and what they had drunk, and somehow Solomon had absorbed the knowledge that Constance had been deliberately poisoned. The importance was very much secondary, however. None of it mattered if she did not live.

Until Elena Savelli arrived, and abruptly every nerve seemed to scream with alarm.

Yet it was her questions that aroused him from his torpor: *"Where? When? Who was there?"* More importantly, they seemed to waken Constance from hers. Although appallingly weak, she was still his Constance, flooding him with hope. And the fact that she did not object to Elena's presence made him think.

Elena was right. Constance's death in her presence would see Elena arrested, rightly or wrongly.

Struggling over his own exhausted fears, he recognized finally that the doctor would not have left the house if he truly feared still for his patient's life.

"Her heart is still strong. She can't have ingested much, and much of what she did take must have been expelled. She needs sleep…"

Solomon had barely taken in the words at the time. He was too busy willing her to live.

Leaving his hand in Constance's relaxed fingers, he turned his head slowly to regard the widow. "Where? When? Who was there?" he repeated. "We were at a reception at the British consulate, and the poison must have been in the wine."

"*You* were not ill. Neither was anyone else, or Donati would have told me. The poison was in *her* wine. Why?"

"Because we are asking questions about your husband's murder," he said. "Someone is trying to scare us away before we reach the truth… Should they not be poisoning the police also?"

She shrugged. "The police have an agenda that is not necessarily yours. Who was at the consulate?"

More to the point, who was close enough to put poison in Constance's glass? "Kellar. Premarin. Giusti."

Her eyes flickered. "And the staff?"

He almost groaned. Then the memory flashed through his mind—the girl in the white apron and the slightly crooked cap, flitting around collecting used glasses. "Rossi's girl… Adriana."

Elena frowned. "Why would Rossi's model poison your wife?"

"For Rossi. If he killed your husband." Perhaps he had accepted Solomon's commission only to get close enough to hurt them…then got cold feet and left it to the girl instead.

"Rossi is a drunk. But a talented one. He would rather paint your wife than kill her."

Solomon turned back to Constance. Was he imagining the hint of color in her cheek, the peace of her sleep? "It didn't kill her. Perhaps it was never intended to. Just to frighten."

"I hope you are frightened."

"Oh, I am."

Her brow twitched. "You mentioned Kellar. Sebastian Kellar? Why should he wish your wife—or my husband—ill?"

Because he had confessed his disreputable past to Constance just by asking after her mother? If it bothered him, why mention Juliet at all? He was a subtle and possibly dangerous man, but did he carry poison around in his pocket just in case he ran into someone he wanted rid of?

"I doubt he does," Solomon admitted. "And if he did, he should have dealt with me in the same way."

"But you will take her away now, won't you? You will both leave the city and never come back. And the police will pick some criminal at random to execute for Angelo's murder."

Solomon rubbed the back of his neck, easing an ache he hadn't noticed before. "Why wouldn't they want the truth?"

"Oh, I'm sure they do. They just don't insist on it. Someone will pay, preferably someone who is guilty of *something*."

He dropped his hand back into his lap. "You are cynical."

"I am realistic. And I mistrust Austrian oversight in this case. It means they want a quick result, and Foscolo will go along with it. They must discourage people from doing away with Venetian allies of Austria."

"You are saying that even if the murder is not political, its investigation is?"

"Of course. Signor Grey, let me order some food for you, and then you must rest. I will sit with your wife and call you when she wakes, or if there is any change."

He opened his mouth to speak, his gaze straying to the other side of the bed where he had slept since they had arrived in Venice. He wanted nothing more than to crawl in beside Constance and hold her.

But this was not about him. He needed to do what was best for Constance.

He glanced back to Elena. The woman's rather hard eyes softened, though she must have read the suspicion in his own.

"Whichever maid you trust most, have her sit in here too. Just for an hour or two."

EVERY PART OF Constance ached, outside and in. Behind her was a nightmare of sickness and purging and general awfulness. She felt too weak even to move. Yet she was no longer afraid. For a moment, in fact, she felt so peaceful that she wondered if she had died, and quickly opened her eyes.

If she was dead, so was Elena Savelli, who regarded her over the top of the book in her hands. The book lowered. "You look better. How are you?"

"Not dead. Where is Solomon?"

"In the dressing room. I persuade him to rest."

"That is good… What time is it?"

"Just after two of the clock."

"In the afternoon," Constance said cautiously. "The afternoon *after* I was taken ill?"

"Exactly." Elena spoke in rapid Italian, and the maid Constance had not even noticed—her name was Maria, and she had occasionally helped Constance to dress when Solomon was otherwise engaged—rose and went out with a quick, tremulous smile. "She goes to fetch fresh wine and water, which is all the doctor will allow you."

"I am so thirsty. What is in the glass?" Constance looked at the bedside table.

"The same, but you'll forgive me if I don't let you drink it."

"You were not at the consulate."

"I see you understand what happened to you."

To her horror, weak tears started in her eyes. Fortunately, Solomon emerged from the dressing room with his hair on end and his shirt open at the throat, and she tried to lift her arms toward him. And then he was on the bed with her, cradling her against him.

"I thought I was with child," she wept, and he stroked her hair and kissed her temple until the door clicked and Elena was no longer there. Constance sniffed and gave a watery laugh. "I scared her off. Why did she come?"

"Because she felt sorry for you, I think. And you told her to look after me."

"I thought I dreamed that," Constance said, allowing Solomon to lay her gently back against the pillows in a more upright position, which seemed to help her aching head. "I must trust her."

"So must I, though I left Maria here with her to be sure."

"She doesn't seem to feel insulted."

"No, she expects it. She understands a great deal. I just wish she would trust us in return."

"Does she know who poisoned me?"

"No, I don't think so. But she knows more about her husband's death than she told us."

Maria entered with a jug of water, a tall, clean glass, and a bottle of wine.

"Thank you," Solomon said as she took the old glass away. "You can return to your other duties now."

In the doorway, the girl stood back to allow Elena to re-enter the room.

"Domenico Rossi is here," she said. "He claims to have an appointment to paint you. I told him you were indisposed, but it struck me that you might want to speak to him."

"I'll go down in a few minutes," Solomon said, opening the wine bottle to add a splash to the water in the glass. "My thanks, signora, for your help today."

"And mine," Constance said. "I hope you will come again."

Elena inclined her head. "As I hope you will call on me. In the meantime, send for me if you need me."

WITH RELUCTANCE, SOLOMON left Constance alone, sipping her water, while he went downstairs to the drawing room to find Rossi seated on a stool behind his easel, which he had placed in the same spot as yesterday, right in front of the open, right-hand window.

"Sit," Rossi commanded. "Quickly. Just there."

Solomon sat. After all, he had to be somewhere, and this way, he looked directly into the artist's face.

"Where is the lady?" Rossi asked with undisguised impatience. "I need her too."

"She is indisposed. I saw your Adriana last night. Or, at least, yesterday afternoon."

"She said so." Rossi clearly wasn't interested. "She gets occasional work through an agency. Signor, you wear different clothes!"

"Does it matter?"

Rossi shrugged irritably. "Not for today. You don't look so well. But you'll do. The afternoon light is better here."

"Does Adriana often work at the British consulate?"

"Once or twice before, I think. They have staid parties there to introduce British merchants to Venetians. Or just to be important. Adrianna clears up after them."

"Did you send her there?" Solomon asked steadily.

To his surprise, Rossi laughed. "No one sends Adriana anywhere. I prefer her in the house, but..." He shrugged. "The money is useful." He scowled at his picture and then at Solomon, then picked up his brush. His brow cleared slowly. As though he could now think about something else, he asked, "How is Signora Grey indisposed? What is the matter with her?"

"I believe she was poisoned."

The brush stilled. *"Poisoned?* Who would poison that beautiful lady? It is a crime against nature, against God. I expect she ate the clams. She will be fine by tonight."

If Rossi was an actor, he was a damned good one.

But then, Solomon reflected, one could say the same about Elena.

Neither of them had been at the consulate, and his instinct was to look more closely at exactly what had happened around Constance's glass. Someone there had put something in her wine, and they needed to know who quite urgently.

When Rossi had stomped off, irritated by Constance's absence, Solomon raked in the desk for Constance's notes and, taking them with him, retreated back to the bedroom. If she was up to the task, it was time to compare notes and work out who had poisoned her. Once they knew that, surely they would find Savelli's murderer too.

CHAPTER ELEVEN

CONSTANCE HAD FALLEN asleep again, her water glass, drained, on the bedside table. For a moment, Solomon stood looking down at her. A year ago, he had never even spoken to her, and yet now, she was everything. A fresh surge of fear washed over him, for she was so weak, he knew he could still lose her.

It was not the first time she had been hurt in the course of one of their investigations. She had been hit on the head, almost burned alive...but he would not think of that. Because, always, she bounced back, going blithely on with the investigation, approaching the next with excitement and the same vital curiosity that had first drawn him to her. It was something they shared.

Part of him was still screaming that it was madness to expose her to these dangers, whatever risks he took on his own account. Of course, it was Constance's decision, not his, and she had made it clear he had no right to dictate to her, only to discuss. Theirs was a partnership.

Not now. Since they had married, he had every right to rule her. Though he could just imagine her reaction if he tried to do so. Laughter surged into his throat, catching at his breath, and turned abruptly into tears.

"Oh, Constance," he whispered, sinking down on the bed. "Why are you so impossible, so wonderful, so *necessary*..."

A knock sounded at the door, and he hastily dashed his sleeve across his face. Rossi was right—he should change his clothes, though the matter seemed the least important in the world right now.

"*Avanti,*" he called, and Maria came in with the doctor.

Disturbed, Constance woke again and was given more to drink from Donati's own hand. Watching him almost as closely as he watched Constance, Solomon found his hopes rose, for there was a definite spark of approval in the doctor's eyes.

He asked her questions, listened to her heart, then sent her to the privy with Maria's support. It broke Solomon's heart to see her walking like an old woman.

"Is the danger past?" he asked when he and Donati were alone.

"No," said the doctor, "but I would say it is definitely reduced. Her body is shocked and severely weakened and will take some time and care to recover. But she is a healthy young woman. And a lucky one. I would guess she ingested very little of the poison."

"Do you have any idea what the poison was?"

Donati sighed. "I cannot be sure. It could be one of several." Deliberately, he met Solomon's gaze. "I reported the incident to the police."

Solomon nodded. "I am surprised they have not called."

"They may be suspicious of you, Signor Grey," Donati said bluntly.

Solomon nodded. He had expected that, and it scarcely mattered.

Constance returned and answered a few more probing questions from the doctor, while he pushed the glass back into her hands and gestured to her to drink.

"No food until tomorrow," he said at last.

Constance gave a tired smile. "That will be no hardship."

"And then only the lightest gruel, or thinned soup," Donati instructed her, rising to his feet. "I will speak to your cook on my way out."

Maria went with him to show him the way.

Constance leaned her head back against the pillows and reached for Solomon's hand. "I feel as if I've marched for miles across London, and I only walked a few yards to the next room and back."

"They are big rooms," he said encouragingly.

She laughed, and it sounded to him like the finest music. Then she said, "Will you open the curtains and the window, let me see the city? I don't want to waste this time."

He rose and obeyed, letting the light flood in. The afternoon sun was still shining on the water and the bridges and streets, the old and beautiful buildings, the passing boats. Somewhere close by, a blackbird sang, and in the distance, he could make out a gondolier's song.

He returned to the bed and kicked off his shoes so that he could stretch out beside Constance. She leaned against him, and he put his arm around her. She had always felt surprisingly delicate in his hold, but now she felt fragile like glass. Very thin, fine glass. *Foolish imagination, of course.*

She said, "How was it done, Solomon? I only had one glass of wine."

"Premarin topped it up."

She turned her face up to his, her eyes wide. "So he did. And it was just after that I began to feel ill. Within a few minutes."

"Would it have acted quite so quickly, though? Let's try to follow your glass and work out when it could have happened without either of us or anyone else seeing it. Simons gave us each a glass from a tray. It must have been a random choice, for other people were taking glasses at the same time. In those first minutes, there was only you and me and Simons. And then Mrs. Hargreaves."

"What with her skirts and mine, we never got very close to each other." Her brow twitched. "She said the police here were *secret* police, spies of the kind that read letters and listen to conversations. Especially Lampl."

"I'm sure some of them are. Austria has a vast and seething

empire of discontent to keep together. What happened in 1848 gave the government a huge fright."

"It's hard to reconcile that the government of this charming city is the same one Dragan Tizsa fought against."

Dragan Tizsa, the revolutionary Hungarian husband of a duke's daughter. Both had attended Constance and Solomon's wedding back in what seemed like another lifetime, and both were quite gifted amateur sleuths.

Solomon said, "It is definitely worth remembering."

But Constance had moved on. "Are they trying to cover up the truth of Savelli's murder?" she said, doubt in her voice. "Are we getting too close to a culprit they don't want accused?"

"We don't seem to be very close to anything at all," Solomon said wryly. "And I very much doubt the police would go about poisoning prominent foreign citizens."

"Bad for business," Constance said.

"Precisely. Whom did you speak to after Mrs. Hargreaves? And did you put your glass down anywhere during this time?"

"No, I don't think I did. I spoke to a few people—well, listened, mostly—but no one came too close. And then I bumped into Mrs. Hargreaves again. That was when she more or less told me Lampl was a secret policeman. And then I went up to Kellar…"

"Now there is an interesting man. Do you think he really does know your mother?"

He passed her the glass of water, and she sat with it in her hand for a moment, frowning, before she raised it to her lips.

"Do you mean he lied? Used it as an excuse to speak to me? But I approached *him*, and I could swear he was…taken aback. Unprepared. Almost alarmed. Ha! Maybe he does know her after all." She took another sip of water, then added with some difficulty, "I wondered, you know, just for a moment, if he could be my father. And I really think he was wondering the same thing, because apparently I look very much like her as she was then. But it has been thirty years since he saw her."

"I wonder," Solomon said, distracted from his main concern, "if she was respectable then?"

"*Juliet?*"

"Think about it. Would he have been so interested in the daughter of a whore? Would he even have remembered her, let alone brought her into conversation in respectable Society? Your mother taught you to read and write. How many other girls did you meet in your early years who could do so?"

"None. I made money out of it." She spoke absently, clearly still mulling over this different view of her outrageous parent that she had never considered before. Of course, children tended to accept their parents with all their peculiarities—criticizing, perhaps, but not questioning. "You mean, Juliet could be a fallen lady, like Elizabeth Maule?"

Discussing Elizabeth, whom Constance had saved from the streets and then from a murder charge, was too far removed from the urgency in Solomon's mind.

"That is for later," he said firmly. "When I saw you with Kellar, he was quite close to you, although whether or not he could have dropped something in your glass without your noticing—"

"He grasped it," Constance interrupted, staring at him. "When he said, *I knew your mother,* I was so stunned that I almost dropped the glass, and he grabbed my hand to steady it. I was so distracted... If he was quick, he could have dropped something in then. I would never have seen. But why would he? He brought up the subject of Juliet, after all, not I..."

"A roving diplomat," Solomon said thoughtfully. "Perhaps it does not suit the British government to have us asking questions about someone."

"Nationalists. The British support the cause of Italian nationalism and unity."

"But would they murder their own people to prevent a little scandal in the camp?"

"I am not dead," Constance pointed out, and Solomon's

blood chilled all over again at how close she had come.

He had to force his mind onward. "Well, let us allow that Kellar had an opportunity. What happened then?"

"You joined us." Her free hand plucked at the bedclothes. "And when I turned away from Kellar, I almost bumped into Giusti."

"Or he bumped into you," Solomon said slowly. "Deliberately? I couldn't see your glass at the time, but when I stepped around you, your wine seemed in danger of spilling over the side. Could Giusti have done it?"

Constance sighed. "I suppose he could have. Again, if he was quick and prepared. But why? Everyone suspects him of Savelli's murder."

"Apart from those who think it was Elena. I took the glass from you and put it on the table." He shook his head in annoyance. "I never even glanced at it after that. Anyone could have passed and dropped the poison in, and I wouldn't even have noticed."

"Neither would I. We were too busy talking to Giusti, and then to Lampl, and trying not to be embarrassed by Lampl's reaction to Foscolo's presence. But I don't remember anyone coming close to the table. Until you picked it up again for me when we went to join Premarin."

"Premarin," Solomon repeated. "Everyone's friend. Who poured wine into your glass. Perhaps that diluted the poison that was already there."

"Or he somehow dropped something in when he poured." She shifted restlessly. "And we talked to him and his friends for some time. We can't rule him out. And there's someone else, Sol. Rossi's girl, Adriana, was there, the maid collecting glasses."

"I know. I saw her. An odd coincidence, perhaps, but Rossi tells me she takes such work from an agency as it offers. She has worked at the consulate before, apparently. He was neither embarrassed nor put out by the fact that I'd seen her there. He didn't appear remotely interested."

"He must know we are investigating Savelli's murder. He could easily have guessed we suspect him."

"He won't have many clients if he keeps murdering them. Again, we have no evidence one way or the other. I didn't see Adriana anywhere near you or your glass, but I didn't watch her all the time. I can't rule her out."

"Neither can I," Constance said. "She *did* pick up some glasses close to where we stood with Premarin." She shook her head. "Only… While she clearly puts up with a lot from Rossi, she doesn't strike me as someone who blindly follows orders. She would not poison someone just because he told her to."

"She could think she was protecting him without orders."

Constance made a little gesture of frustration. "We are no further forward. We have the same suspects as for the Savelli murder. Giusti, Premarin, Rossi, or Adriana. And now we have added Kellar."

"But not Elena," Solomon pointed out. "And she alone came to help. Though I admit I was suspicious at first."

"I think she is lonely and unhappy, and was so even before her husband's death."

Solomon nodded agreement. "She has motive and, perhaps, opportunity in Savelli's case. But I don't think she has the character. *And* she was nowhere near the reception to poison you."

Part of him could not believe he was discussing the poisoning of his wife so calmly. Perhaps that was the only way to deal with the horrific—by treating it as normal. Though that idea was horrific in itself. Murder and attempted murder were not normal, and when they started finding it so, they would have to dissolve Silver and Grey and stop…

There was a faint flush on Constance's cheeks. She looked exhausted.

"We've talked too long," he said with contrition. "Take a last drink and go to sleep."

She obeyed like a child, and he set down the glass for her and helped her to lie down. She was already half asleep. Only when he moved to sit in the chair did she grasp his hand weakly.

"Will you stay with me, Sol?"

"Always," he said, and his voice cracked. Her fingers tightened, but she smiled, and he sat on the bed beside her, watching her sleep while his heart ached.

THE POLICE FINALLY came the following morning.

Constance had woken from a long sleep feeling very wooly, and she was still physically as weak as a kitten, but at some point, she had been aware of Solomon asleep in bed by her side and was glad. She knew how this had devasted him—it was still a matter of wonder, but his care moved her even as she worried for his own health.

He was walking toward the bed looking much refreshed and more his usual elegant self in a light suit and crisp shirt.

"Foscolo and Lampl are here. I have told them what we know of the poisoning, and they have obviously spoken to Dr. Donati, but they want to see you, too. Are you up to it?"

The wooliness began to recede. "If can wear my dressing gown and a cap and sit in the chair covered with blankets like an old, invalid lady, then yes."

Solomon's eyes lightened at her tone, and he helped her out of bed. She felt ridiculously proud that she could deal with her own comfort and basic ablutions for herself, although she was very glad of his aid in wrapping her in dressing gown and shawls while she sat exhausted again in the chair. She drank some more water with its flavoring of wine and realized she was hungry. That cheered her further, although she rather dreaded tempting providence by actually eating. She was glad of the delay offered by the policemen.

Inevitably, Lampl entered first. He bowed very correctly.

"Signora, how are you? I am so sorry to hear of your illness." He certainly gave her a cold, hard look, as though making sure any illness had been involved.

Behind him came Foscolo, who behaved in much the same way.

Solomon set chairs for them opposite her, and then he stood at her shoulder, a comforting and protective presence.

"And so you believe you were poisoned at the consulate reception?" Foscolo said.

"Dr. Donati believes it," Constance said mildly.

"Why do you think anyone would want to hurt you?"

"Probably because we have been asking questions about Signor Savelli's murder. But then, so have you, I imagine, and you both look perfectly healthy."

"Your husband," Lampl intervened, "has given us a very detailed description of your movements and those near you at the reception. Perhaps you could tell us your own recollections."

Talking about it last night had helped clarify events in her mind, so she could tell them accurately and concisely. "Some of this you witnessed yourself," she added.

Lampl glanced from her to Solomon and back.

Foscolo said, "And what have you learned from this experience?"

"Very little that is of practical use."

"That it can be dangerous to pry into police matters," Foscolo said severely. "That you should leave the questioning to us. *Those are the lessons you must take from this.*"

"You mean give in and be frightened off?" Constance retorted.

"Yes," Foscolo said. He all but glared at Solomon. "Sir, you have a duty to your wife—"

"We all have duties," Solomon interrupted. "I wonder if, in the course of yours, you have come across the Englishman, Sebastian Kellar?"

A tiny frown formed on Lampl's brow and vanished. "He is a

respected diplomat, here in Venice and all over Italy."

"Is that his only function?"

"He might dabble in trade. I honestly don't know."

"He does not commit crimes, nor get drunk and embarrass himself," Foscolo added. "What more do you want?"

"Does he have a connection to Savelli?" Constance asked.

Lampl leaned back in his chair. Foscolo leaned forward. Both looked baffled. They did not look at each other.

"Not that we know of," Foscolo said at last. "We know nothing against him at all."

"Does the Austrian government regard him as a threat?" Solomon asked Lampl.

"If it does, it has neglected to inform me," Lampl said. "Look, I cannot tell you to leave Venice, but I would advise you to do so until we get at the truth."

"Then you no longer suspect my husband or me of killing Savelli?" Constance said.

"We have made inquiries," Lampl said stiffly, "and have come to the conclusion that it is not likely."

"Much more likely are the thugs he chose to surround himself with," Foscolo growled, and received an annoyed glare from his superior. As if he didn't notice, he continued steadily. "They give each other alibis, but all we need is one witness."

"One witness at three, four, or five in morning?" Lampl said scornfully. "There are none."

"There is bound to be one," Foscolo said stubbornly.

Lampl opened his mouth to retort, but Solomon intervened. "My wife is tired."

They pulled themselves back to order and Lampl rose. "Thank you for your time. I wish you a quick recovery, signora. And please believe we will pursue the matter to the utmost, whether or not it is connected to the Savelli murder. Good day."

"They argue almost like an old married couple," Constance said when the door closed behind them.

"A married couple with years of acrimony behind them and

no common cause."

She twisted her neck to look at Solomon. "You don't think finding the murderer is their common cause?"

He shook his head in an impatient kind of way. "Perhaps they just disagree on methods. But they are not a team. They don't pull together." He came around to face her and crouched at her knee.

"Constance, shall we go?" he asked urgently. "As soon as you are well enough. We can go to Florence, Pisa, Rome…"

"Later," she said vaguely. She reached out and caressed his cheek. "If this was a warning, we are warned. I could not bear to lose you over this or anything else, but…I am safe here for now. And, surely, so are you. Our culprit won't want to draw attention to himself—or herself—by risking another attack so soon."

"That is sheer speculation," he pointed out.

"It is. Let's look at my notes and update them."

"I think I added everything yesterday and this morning," he said, rising to fetch said notes from the little bureau beneath the window.

Maria brought breakfast then—a thin soup for Constance that smelled of chicken and vegetables, and something heartier for Solomon. While they ate, they went over the facts, the opportunities, and the questions thrown up by what they had written, and soon the papers were spread all over the floor with arrows joining one point to another.

Constance warily swallowed a morsel of soup. It was watery but tasty and quite unthreatening, so she took another, and then a larger spoonful, and decided to wait. Her stomach felt odd, but did not actively rebel. She was able to concentrate on the discussion until tiredness overtook her again and the thoughts in her head disintegrated. She blinked, trying to get it back.

But already, Solomon had waded through the papers and was lifting her in his arms. It was sweet to be carried to bed, even if she only slept.

CHAPTER TWELVE

S OLOMON HESITATED BEFORE leaving the Palazzo Zulian. It went against his nature to leave her, even safe, asleep, and guarded by a houseful of servants who seemed to have taken the attack on her as a slight to their honor. It struck Solomon that if he had tried to on the night of her abduction, he could have whipped up an army to storm the Palazzo Savelli and take her back. Fortunately, that had not been necessary, but it was a comfort to know.

As Alvise rowed him to Premarin's house, it struck Solomon that he and Giusti and Savelli all lived close to each other, on or around the same length of the Grand Canal. One could walk the distance easily, but the back door, opening almost directly onto the water, was only accessible by boat. Without a boat, Savelli's murderer would have had to go through the house.

Had he? Had Savelli let him—or her—in, and then tried to send them home by boat, at which time his visitor simply stabbed him? Such evidence as they had was against it. Elena had heard no one in the house, and the Savelli boatman had not been summoned. He doubted any other had either, or the police would probably have found them.

Premarin, it turned out, was not at home. Impulsively, Solomon asked for Signora Premarin and was admitted at once.

Constance had found the young lady difficult to talk to, and rather strange. She also suspected her of harboring illicit feelings for Savelli. If the murder was about love, it didn't *have* to be the love of Giusti and Elena.

Signora Premarin received him with surprise but unexpected delight. When he smiled, her face became animated, as now when she gave him her hand, her plainness vanishing into something almost pretty. Solomon, fastidious and hopelessly devoted to his own wife, could still see her attractiveness, though whether it had been enough to drag the similarly devoted Savelli from *his* wife was another matter.

"Forgive the intrusion," Solomon said politely in careful Italian. "I hope you don't mind my calling when your husband is from home?"

"Of course not. You are very welcome. Please, sit down." She cast aside the needlework she had abandoned on the sofa, as though she expected him to sit next to her. Solomon, wary by nature and not unused to certain women's wiles, pretended not to notice and took a chair close enough to talk, but far enough away to avoid touching.

A servant brought the inevitable wine and cicchetti. Solomon felt obliged to accept, although the hairs stood up on the back of his neck as he remembered Premarin pouring wine into Constance's glass.

Since Signora Premarin poured it herself from the same bottle, and drank happily, he risked a sip of his own and politely took a small savory with anchovy and cream.

"We were sorry not to see you with your husband at the British consulate reception," Solomon said.

She wrinkled her nose. "I am too stupid to enjoy such affairs, and I cannot speak English. I like the way you speak Italian."

"I try my poor best, but feel free to laugh and correct me at will. How is your husband?"

"He is well. Busy."

Solomon waited for her to ask after Constance, but she didn't. So he abandoned subtlety. "I am glad to hear it. My wife was taken ill after the reception, so I was hoping he was not affected."

"Oh no, Nicolo is never ill. I expect it was the clams. Some cooks are not careful enough with them."

"Thankfully, we did not eat the clams. You did not hear about anyone else being ill from the event?"

She shook her head. After a moment, as though the thought had just occurred to her, she said, "Is your wife recovered?"

"Not entirely. But she is better than she was."

"Oh, good. You have not been married for long, have you?"

"No, just—"

"Your wife is very beautiful. Do you love her?"

Solomon blinked. "Yes. Do you love your husband?"

"Of course." Her eyes fell to her wine, and she took a sip, then reached nervously for one of the savories. "He is a good man and kind to me. Not every man is kind."

"That is sadly true. Who has been unkind to you, signora?"

"Oh, no one in particular."

Constance was right—conversing with the girl was frustrating to the point of impossibility. She was an odd mixture of blunt and secretive. But with the attack on Constance, their inquiry had become urgent. They needed the truth *immediately* and the culprit safely behind bars. For everyone's sake.

"Was Signor Savelli kind or unkind?"

Her eyes shone quite startlingly for an instant, then faded into sadness. "Kind, of course. She did not deserve him."

"Why not?"

"She is cold."

"What makes you say that?"

"I watched her—watched them both when we dined. I could tell she made him unhappy. She did not hang on his every word, as I did." She blushed furiously, then met his gaze with sudden boldness. She even tossed her head in an odd, coquettish gesture that was truly disturbing. "Do you think I am an unfaithful wife, Signor Grey?"

"No," he said at once, and her shoulders drooped.

"I am in my mind. Still. I am a sinful woman."

"In what way?" he asked. He almost wished Premarin would come. At the same time, he was afraid he would, thus ruining whatever confidence was imminent.

She lowered her eyes, a secretive little smile playing about her lips as she pleated the silk of her skirt with her fingers.

"I went to his house," she said huskily. "At night."

WHEN CONSTANCE WOKE up, Solomon was not beside her. Elena Savelli sat in the chair by the bed, reading her book in the sunlight shining through the half-open window. In sudden panic, Constance cast her gaze around the floor, which she had last seen strewn with her own and Solomon's jottings about everyone, including Elena.

Of course, Solomon had tidied them away out of sight.

"You look better," Elena said.

"I ate three spoonfuls of soup and they all stayed in my stomach."

"Congratulations. I believe they are bringing you more. Try for four spoonfuls."

"I don't know if I am quite so ambitious. Where is Solomon?"

"I don't know. They tell me he went out in the boat. Do you want help to sit up?"

"No. I think I can manage that." Constance sat up with caution, mainly to avoid the return of the headache that had plagued her, especially with sudden movements. It remained blessedly absent, so she regarded the other woman more cheerfully. "It is kind of you to come back."

"It's hard to be ill without female relatives to look after you and spoil you."

"I never had that. Just friends. You miss your family."

Elena nodded and seemed about to speak when Maria came in with the promised bowl of soup, and yet more water with wine. Behind her came another maid, who set a little table for Elena with a glass of wine and a plate of cicchetti.

Constance waited until the servants had gone and she taken a drink and a spoonful of soup. Then she said, "Your family truly never forgave you for your marriage?"

Elena swallowed her first bite before she answered. "I thought they would in time, when everything settled down again and they realized Angelo was good for me and for Venice. I thought my sister at least would come secretly and maybe talk the others around. She didn't. To them, I am a traitress. I betrayed them and Venice and Ludovico Giusti."

"You must have loved your husband very much."

Elena's gaze was on her food, which she ate, perhaps to give herself time to change the subject. Constance, since her stomach didn't seem notice the soup, took another spoonful.

Unexpectedly, Elena said, "I'm not very sure I know what love is. I thought I was madly in love with Ludovico—all that excitement and desperation to be together, so overwhelming when mingled with our noble cause. Democracy, independence, a united Italy. It was childish. I understood that during the siege."

"It must have been awful."

"Men died all the time. And then there was cholera, other diseases, and everyone began to die, even children... I felt responsible. I kept thinking, *What have I done?* And then, *What is Ludo doing?* Fighting to the bitter end, always at the front, leading raiding parties into the countryside against the Austrians and their allies. The city was hell, and *we* had done that to it. No one else seemed to see that. Except Angelo Savelli. He wrote to me from the beginning, you understand, because he and Ludo had fallen out when we pushed the Austrians from the city. When Ludo was reported lost during one of his raids, it was just part of the hell. And then Venice surrendered, and the Austrians came back. My family—those who were still alive—fled to our country house, but I stayed behind."

"Why?" Constance asked.

Elena shrugged and sipped her wine. "I don't know. Because I deserved the hell, I think, and I felt somehow that I had to see it through to the very end. And Angelo was still that one sane voice amongst the horror."

"You married him for protection," Constance guessed.

"Protection," Elena agreed. "And sanity and respect. And love, I thought, a more mature love this time, not the madness that was Ludo, which had brough us all to hell." She gave a twisted smile. "But Venice survives, as you see. Divisions remain, ill feeling, betrayal, but mostly, everything goes on as it did before 1848." Her smile, such as it was, faded, and she took another sip of wine. "Ludovic came back, of course, because he was not dead but severely injured and in hiding from the Austrians. Everyone pretended not to notice so that he could stay. Only I was forced to decide between him and Angelo, because by that time I was betrothed to both of them."

"You no longer loved Giusti?"

"I hated Giusti like myself, for what we had done. We were bad for each other, and I was no longer some innocent, melted by a dashing smile and a few passionate kisses. There is nothing important in those things. So I chose Angelo."

"Were you happy?"

She considered. "Individually, neither of us was happy. Together we survived, and Angelo's business thrived. I entertained his friends and his rivals, kept his house. The city's scars began to heal. Was it love? I don't know. I don't think I ever understood him any more than he understood me." She gave a small, hard laugh. "A sad tale, is it not?"

"Yes," Constance said with pity. "I think...I think you did your best, which is all any of us can do, whatever the situation. And I think you loved them both—in different ways, perhaps—as they loved you."

Elena met her gaze. "I might have thought so, except that I have seen *you* with *him*. Your husband. No one has ever looked at me as he watched you, so devastated by your illness, such stark, raw emotion. *That* is love. And I have never known it. I doubt I am capable of feeling it or inspiring it."

Constance felt her face warm. In return for the other woman's confession, she said, "I do love him. I always did, though I didn't always recognize it. Nor could I believe he would ever feel the same for me."

"Why not? You are one of the most beautiful creatures I have ever seen. You have warmth and wit and intelligence. I think men must find you fascinating."

Constance smiled. "I worked at that. Let us just say that I have a past."

"And he forgave you?" Elena asked with sudden intensity.

"Not so much forgave as... It ceased to matter very quickly. There is a bond between us. I think it was there from the first time we met, when we never even spoke. The feeling terrified me."

Absently, Constance ate her soup, aware of the other woman's curious gaze.

"Who do you think killed my husband?" Elena asked.

"I was going to ask you the same question."

Elena sighed, and Constance laid her spoon in the bowl. She seemed to have eaten almost all the soup, which surprised her. She hoped her stomach would not mind.

"To be honest," she said, "I like nearly everyone we have found with a motive and even the vaguest opportunity. The most likely suspects are surely the men your husband hired to protect you."

"To watch me," Elena said bitterly. "I think he imagined Giusti would kidnap me—after four years—or perhaps that I would run away with him. And that was why Giusti kept the jewels—to keep *me*."

"Jealousy comes with love. I am not immune. Nor is Solomon."

"Excess, obsession, was not something I ever suspected of Angelo. Giusti, yes. But not *him*."

"Are you not afraid to live in the same house as those men?"

"I pay them, so no. Besides, I want them where they can be found, even kicking their heels with boredom."

"And if your husband refused to pay them for something?" Constance persisted. "It is the most easily explained solution."

"Except that whoever killed Angelo probably poisoned you too, and our men have no access to the British consulate. And in any case, no one saw any of them leave the house the night Angelo died, let alone skulk at the back door."

Constance shifted restlessly. "But then, no one saw or heard anything or anyone."

Elena's eyes fell, as though involuntarily, and Constance stared at her.

"You don't sleep well," she said slowly. "Even before your husband's death, you didn't sleep well. Elena, did you see someone outside the house?"

"No. I saw no one."

You are lying again. It seemed the unexpected confidences were over. But Constance could not allow that. If she was in danger still—if Solomon was—this mystery could not be allowed to drift on unsolved. She needed to press Elena, make her tell the truth. Yet she knew instinctively that this was not the kind of woman who responded to bullying or nagging. Her trust, this apparently greater trust, had to be won more subtly.

Forcing herself, she changed the subject.

"Tell me about the Premarins. I believe they are friends of yours. You dined in each other's homes. Did this friendship survive the government contract that your husband won against Premarin?"

Elena's brow twitched. "Oh, that. It had only just been signed, but I can't imagine Nicolo Premarin bearing a grudge. He is the most pragmatic of men, and I doubt he needed the money. I certainly can't imagine it driving him to murder Angelo in the middle of the night."

"But his wife is a curious lady, is she not?"

"Bianca?" Elena said in disbelief. "She must be the least curi-ous person I have ever met."

"Then she is not a friend of yours?"

"She was often around. Like a shawl you don't much like, but it serves its basic purpose."

Definitely not a friend. "She does not like you either," Con-stance remarked.

Elena shrugged. "She wouldn't. She knows Nicolo proposed to me."

"*Did* he, now?" Constance leaned forward eagerly. "When did he do that?"

"Oh, around the time the Austrians retook the city. He want-ed a mother for his children, I think. I turned him down."

"And subsequently became engaged to Angelo..." There were possibilities there they had not considered. Personal jealousy added much to annoyance over a contract. Surely together they *did* constitute a serious motive?

"I suppose Bianca cannot forgive me. She liked Angelo, though."

"I had that impression," Constance said carefully.

Elena, who was not slow, widened her eyes. "Seriously? She had a *tendre* for Angelo?"

"He never mentioned it?"

"I doubt he noticed. I certainly didn't, though now you men-tion it, she was always more animated around him, and she did gaze at him as though he were some kind of oracle. Or god. I thought she looked at all men like that."

"Perhaps she does. But would it be possible that she some-how inveigled Angelo into an affair with her?"

Elena opened her mouth, surely to annihilate the preposter-ous idea. But then she only stared blindly at Constance, clearly considering it. "A woman who was no threat to his pride or his sanity," she said slowly. "He need not even consider it betrayal in his mind... Which would be wrong, so wrong, to both of us, and to Nicolo. No, I cannot imagine it. You do know that she tells lies? Fantasies, probably."

BIANCA PREMARIN'S WORDS flabbergasted Solomon. He could only stare at her.

"I went to his house. At night."

"Which night?" he managed at last.

"Lots of nights."

His heart had begun to beat with slightly horrified excitement. "Including the night he died?"

She nodded.

Careful to sound neither shocked nor urgent, Solomon asked casually, "What did you do there?"

"I watched for him. Sometimes I saw him."

"Did you speak to him?"

"Not yet," she said dreamily, as though she had forgotten that he was dead.

Tears started in her eyes. The pretense of the coquette, the sophisticated woman of love affairs, crumbled so quickly and so hopelessly that Solomon felt both appalled and desperately sorry for her.

He moved hastily on. "Did you see him the night he died?"

She shook her head. "I did not even see him at the window."

"Did you see my wife or me?" he asked curiously.

She stared at him. "No."

"What time was this, signora? When you were watching? Was it after midnight? It is important to me."

She smiled. "Then yes. I must have been there around three in the morning."

"Three? How did you get there?"

She lifted her eyebrows. "I walked. It is easy enough. The house—this house—is quiet then. The children are asleep, and the servants are abed. I have all the keys."

Solomon felt a pang of disappointment. "You walked. Then you watched the Palazzo Savelli at the front of the house."

"No one ever saw me," she said anxiously. "I wore a veil and the hood of my cloak, and in the dark I could blend in with the tree at the side of the canal. I hoped he alone would see me there and come to me. But he never did."

"Did you hear anything that might have come from the back of the house? Voices? The splashing of oars, perhaps? A fight?"

"No," she said with a vagueness that told him she wouldn't have noticed a major battle taking place out of her immediate line of vision.

"So, you went home again without seeing anyone?"

Her gaze refocused on him with a spark of triumph. "Oh, I saw someone. As I was going home, someone passed me in a boat, turning out of the canal that runs along the back of the Palazzo Savelli."

"Did you see his face?" Solomon asked without much hope.

"Oh yes, it was Ludovico Giusti, and he could only have been coming from his lover. Elena."

CHAPTER THIRTEEN

UNDER NORMAL CIRCUMSTANCES, Solomon would have gone straight to Giusti, but he had already been away from Constance too long in her current condition. On top of which, the stupid feeling that she could not be safe without his presence never quite left him, which was ridiculous considering she had been poisoned right under his nose.

Still, he willed Alvise to row faster.

Entering the Palazzo Zulian, he went straight upstairs without questioning the servants and strode through the private sitting room to their bedroom.

It gave him a small shock to see Elena Savelli there in the chair by the bed. But his attention was all on his wife, who looked considerably brighter. She was still terribly pale and the great shadows around her eyes would take time to fade, but her eyes sparked once more in the way that told him she had much to discuss.

"Solomon," she said, holding out her hand at once.

He went to her, sitting on the bed to take her hand and kiss it. "Have you eaten more?"

"Yes."

"She ate almost an entire bowl of soup," Elena said, rising to her feet, "and should be congratulated. I must go."

"Will you come back tomorrow?" Constance said.

"If you wish."

A friendship had begun to form between the two women,

and that made him uneasy. Because Elena was still a suspect in her husband's murder, if not the attack on Constance. And because of what Bianca Premarin had said about Giusti. It was Constance's instinct to befriend and defend other women, which had proved dangerous on at least one other occasion.

Of course, Solomon bowed to Elena and thanked her for coming. But he was glad to be alone with his wife.

"How are you? Are you tired?"

"No, I am doing nothing but sleeping and eating and talking. I've had a most interesting hour with Elena."

"I've had quite an interesting time with Bianca Premarin."

"Have you indeed?" As he settled beside her again, she leaned against him, her arm across his waist. "Elena says she lies."

"She probably would say that. Bianca says she saw Giusti on his way back from the Savelli Palace on the night of the murder."

Constance's eyes widened. "Is that what she's not telling me?"

"Who?" Solomon asked, confused.

"Elena. She sleeps poorly, and I'm sure she saw something, someone, that night that she doesn't want to admit. We thought that before, but now I'm sure. If what you're saying is true, then she saw Giusti. Old loyalties are keeping her silent. It makes sense."

"Or she could be lying because it was her husband she saw when she stabbed him."

Constance shook her head. "Or Bianca could be lying. From what Elena said, Bianca talks sometimes as though her fantasies are real."

"As though she's lying to herself," Solomon said. "*That* is probably true. She began by trying to make me believe she was some sophisticated temptress, that she had indulged in some affair with Savelli, going to his house every night. But from what she said later, she only ever stood outside the front of the house, watching pathetically for a glimpse of him. She never even spoke to him. But she says she was there on the night he died."

"Can we believe her?" Constance said doubtfully.

"Not without corroboration. The other thing to consider is…the girl is unstable. What she told me could easily be another fantasy to hide the fact that she went by boat to the back of the house and killed Savelli for ignoring her, or rejecting her, or for some other reason the rest of us will never understand."

"Do you think she is mad?" Constance asked uneasily.

"I would say she's on the verge of it. Would Premarin protect her?"

"That's the other thing," Constance said. "Premarin proposed to Elena first, but she chose Savelli." She sat up straighter. "Bianca could have told her husband any old story that might have made him jealous enough and angry enough to kill."

"But did she? Why would Constance protect Premarin or Bianca?"

"It has to be Giusti," Constance said unhappily. "I really don't believe she would have killed her husband. She thought both too much of him and too little."

Solomon raised one eyebrow. "What does that mean?"

"That she loved him in a quiet way, not a way that is all-consuming, angry, or jealous."

Distracted, he found himself saying, "How do you love me?"

She smiled. "All ways."

He had to kiss her for that, but, very aware of her health, he kept it gentle if not quite chaste. Then, unaided, she rose from the bed, donned her dressing gown, and walked into the sitting room, where she sat on the sofa with an air of triumph that warmed him and made him smile. Could he allow himself to believe she was on the mend? She believed it, clearly, and he grasped that with painful gratitude.

"This is not quite the trip we planned, is it?" she said ruefully.

"I'm not sure I care for the unexpected anymore."

"Not *this* unexpected. I have never felt so dreadful in my life." She tried to keep her voice light, but there was a catch in it that brought him quickly down beside her.

He put his arm around her, burying his lips in her hair.

She gave a little gasp. "This is different. We've been hit and hurt before and I never truly cared because it was done in a moment of fear or anger, but this... It is deliberate, personal, *hateful*..."

He tightened his arm around her. "Shall we leave?"

She shook her head. Was ever a woman so stubborn? So maddening and brave and wonderful...

"We can't," she said. "I refuse to let such a person go on. They stabbed a man—a good man, by all we have learned—with his own weapon, and poisoned me just when you and I..."

"Hush," he whispered, kissing her temples, her cheeks. "Hush. I know. I am angry and afraid as I have never been. I don't understand these people. I don't understand the crime. It's like blundering through a blinding fog in an unknown place."

She gave a watery laugh. "No, it isn't." She sat up, wiping her eye. "People are just people, the world over. They are poisoned in England, too. I know I'm taking this too personally, probably because I like whoever did it. That hurts."

"It hurts," he repeated. "There is a lot of hurt in this city. What if Savelli was not killed for revenge or greed or politics, but simply from unbearable hurt?"

"Then we come back, surely, to Giusti and Elena."

"Or the Premarins, although that theory still feels ridiculous and far-fetched." He rose and strode over to the cabinet where he had tidied away their notes before going out. "The whole of Venice hurts from the recent revolution and war. But the greatest personal pain in this case is all between Giusti and Savelli and Elena..."

Hastily, he spread their notes around, rearranging as he spoke. "The murder weapon—the only physical evidence that exists, although we have never even seen it—is from Savelli's own house. His bodyguards, who obey Elena as far as we know. Giusti, Savelli's enemy but one-time friend and Elena's jilted betrothed. Premarin, who also proposed to Elena. Premarin's wife, who hates Elena because she was foolishly obsessed with

Savelli. Rossi, according to the awful Mrs. Collins at the consulate, could have been Elena's lover. Was that the real reason Savelli dismissed him?"

He stood back with the papers arranged and sank back down beside Constance, who was gazing at them. They looked like a bizarre kind of star, with everyone and everything emanating from a central point—Elena.

"It doesn't make her the murderer," Constance said slowly. "But you are right that everything seems to connect to her, stem from her. In fact, rather than being the perpetrator, she has to be the motive. Someone killed Savelli for Elena."

"With or without her knowledge," Solomon said. He frowned, dragging his fingers through his short hair, then bent and picked up the abandoned paper with their notes on Sebastian Kellar. "Except for him. He knew Savelli and his wife but was not involved with them. If he hadn't talked to you, been so close to your wine, we wouldn't even have considered him."

"Then we can rule him out?"

"If the murder was about Elena and hurt."

"And he is not a political assassin," Constance pointed out.

"There is no evidence of that, just the speculation of our fevered imaginations, which seem to have taken us back to the days of the Borgias."

Constance said, "Elena spoke of Giusti as in the past. I really don't think they were having an affair. In which case, why would Giusti kill Savelli now?"

"Because of the street attack? Because he had had enough? Remember, they used to be friends. There is the hurt of betrayal between them. And if we can believe Bianca, Giusti was rowing from the back of Palazzo Savelli that night."

Constance shifted impatiently, bumping her hip against Solomon's. "If this is right, if Elena is at the center of this maelstrom of feeling... I don't think she's aware of it. I don't believe she has affairs with anyone, not Giusti and certainly not Premarin or Rossi. It gets us no further forward. At least until we talk to Giusti again."

Solomon glanced at the window. There was plenty of daylight left, although the sky was clouding over. "I could go and see him now." He didn't want to leave Constance again. And besides… "But it might be better if we could both be there. We work better together."

She snuggled against him. "We do, don't we?" she said complacently. "We could send him a note, invite him to call."

Solomon regarded her, taking in the bruised eyes and the obvious exhaustion of her body, weighing her condition against the urgency of finding and arresting the murderer. "In the morning," he said reluctantly. "When we are fresher and you, hopefully, will be even stronger."

"I might be able to eat solid food tomorrow," she said hopefully, and his lips tightened in fresh fury.

Whatever the motive of the killer, this was *damnably* personal for Solomon.

⤜⤜⤜⊁⫷⫷⫷

CONSTANCE FELT SO much better in the morning that she nibbled some bread with her clear beef soup, and insisted on bathing and dressing, after which she walked downstairs on Solomon's arm and ensconced herself in the drawing room, from where she could look out over the canal.

The magic of Venice had not faded, she decided. It had just acquired more facets. Like people. Like London.

Rather to her own and Solomon's surprise, Giusti presented himself punctually at half past ten as Solomon had suggested in his note. He entered looking almost fearful, though his face lightened considerably at the sight of Constance.

"Signora!" he said, striding forward with his arm outstretched. "I am so glad to see you up and about."

She gave him her hand without rising. "I am definitely recovering, though lamentably weaker than a newborn kitten!"

"I called when I first heard the rumors—which are flying around the city, by the way. Surely you cannot have been poisoned at the British consulate!"

Solomon waved him to a chair. "Sadly, there is no doubt about it. The doctor is convinced."

"But this is shocking! Could it have been an accident?"

"An accident affecting only my wife's glass?"

Giusti grimaced. "But why?"

"The only reason we can think of is because we were asking questions about Savelli's death," Solomon said.

Giusti nodded, frowning. "Attack your wife and ensure you both leave… But that still leaves the police, who are asking much the same questions. And Foscolo was there for some of the time, at least. I suppose that would be too obvious… But this is terrible! Is that why you asked me to call? To say farewell?"

"Oh, we are not leaving just yet," Constance said.

His eyes widened with surprise but no obvious chagrin. "You are a brave lady," he said warmly. He cast a quick glance at Solomon. "Could you not persuade her?"

"No one is more stubborn than my wife," Solomon said evasively.

"Coffee?" Constance offered. The idea of drinking wine so early in the morning still went against her nature, although the Venetians seemed happy to do so throughout the day.

The servants brought coffee in and served it, for which Constance, ridiculously exhausted after coming all the way down the stairs, was grateful.

"Guisti," Solomon said, once they were all comfortable, "on the night of Savelli's death, after you and I collected Constance from his palazzo, you went straight to your own home and stayed there, yes?"

Giusti regarded him, his face suddenly, deliberately blank. Constance caught her breath.

And then, to her annoyance, the door opened again and Mario the manservant announced, "Signora Savelli."

It was as though a bolt of lightning shot through the room. Giusti leapt to his feet. Elena walked in and stopped dead just inside the door. Her gaze locked on Giusti and the blood seemed to drain from her face.

Giusti, grasping the back of his chair so tightly that his knuckles turned white, stared at her for one tense moment, then tore his gaze free and flung words over his shoulder at Solomon.

"Yes. I was at home all night." Only then did he bow to Elena.

She, however, was no longer looking at him, but at Constance. "I have called at a bad time. But I am glad to see you up and about. I shall come back in the afternoon."

She spun around to go, but Constance would not allow it. It suddenly angered her that they, surely the people at the center of this tangled mystery of murder and hate and lies, should try to drag it out further.

"Stay," she said peremptorily.

Elena was so surprised that she glanced back, her brows raised. "Seriously?"

"I have never been more serious in my life. Please, sit and talk to us. And in the name of God, please tell us the truth. Who was there the night of your husband's death? I know you saw or heard someone and you lied to us."

"I saw no one," she said. Her lips were stiff and bloodless, and yet she sank into the chair as far from Giusti's as was possible.

"You are both lying," Constance said, astonished by the hardness in her voice. "And we have had enough. Signor Giusti, would it surprise you to know that you were seen after three o'clock that morning, rowing in the canal that runs along the back of the Palazzo Savelli?"

"Yes," he said firmly, then, as an afterthought, "By whom?"

"Signora Premarin."

"She lies," Giusti said quickly. "Everyone knows that. Besides, what the devil was she doing out at that time of the night?"

"She was watching my husband," Elena said slowly. "I saw her there once before, last month. She hides imperfectly in the shadow of the tree between the canal and the piazza, as though she wants to be seen. She wanted *me* to see her, to think she was waiting for Angelo. Silly girl. He barely noticed her beyond politeness. I told her to go home, that she was putting herself in danger. She probably imagined I was jealous."

"What time would this have been?" Solomon asked.

Elena shrugged. "Two o'clock? Three?"

"You don't sleep," Constance said, ignoring the sense of guilt at betraying confidences because this was much, much more important. "You look out of windows to pass the time. Who did you see the night of your husband's murder?"

Elena stared at her and said nothing.

"Me," Giusti said. "She saw me. From the back window of the second floor. I know, because I saw her."

"He didn't stop," Elen said, her shoulders relaxing so suddenly that they drooped. "He rowed straight past."

"How long did you stand at the window, watching him?" Solomon asked.

"Not long," Elena replied, her voice curiously hollow now. "Only a minute."

Then Giusti could have come back...

Solomon swung on Giusti. "And you—what were you doing there?"

Giusti dropped his head into his hands and tugged furiously at his hair. "God help me, I don't know. Savelli worried me. To attack me in the street, to abduct Signora Grey—it was madness for anyone to do these things. For him, it was bizarre."

"Yet you did not stop to ask after his health?" Solomon asked without troubling to hide his disbelief.

"It was not *his* health that bothered me," Giusti retorted.

"It was Elena's," Constance said. "You were afraid he would hurt her in his...unbalanced state."

Giusti nodded wordlessly. He looked at no one, but Elena

was watching him.

"Give us more, Giusti," Solomon said.

The young man shrugged, almost helplessly. "There is no more. I saw her at the window and had to be content. I was in no state to take on her husband and his bravos again in any case. Every bit of me hurt. I could barely row. I went home."

Solomon scowled at him. "Do you know the time we could have saved if you had told us this in the first place?"

"He couldn't, could he?" Elena said unexpectedly. "It would have proved that I was up, not asleep."

At last, Giusti took his head out of his hands and met her gaze.

"You were protecting each other," Constance said, and drew in a breath. "Do you suspect each other?"

As one, they shook their heads.

With what was apparently a great effort, Giusti dragged his gaze free and looked directly at Constance. "Whether or not I suspected her, even if I had done it myself, I would not have poisoned you. I didn't, for whatever that is worth. Do you have any idea who did?"

"There were times when the glass was out of our sight," Solomon said. "And neither of us were paying attention. But the people we knew who could have done it were you, Premarin, Sebastian Kellar, and Adriana, the girl clearing away the glasses."

Giusti frowned, shaking his head. "I doubt it—unless the girl was coerced, though who on earth by?"

"She is Rossi's girl."

"Rossi? The artist? I thought he was painting you both."

"He had a grudge against Savelli."

"Hardly one worth killing for," Elena snapped.

But Giusti sat up straighter. "The man has a drink problem. I have run across him in some shocking states. I reminded him once of trying to punch me in a tavern one night, and he looked at me blankly as though he had no idea what I was talking out."

Elena looked at him. "You mean he could have got vilely

drunk and taken everything out of proportion, as drunks do, and decided Angelo had treated him so abominably that he deserved to die?"

"Something like that. And then not remembered anything about it."

Constance met Solomon's gaze. "He didn't come today. Perhaps he started to remember."

"And perhaps he just decided there was no point in coming while you were ill," Solomon said.

"Or he was drunk in some tavern," Giusti added. "I'll go and get the truth out of him for you."

"No," Constance and Solomon said together.

Solomon's lips twitched. "We'll send for him. I don't want him to close up like a clam. But thank you for the offer." He adjusted his gaze to encompass Elena as well. "And thank you for telling us the truth at last."

An instinctive, surreptitious glance passed between Giusti and Elena. It might have been permission, for he said, "There is one thing more. I sort of called on Signora Savelli the next night."

"Sort of?" Constance repeated.

"He climbed up the building," Elena said without expression, and yet Constance had the idea that it both impressed and terrified her, "and entered by a first-floor window that was unlocked."

"Why?" Constance asked.

"Because he was dead," Giusti said. "I needed to know she was well. Again. And..."

"And what?" Constance prompted him.

"Condolences," Giusti muttered. "I needed to offer condolences. He was her husband."

"And your friend," Elena said in little more than a whisper.

Giusti swallowed. "Once."

Solomon said, "Forgive me, but I have to ask. Was that the only time you—er...scaled the walls?"

Giusti's fingers curled involuntarily. Then he gave a shrug

and an odd, crooked smile. He met Solomon's gaze with an expression of reckless defiance, as though he were about to charge into battle or fight a duel.

"I had done it before as a boy. With Savelli. It was my only time as an adult. But since it is a day for confession, it is not the only time I rowed past the palazzo."

"Were you looking for a fight?" Solomon asked. "Or reconciliation with an old friend?"

Giusti shook his head. "No. Just a glimpse."

Of her. Of Elena. *Poor, foolish, lonely boy…*

He sprang to his feet. "I'm sorry. I will go. But let me know if I can help. You are doing more than the police. And suffering more."

"Not now," said Constance, who felt suddenly much more cheerful about the whole case.

Extracting the admissions they had from Giusti and Elena was like an achievement. They were nearing some truth, at last. And judging from the queer expression in the widow's eyes when she looked at Giusti, so was Elena.

CHAPTER FOURTEEN

F OR THE FIRST time since she had been ill, Constance didn't have the urge to sleep every half-hour. She sat on the drawing room balcony in the surprisingly warm spring sunshine and flexed her fingers and toes. She felt as if she were absorbing the light like a sickly plant and growing stronger with every moment.

Solomon sat beside her as they watched the passing boats and the lively interactions of the people below. Folk were much less inhibited here. Even the wealthy seemed to call loud greetings and jokes from windows to boats, or even hold long conversations. Yet it all felt curiously peaceful.

She and Solomon did not discuss the case for some time, though she was mulling over the recent conversation with Giusti and Elena, and suspected Solomon was doing the same. The gentle companionship was precious. This was still their honeymoon.

Solomon said, "Do you believe them?"

"Yes," she replied, knowing exactly whom and what he meant. "I want to, of course, but I do think it was the truth at last."

He nodded. "It seemed so to me. So, if we rule them out, what is our next step?"

"Premarin. If he will talk to us. And Rossi, when he comes. I also think we need to exchange views with the police."

"With Foscolo," Solomon said, "while Lampl is

not…*overseeing* him."

It made sense. Foscolo was the man who did the work, who knew about crime. Lampl was there to serve Austria's interests, whatever that entailed. Since Savelli had been Austria's friend, she presumed the two men were pulling in the same direction, however irritably. But perhaps that depended on who the culprit was.

Solomon said, "Look. It's Kellar."

Following his gaze, she saw the Englishman in his gondola, shaded from the sun, being rowed along the canal. He looked immensely comfortable, but he appeared to be gazing in their direction.

Solomon lifted his hand in greeting, and won an immediate response. "Shall we invite him up?"

During the worst of Constance's illness, her mother had often crept into her mind. Odd memories of childhood comfort that she thought she had forgotten, maddening incidents of neglect and quarrels, and the guilty recognition that she knew nothing of Juliet's life *before*. She had been more interested in her unknown and mysterious father.

"Yes," she said, "if he will come."

Solomon stood and leaned over the balcony, beckoning. The boatman steered closer to the side and Kellar, presumably absorbing the habits of the natives, called up, "How is Mrs. Grey?"

Constance waved and smiled, and Solomon called back, "Come and see, if you have time."

Apparently Kellar had time, for the boatman eased his vessel against the steps and Kellar rose from his comfortable seat and stepped ashore with the ease of long practice.

"Are you sure you are up to this?" Solomon asked her. "I can take him somewhere else while you rest here."

"I am bored with resting. And I'm curious."

He smiled, her answer clearly pleasing him. "I daresay it is a civilized hour now for wine and cicchetti."

He went into the room to greet Kellar, who sounded both jovial and anxious about Constance's health. Solomon placed a chair for him in the balcony doorway, as he requested.

"Even at this time of year, the direct sun bothers my eyes," he said. "Old age is both a blessing and a curse."

"You are hardly old," Constance scoffed.

"I am six and fifty, so I am hardly young." His piercing gray eyes fixed on her face. "You have had a bad time. There are all sorts of rumors flying around Venice. The consul is appalled, and not a little frightened."

"Fortunately, no one else seemed to be affected," Solomon said.

"Which is significant," Kellar said, meeting his gaze. "I have a country house in Tuscany that you are welcome to use, once you are fit to travel."

"That is very kind of you," Solomon said.

"It is a most disturbing event. I suppose there is no doubt that it was poison?"

"Not according to the doctor—who believes she only survived because she ingested so little."

"Or because no one intended me to die in the first place," Constance said. "Just to frighten me away."

Kellar regarded her. "And they haven't, have they?" he said slowly. "Is that because you are foolishly brave? Just foolish? Or because you know who did it?"

"We have a few theories," Solomon said.

Kellar grimaced. "I imagine I must feature there."

"Your name was on the list," Constance said, "but we could find no motive."

His eyes twinkled at her bluntness. "I have none," he assured her. "I wanted to marry your mother, you know."

"*Juliet?*" Constance said in disbelief, before she could stop herself.

Kellar smiled. "Why should that surprise you? Presumably she married *someone*."

Constance, thinking of Solomon, merely smiled back and kept the truth to herself, although curiosity surged. "How did you meet my mother?"

"At a garden party. The sun shone on her hair like a halo." Kellar inclined his head. "Much as it does on yours now. I all but forced our hostess to introduce us, and I courted your mother most assiduously."

This sounded like respectability of a kind totally alien to Juliet—or at least Constance's knowledge of her. Suspicions rose.

"Did her family approve?" she asked lightly.

Kellar's mouth quirked. "You are trying to catch me out. I don't blame you for your suspicion, considering what happened to you. But we both know she had no family. She was the companion of a rather terrifying old lady. Or, at least, she seemed old to me at the time. She was probably forty years old. In any case, I was young and brash and I was not interested in anyone's approval except Juliet's. And I thought I had it."

Just for an instant, his sharp eyes softened with reminiscence. But he was not, it seemed, a man who dwelled in the past or wallowed in regrets, for when he blinked, the tender expression had vanished.

"But you did not?" Constance prompted him.

"Have her approval? Yes, I think I did. Just not…enough."

"Why was that?" Constance asked, aware she was going beyond interest to inquisitiveness.

"Honestly? I never discovered. The best I can think of myself is that my posting to America loomed. I was swept off my feet and assumed she would prefer the adventure of marriage as a diplomat's wife to the respectable drudgery of her present life. I think it was too quick for her, an irretrievable decision she was not yet ready to make. She refused my offer and I went to America alone. She never answered my letters. But I never forgot her."

There was genuine feeling in his voice, but he was not, somehow, the kind of man one felt sorry for. He was not inviting sympathy or reciprocal confidences. Constance, who hadn't quite got past the idea of Juliet as companion to a respectable old lady, could think of nothing to say.

He was watching her steadily. "I think you too are a remarkable woman. You must tell me about your father one day."

"One day," she said, "I might. A glass of wine, Mr. Kellar?"

"Why not?" He sighed with contentment as the servants brought the usual wine and savories. "There are reasons Venice is my favorite city in Italy." He raised his glass to them. "To *La Serenissima*, and your continued recovery, Mrs. Grey."

Constance mixed a small amount of wine with water, and risked nibbling at the plainest savory on offer, something with ham and apple.

"We would value your help, sir," Solomon said. "Is there anything you can tell us about Angelo Savelli that might shed light on his murder?"

"I did not know him well anyway, but no, I know nothing to his discredit—save his enmity with Giusti, which was mostly habit and instinct, from all I can gather. I liked him." Kellar gave a wry smile. "There was something almost British about his reserve. And like most people, I found his wife fascinating."

"What about Nicolo Premarin and his wife?"

"All things to all men. A pragmatist and a danger to no one. I'm not sure I have met his wife, though gossip says she is younger." He cocked an eyebrow. "You are seriously considering them for the murder? And the poisoning, since I presume they are connected."

"We presume so, too."

"For what it is worth," Kellar said slowly, "I have heard that he is a worried man. There is no obvious sign of business difficulties and he did survive revolution and war. But I do wonder if everything is as safe for him as most people assume."

"He lost a valuable government contract to Savelli," Constance said.

Kellar, probably more used to absorbing gossip than spreading it, merely gave a thoughtful nod.

"Worried men make bad decisions," Solomon remarked, "and can act quite out of character."

Kellar gazed out over the canal. "He has many friends in Venice. And all over Italy."

A shiver passed over Constance. She stared at Kellar's half-averted face. Was that a warning?

AFTER A LIGHT luncheon, Solomon went out to try again to see Premarin. In the light of Kellar's warning—if that was what it was—Constance felt uneasy about his going alone. On the other hand, while she was happy to take short walks and long rests in the little garden at the side of the house, she doubted she was up to visiting.

It annoyed her, because this was, presumably, what the poisoner had wanted. To slow them down and halt their inquiries. If only she knew what it was that had frightened the murderer into such a risky attack, something she or Solomon had said or done that the police had not...

Solomon left her with the notes when he escorted her into the little courtyard garden. She did not spread them about this time—for one thing, the wind was likely to carry them off, and for another, she just wanted to read them straight through, with all their thoughts and speculations.

She paused quite close to the beginning. The weapon that had killed Angelo Savelli was a long-bladed dagger, according to the police. Constance had never seen it. She wondered if the police had returned it to Elena, along with her husband's body...

"Signora!"

The call startled her out of her thoughts, and she peered toward the noise. Domenico Rossi stood on the other side of the tall wrought-iron gate that covered the opening between the

Palazzo Zulian and the building next to it.

She laid down the papers on the bench beside her and rose without thinking to unlock the gate and let him in. As he strode past her into the garden, she caught a whiff of wine on his breath. But then, small amounts of wine were drunk all the time here by most people. She was just more sensitive to it because she was barely drinking it at all right now.

He spun around and spread his arms with pleasure. "I came to see how you are, but how wonderful to see you looking so well! When I last saw your husband, he scared me witless. You *are* better?"

"Much better, though still annoyingly weak. It has rather interfered with our portrait, I'm afraid. I don't think I want to be painted looking exhausted and ill!"

"Who would? But in my picture, you will shine as you still do."

"Hmm." As she sat back down, he bent and picked up the papers from the bench, presumably so he could sit beside her. She could not help the speed with which she grasped them. "Let me take these out of your way…"

Over the notes, their eyes met for an instant and she saw that he knew what they were. He must have glimpsed something of what was written there. She couldn't recall what was on the top sheet, apart from that one brief mention of the weapon. She just hoped it was not littered with suspicions of Rossi and Adriana.

After a frozen instant, his grip loosened, and he sat down as though he did not care. She placed the pile of notes on her lap, face down, and folded her hands over them.

"We did not expect you today," she said lightly. "I'm afraid Solomon has gone out."

"Making inquiries like a policeman?" Rossi said, a sudden spark in his eyes. "Or a spy."

"Or a concerned husband," she said evenly.

His eyes narrowed and she became aware that the smell of drink was really quite strong and sour. "But it's about more than your eating something that disagreed with you, isn't it? It's about me. Why? Did someone tell you I drink too much and forget things?"

She met his gaze because she never backed down. "Such as whom you last fought with?"

Nicolo Premarin was at home, alone in his comfortable, blessedly masculine study, gazing bleakly into space and wondering what the devil he was going to do. He did not even hear the door open until the servant spoke.

"It is the Englishman again."

Relief at this distraction hit him in waves. Besides, his ambition to rope Solomon Grey into some—any—kind of partnership had not abated one iota. He bounced to his feet, hurrying into the hall to capture his prize before Bianca discovered him.

Greeting the Englishman effusively, he bore him off to the study rather than to the drawing room and his wife.

"My wife told me you called yesterday," he said. "I was so annoyed to have missed you. I would have come to you, only I don't like to intrude when your wife is ill."

"I believe she is mending, although we had a serious fright." Grey sat in the comfortable chair Premarin indicated.

Premarin decided to do him a favor. "You should know," he said confidentially, "that words like *poison* are being bandied about."

"Indeed," Grey said without obvious surprise. He met Premarin's serious gaze with cool, clear, dark eyes.

It gave Premarin pause, that look, reminding him that Grey was not a man to trifle with. He had not achieved what he had by stupidity or even luck. He was a polite, elegant force of nature.

Grey added, "We believe the poison to have been in her wine glass at the reception, for she ate nothing."

Premarin felt the blood drain from his face. "But…you cannot think… I poured her wine from a fresh, open bottle, but I drank the same wine myself. So did you!" He had to control the panic before his voice gave him away. There was too much at stake here.

"I know," Grey replied, much to Premarin's relief. "You might even have saved her by diluting the poison that was already in her glass. The trouble is, we cannot tell when or by whom the poison was placed there."

"But my dear fellow…! I cannot conceive… This is truly shocking, utterly dreadful."

"It is," Grey agreed, unblinking. "Have the police not asked you what you witnessed?"

Premarin shook his head. "No. I know of no one who has been questioned, in fact, which is why I did not believe the rumors could be true. Perhaps the authorities were satisfied after talking to the consulate staff."

But how could they be satisfied without a culprit? As far as he knew, they did not have one. And yet they hadn't spoken to himself or Giusti, or anyone else he knew who had been there.

Clearly this had already occurred to Grey. Premarin, doing his best for his countrymen, said, "I suppose, since your wife recovered, they have gone back to the murder of poor Savelli."

"Don't they believe the matters are related?"

Premarin shrugged. "Who knows what they believe?" He hesitated, searching Grey's face, which, now he looked more carefully, was all suppressed anger and nigh-intolerable anxiety. He didn't even try to hide it. Premarin, veteran of a thousand successful negotiations, found himself hurrying into unplanned speech. "It is difficult. Everything is difficult now. I know for a fact the government wants the murderer found, but the attack on your wife could easily become a diplomatic incident. If they find Savelli's killer, then presumably they have your wife's poisoner too, and justice will be served. Though I myself see no obvious connection."

Grey lifted his brows in blatant disbelief, and Premarin could have kicked himself.

"Don't you?" Grey said. "My wife and I have been asking questions, at first because we were once under suspicion ourselves. But we don't like to leave such matters unsolved, and I owe Giusti—another suspect—a debt of gratitude. I don't believe he killed Savelli."

"I find it hard to believe too." Premarin spread his hands. "Anything I can do to help you," he said with sincerity, "I will."

Grey held his gaze, and pounced. "Did you know that your wife has been seen late at night outside the Palazzo Savelli? Including on the night of the murder."

Premarin closed his eyes as though that could shut out this suddenly relentless man and his own burning shame. And Bianca's. He had to say something, make some kind of defense.

Then he remembered quite suddenly whom he was dealing with. Premarin was good at reading men. He'd had to be. And he had already assessed Solomon Grey as a clever, driven, but basically honest man. He was not unkind, but he would not tolerate deceit.

And so Premarin's defense, like any future negotiations—and he refused to give up on those even now—depended on his own honesty. And on Grey's goodwill and understanding. He had to risk it.

He opened his eyes in time to catch the hint of pity in Grey's, quickly veiled. But there would be no quarter. The man wanted, *needed*, an answer.

"I was not aware she had been seen," Premarin said with what dignity he could muster. "But I know she was there. So was I."

Grey's brow twitched, ever so slightly, his only betrayal of surprise. "You were? No one told me that."

He was not here for blame or accusations, Premarin saw with considerable relief, just truth. So that was what he would give him, since he had no choice now.

"I am an ageing man, Signor Grey, with a young wife. I married her when she was but eighteen, mainly as a mother for my children. It did not enter my head that she was little more than a child herself. To me, it was a matter of convenience. To her…a girl has the right to expect some romance in her life." He shrugged. "But I work too hard, I make assumptions, and while I am never unkind, I certainly make few allowances for her youth. For anything. Until I saw her slipping out of the house one night."

With a self-deprecating smile, he mocked himself. "Now I notice. My honor is at stake. I think she has a lover, so I follow her. She does not go far. She just stands in the shadows outside the Palazzo Savelli and waits for him to appear at a window. He never acknowledged her. I don't believe he ever noticed her, but that first time I waited. I too saw him at a window. When he had gone, when the last light was doused, she left, and again I followed. She returned straight home."

Saying it all was ridiculously easy. The earth did not swallow him up. No monster ate him. Grey did not even look at him with scorn, just those steady, unblinking eyes, taking in every nuance of his face and voice.

"Savelli was a handsome young man," Premarin continued, "everything I am not. He even made an effort to talk to her, to listen. Which I did not. Oh, it woke me up to my own behavior, my own frailties as well as hers. In some ways, I am too late. She knows I do not love her."

"How does she know?"

"Because Venice is a small city. Everyone knows I asked Elena first. Elena Savelli, as she is now."

Grey's eyes grew sharper. Premarin doubted he could have hidden if he'd tried. "You were in love with Elena."

"And I could not have her, so I took another, any other, for convenience. Bianca's family were generous. She was convenient. Only she isn't now. She is a worry to me, Signor Grey. The first time, I followed her from suspicion. After that, from fear for her safety. She never noticed me. I only hope no one else noticed either of us."

Grey stirred, as though moving on. "On the night that Savelli died, you followed her to his house as usual. The front of the house?"

Premarin nodded.

"You did not go by boat?"

"It's a simpler walk, and clearly neither of us wished to wake the gondolier."

"What time was this?" Grey asked.

"About two? After three by the time we left."

"Did you see Savelli at his window? Hear his voice? See any of his servants?"

"Nothing. No one."

"What about on the way home? Did you see anyone in the streets? On the canals?"

"There were a couple of boats. I didn't look." Premarin stopped, frowning. "Wait, though—I did see someone in a boat, drinking straight from a bottle and shouting occasional obscenities. The man is a known drunk, so I hurried to catch up with my wife. But he didn't appear to notice her. He seemed to have some fixed purpose, though he could not keep his boat in a straight line. He bumped into several that were tied up and swore at them all."

"Where was this?" Grey asked urgently.

"On the Grand Canal, though I think he turned off because I couldn't see him the next time I glanced over my shoulder."

"Going in which direction?" Grey demanded. "Toward Savelli's house or away?"

"Toward, I suppose."

"And this man was known to you? Who is he?"

Premarin could see that Grey already knew, but he said it anyway. "Rossi. Domenico Rossi."

CHAPTER FIFTEEN

CHALLENGING AN AGGRESSIVE drunk is rarely wise. In the old days, Constance would have found a way to distract him. Perhaps she had grown lazy in recent years, because in her establishment, on the rare occasions a man misbehaved, she had merely to snap her fingers and two burly young footmen would have the transgressor out of the front door before he or anyone else noticed. They never made a fuss in the street. After all, who wanted to be discovered by friends, neighbors, or the police shouting outside a brothel?

This was an entirely different situation. She was alone in a secluded garden with a man who might have killed already and arranged the poisoning that still seemed such a terrible, personal attack.

And Rossi was undoubtedly angry. His eyes had seemed to flare into fury as soon as she mentioned fighting, but there was more there. Fear? Desperation? Although not a particularly large man, he was big enough and unpredictable enough to be a threat. And he was poised, his very stillness unnatural and unnerving.

"I do not fight," he stated with a sudden softness that chilled her. "I am an artist."

"And a very fine one." Flattery was an old and successful weapon, but she was still afraid to release his gaze. "But you are still human. Anyone would resent being dismissed as you were by Signor Savelli. And the signora…such a beautiful lady."

His eyes softened in reminiscence. "Fire and ice and

strength," he said, and then his gaze refocused. "I wanted to paint her very badly."

"Did you love her?"

A moment longer, he stared at her and her healing stomach lurched with fresh fear. She clasped it and her pile of papers and tensed for the blow, whatever it would be.

Then he threw back his head and roared with laughter.

Constance breathed again, but the man was too unpredictable for her to relax entirely. Though he seemed about to disprove one of their theories.

"Her face obsessed me," he said suddenly. "So does yours. I cannot love all my obsessions. I have reality."

"Adriana."

A smile flickered across his lips. "I should marry her." He sighed. "And I should drink less to make her marry me."

"Why don't you?"

"That," said the artist, "is a very good question. I like to drink. And when I don't paint, when my own lack of talent scares me… I drink and it doesn't matter. Until I wake up."

"Do you tell Adriana this?"

He plucked at his coat as though suddenly too warm. "No. But I think she knows. She knows everything."

"Even that you don't always remember?"

It was a risk to bring up that subject again, but he only shrugged. "Probably."

Questions tried to force themselves from her lips, but she knew better than to hurry him at this moment. They *almost* understood each other, and she couldn't take the chance of ruining that.

His gaze swept suddenly back to hers. "You want to know, don't you? If I went back to the palazzo to fight with Savelli? I might have. I might not. When he sent me away that day, I got vilely, stupidly drunk. Adriana shut her door on me, and who can blame her? I woke up in my studio the next morning, as if I hadn't moved. But I had. My clothes were filthy and wet, as if I'd fallen in a canal or a puddle and rolled about the streets. I had bruises, but whether someone punched me or I fell over and hurt myself, I don't know.

"Dreams from that night came back to me, full of my anger against Savelli. There was blood. It didn't feel real, but I don't know if it was or not. Other people were in the dream too. Premarin, trailing after his plain young wife. I knew it was her even though she was veiled and hooded."

"How did you know?" Constance asked.

"The way she moved."

"Where were they when you saw them?"

"Somewhere beside the Grand Canal. On foot." His eyes widened. "Close to the Palazzo Savelli..."

It seemed to Constance that there had been so many people close to the Palazzo Savelli that night, it was a miracle they hadn't fallen over each other. Giusti, Premarin, Bianca Premarin, Rossi. To say nothing of Savelli's wife and the household who had seen and heard nothing.

A few steps forward and then snapped back to the beginning.

And Rossi didn't even know whether or not he was guilty.

"In your dream," she said suddenly, "when you attacked Savelli and there was all that blood, did you have a weapon? How were you hurting him?"

He grimaced but didn't need to think about it. "With my old palette knife. Is it not symbolic?"

At last. Constance smiled at him, and he looked momentarily dazzled. "Symbolic of your innocence. I think we have both been afraid your dream was not a dream but a drunken memory of drunken rage. But it can't have been a true memory because you used a palette knife. That isn't what killed him. Your dream was only a dream. You didn't actually kill Savelli. It is quite a distinction, since the evidence seems to rule out no one else in Venice."

"HE COULD BE lying," Solomon said judiciously.

He had come home in something of a panic, shortly after Rossi's departure, and Constance, back indoors in the drawing room and sipping weak tea, had immediately poured out her encounter with the artist.

"I don't believe he is," she said.

"You are usually right," he allowed. "And we don't believe either Elena or Giusti were lying either. We just have to bear in mind that we like these people and don't want them to be guilty."

She had not told him of her sudden sense of threat in Rossi's company. It no longer seemed important, since it had vanished like a summer rain shower. "What of Premarin?"

"Oh, he was there, following his wife, whose oddities he appears to be well aware of. He might even be taking responsibility for some of them. He claims to be jealous no longer, merely ashamed, and both he and Bianca seem to have been heading homeward when they and Rossi saw each other."

"He could have taken a few minutes away from watching his wife in order to entice Savelli outside," Constance said.

"He would need to have gone through the house, without his wife seeing Savelli letting him in. And even if that were possible, why would Savelli show him out the back way, where he has no means of transport?"

"Savelli's own boats were there." She sighed. "You're right, though, it doesn't make any sense. Have we finally reduced our suspects to none?"

"It would seem so."

They were silent for a little while, gazing out of the window at the breathtaking view. Not as magnificent as the Grand Canal, but with its own quieter, more *real* beauty.

"The weapon," Constance said suddenly. "That's what I was trying to think about when Rossi distracted me. We have not seen it. Do you suppose the police gave it back to Elena?"

"We can ask her. Though I don't see what we can learn from it at this stage. It was Savelli's own weapon and left in his body."

She reached out and took his hand. "Is this our first failure, Solomon? On our first case since our marriage?"

His thumb caressed her wrist. "Perhaps one should not go investigating on one's honeymoon. There are too many other distractions."

"I have so loved those distractions," she said, carrying his hand to her cheek.

"So have I," he said, just a little huskily. "God, so have I."

"I am very much better," she said.

He smiled, sliding his hand from her cheek to her nape and making her shiver. "Temptress."

They stayed like that as the afternoon wore on, and though she waited with her heart skittering, she knew he would not take her to bed. Not yet.

In present circumstances, his abstinence only emphasized his care of her. And in any case, just being with him like this as the afternoon drew to a close, and an unsolved and apparently insoluble mystery hung over them, was strangely sweet, and more, much more, than enough.

IN THE MORNING, Constance woke up feeling much more like herself. She was frustrated that Solomon insisted she drink a cup of coffee before she rose and then insisted on helping her dress. But the anxiety in his eyes—how long had it taken her to recognize all those expressions she had once found so veiled and difficult?—lightened to approval as she ate her egg and bread for breakfast.

"I shall come with you to call on Elena," she said firmly, and he merely nodded. If anything, he seemed amused by the challenge in her manner.

Alvise grinned as he helped her into the boat, and he sang all the way to the Palazzo Savelli.

Although the servant let them into the foyer at once, he left them there while he carried their names to his mistress. Pellini, one of the bodyguards who had abducted Constance, lounged near the front door, watching them in a surly manner, as though he expected them to steal the silver.

"If *he* didn't kill Savelli himself," Constance murmured, observing him in return, "he probably still thinks you did."

"I'm a possibility to him, no doubt, but so is Giusti, whom his fellows were busy beating to a pulp when we first saw them. Unless, as you say, he did it himself. The bodyguards are about the only suspects we have left."

The servant came back and conducted them solemnly to the drawing room, where Elena sat not in splendid isolation but in the company of the Venetian policeman Foscolo, who scowled at the very sight of Solomon and Constance.

Elena, on the other hand, was openly delighted to see them, coming forward at once with her hand outstretched. "Signora, should you be out so soon?"

"It's an experiment," Constant said lightly. "I feel I will go mad trapped indoors."

"I know the feeling. You have met Signor Foscolo, of course."

Foscolo nodded curtly. He looked undecided as to whether to vacate the premises in disgust or stay where he was in the hope of discovering the point of their visit.

"Wine?" Elena asked. "Or is it too early for your English sensibilities?"

Constance shuddered. "Certainly for this English stomach."

"Sit, my dear. Every time I see you, you look better."

Foscolo, clearly tired of the small talk, said abruptly, "What brings you here?"

"Actually," Solomon said, with a quick, apologetic glance at Elena, "we wanted to know if the police had returned Signor

Savelli's dagger, and if so, if we could see it."

A spark of anger lit Foscolo's face. "I could have told you that without the need to distress the signora. The weapon is still in our possession, and no, you may not see it, because it is none of your concern."

"Then how fares your inquiry into my wife's poisoning?" Solomon asked steadily. "I presume there is one?"

Pinkness seeped into the policeman's face. "Naturally. I will keep you informed." He nodded stiffly to Elena, all but clicking his heels as wishing them all good day, and stalked out.

Constance, who had always preferred him to his Austrian superior, was taken aback by this apparent hostility. "Does he suspect us again?" she wondered aloud.

"Oh, no, Lampl is probably hampering the natural course of his inquiries," Elena replied. "It must be like working with one's hands tied."

"But your husband was a friend to the Austrian government," Solomon said. "Surely Lampl wants the culprit brought to justice?"

"Of course."

But did Foscolo? Had Foscolo found the truth and it was somehow unpalatable to him? Or to Lampl and the government of Venice?

"Why did he come?" Constance asked, a new idea struggling into her mind.

"A courtesy, I think. He told me he had found no evidence against the bodyguards Angelo hired, but still he advised me to pay them off."

"Why haven't you?" Solomon asked.

Elena sighed. "I suppose I was wary of them vanishing somewhere we couldn't find them before we discovered they were the culprits."

"That is brave," Solomon said, "and risky. I thought you didn't suspect them?"

"I don't, really. It makes no sense. But nothing does, now."

Elena spoke flatly, without pathos, and yet it struck Constance as poignant.

There was nothing she could say that would ease the loss, the pain.

Solomon said, "Your husband was a collector of antique weapons, was he not? Perhaps you could show us his collection?"

Constance blinked at him in surprise. It seemed unusually insensitive of him, especially when he had already asked about the murder weapon.

Elena's brows lifted, though she did not seem to be particularly disturbed. She led the way across the fine gallery to the study she had shown them on their first visit.

Comfortable, functional, and decorative, it looked exactly the same as before, dominated at one end by the large desk and throne-like chair. At the other side of the enormous fireplace were the glass display cabinets, to which Elena led them without obvious emotion.

To Constance's untrained eye, Savelli's collection looked like a fine historical armory—swords and daggers of all shapes and lengths, both simple and ornate in style, ancient-looking pistols and a musket, a pair of fine, silver-mounted dueling pistols, and, on the wall, a medieval shield with a coat of arms painted upon its curved surface.

As she gazed around with a mixture of awe and distaste, Constance became only slowly aware that Elena was staring fixedly at an object in the second case. Alarmed, Constance went to join her there. There was only one object on display there—a long dagger with a dazzling jeweled hilt and shining blade.

"What is it?" Solomon asked.

Elena stepped back, one hand flying to her mouth, and then falling to her side.

"That is it," she gasped. "That is the dagger that killed him."

CHAPTER SIXTEEN

SOLOMON STARED AT the widow. There was no doubt the sight of the dagger upset her, and he was instantly sorry he had asked to see the collection at all. In fact, he wasn't quite sure why he had suggested it. Perhaps to give him some more idea of the murdered man and at least the *kind* of weapon that had been used against him. Constance had not quite approved, and of course she was right.

He said gently, "According to Foscolo, the police did not return it."

"Then why is it here?" Elena snapped.

"It must have been a different dagger."

She stared at him. "I saw it sticking out of my husband's chest. Do you think that is something I could forget or mistake?"

"No," Constance said, taking her hand and leading her away. "Of course he thinks no such thing. We have to work out how it got back here."

"Foscolo." Pulling free, Elena hurried to the door and called for her servant before hurling English words over her shoulder at Constance and Solomon. "He must have returned it on his way out of the house. He probably came with that purpose and struggled for the right moment, and then you came and—"

Elena broke off, turning on the servant instead. "Did you show Signor Foscolo straight to the front door? Did he go anywhere else in the house? In here?"

"No, signora," said the mystified servant. "I brought him

straight up to you without asking, since he is the police, and I showed him straight out."

"Was he carrying anything when he arrived?" Solomon asked.

"No. Nor when he left."

"What of Signor Lampl?" Solomon said. "Has he ever been here without disturbing the signora?"

"Oh, no," the servant said, apparently shocked. "Well, not after that first day when they were both in this room—Signor Foscolo and Signor Lampl."

That was certainly true. Solomon had been interviewed by them both here.

"Did they pay much attention to these weapons on display?" Constance asked the servant.

"I was not in the room for most of the time."

"Of course not," Elena interrupted sharply. "But I'm sure you know which cases were breathed on and which had fingermarks all over them when they had left."

He flushed and bowed his head. "Actually, none of them, signora. The police seemed more interested in the master's papers."

"You may go," Elena said, and turned slowly back to Solomon. "What are you thinking?"

He wasn't sure that he wanted to tell her that yet, so instead, he said the next thing that came into his head. "That dagger you recognize is a conspicuously beautiful and valuable weapon. Why would your husband have stuck it in his belt when he went outside without his coat at five o'clock in the morning?"

Elena blinked several times, then sank onto the nearest chair. "I don't know. I suppose... I assumed he was polishing it when he was distracted. He often dusted and polished his collection at the oddest times."

"When he was distracted by whoever enticed him outside, you mean?" Solomon said, and Constance, suddenly catching on, hurried to each of the windows to confirm what he already suspected.

"Yes," Elena said helplessly.

"But this room looks onto the side of the house only," Constance said. "You cannot see the back door or the canal running past it from here. Nor can you see the front."

Elena frowned, beginning to look baffled. "Did he *hear* something, then? Even if he did… Surely he would have laid the dagger back in its case, not put it in his belt."

"Unless he was afraid for his life," Constance said.

"Then why go out at all? Why not summon the bodyguard he insisted on hiring?"

"Pride?" Constance suggested.

"But to take that *particular* dagger? When I saw it, when I saw *him*, it never struck me how odd it was, but he would never have taken that out of the house so carelessly. It would be an invitation to be robbed. For protection—" Elena got up suddenly and strode past Constance to the desk, pulling open the second drawer down. From it, she took a plain, clean, much shorter blade and set it carefully down on the surface of the desk. "*This* is what he took to protect himself, ever since he returned to Venice with the Austrians. He cannot have been in such a hurry that he chose *that*"—she pointed toward the case—"over *this*."

"Then we have two more mysteries," Solomon said. "How was he stabbed with *that* dagger? And how the devil did it get back to its case?"

For a while, the three of them stood there, staring at each other in consternation.

Elena finally said, "Either someone put it back, or it never left this case. And it cannot be the latter, because I saw it in his chest."

Constance caught her breath. "Did you?"

Elena's face twisted in distress, in memory, no doubt, and Constance caught her hand again, as if in both comfort and apology. "No, listen. Only two were ever made."

Solomon's skin prickled with excitement. They were on the verge of discovery, of solution. "They were originally a pair."

"*I* told them that," Elena said impatiently. "Angelo grew up knowing it. The dagger has been in his family for centuries, only one. Yet the tradition is that two identical daggers were made for his ancestor for some ceremonial occasion. Angelo traced the ownership of this one through the ages—it has always been in Venice in one branch of the Savelli family or another. But he never found any sign of the other. It might never have existed. Who would want two such daggers?"

"Who would want *one*?" Constance asked, wandering over to stare again at the beautiful, deadly thing. "Surely no one would take into actual battle?"

"It was never about battle, it was about status, wealth, ostentation. Venice was rich and gaudy when this was made. Her merchants ruled the world. Or at least the Mediterranean world. It was the center of Angelo's collection."

"He was proud of it," Solomon said, feeling his way. "Did he ever look for its twin?"

"Not that I know of. It was not in Venice. I expect he kept an ear out, but he assumed the twin had been lost centuries ago, even broken up and sold for its jewels. You are seriously thinking that he was killed with the lost twin of his own dagger? Would that not be rather fanciful coincidence?"

Or a deliberate message of vengeance. "Perhaps... Signora, are these cases kept locked?"

Constance tried the lid and failed to open it.

"Of course," Elena said. "They are all locked. The key is in the safe." She waved at a locked walnut cabinet beneath a beautiful glass vase.

"Would you see if it is still there?" Solomon asked.

Shrugging, Elena took the ring of surprisingly small keys from some hidden pocket of her gown and advanced on the safe. Even the lock of the safe was cleverly disguised, and it seemed to take several turns and half turns of the key to open it.

Clever, thought Solomon, who had recent experience of a much larger and more conspicuously impregnable set of locks. In this case, most people would quickly give up on the correct key as being the wrong one.

Elena put her hand inside and brought out a single, small key. She walked to the nearest glass case, opened and closed it again, then moved to the jeweled dagger's case and did the same.

"How many keys are there for the cases?" Constance asked.

"Just this one. So the theory is wrong. Angelo was *not* polishing the dagger when he was enticed outside. He can't have just shoved it into his belt for quickness. The cabinets were all locked."

"Could anyone have smuggled it back in? Who else has a key to the safe?"

"Just Angelo. The police still have those, too."

Constance's gaze flew to Solomon's.

"Not *his* dagger," Elena mused. "But he is no less dead. What does it mean?"

"I don't know," Solomon said, "but for your own sake, let us keep the matter strictly between ourselves."

Elena frowned. "But the police should be informed..."

"Not yet," Solomon said quickly. He focused on the dagger, trying to memorize every facet, every tiny scratch on the polished blade. "Tomorrow. Tell me, would you recognize your husband's dagger beside its twin?"

"Clearly not," Elena said.

As they left the Palazzo Savelli, Constance was aware of a powerful urge to walk briskly in the fresh air. However, since she doubted her body was up to it, she accepted Solomon's hand and then Alvise's back onto the boat.

While Alvise rowed, she and Solomon sat beneath the awning and talked in low, urgent voices.

"But the fabric of Savelli's clothes was torn by a blade," Constance said. "The dagger *had* to have been in his belt."

"A dagger," Solomon corrected her. "At one time, not necessarily that night. It could even have been after his death. We never saw the body or what he was wearing."

"If it was the same as he wore earlier in the night, which is what his valet told us, then I saw no tear in his clothes when I met him. The threads found on the murder weapon could just as easily have come from the killer's clothes. Or, as you say, the killer could have made the tear himself to mislead the investigation."

"Elena does not have her husband's keys back from the police," Solomon said thoughtfully.

"But they *could* still have returned the dagger without her knowing," Constance said. She shook her head. "Bizarre behavior, but it goes back to what we thought earlier. Elena is the center of all this."

"I think she is," Solomon agreed. "Whether there are two daggers or just one."

The excitement coursing through Constance was oddly chilling. "How could we have overlooked the fact that policemen are human too? Foscolo, who seems the professional, determined investigator, unmoved by politics or social station, had no reason to call on her today. He is almost afraid to look at her, yet he protects her, like a dog with a bone, even when you just say her name. Like Premarin, he must be hopelessly devoted."

"Hopelessly," Solomon repeated. "So why kill her husband? Is it likely she would turn to *Foscolo*? He might be from an old family, but he is nowhere in the current hierarchy. Was he just doing her a favor, as he saw it?"

"An act of temper?" She shook her head impatiently. "It must have been planned. Either he managed to steal and return Savelli's dagger, or he somehow tracked down its twin. That is obsession."

"Or luck. Foscolo fought for Venice against Austria, but like Giusti, he probably went on raiding parties. Before the siege, he could have gone anywhere in Italy, negotiating, conferring, even fighting."

"We don't know him, or anything about him," Constance said restlessly. "He was never a suspect. He was the law."

Solomon took her hand. "Yet he was there, at the consulate reception. He did not stay long, but during his conversation with Lampl, he stood close to your glass on the table. While we could not see it."

"But why? We were floundering. What did we say or do that convinced him we had to be scared off? We did tell him we wanted to solve the mystery and find the culprit, but surely that alone was no threat to him. Certainly not worth the risk of poisoning me! I'm sure I said nothing…"

"It must have been me," Solomon said. "You would remember everything that was said. I must have said something when you were not present."

"Or someone else reported it to him, even in passing." She shivered. "Oh, Solomon, we have been blind…"

Alvise called a greeting to another boatman who was grinning and calling back. All along the waterways, supplies were being unloaded and taken on board. The streets around them bustled with chatter and business and color. And yet Constance shivered because it seemed suddenly that there was evil beneath the faded, almost decadent beauty of the city, and its charming, friendly residents. *Darkness and light.*

Vengeance… "There has to be more than unrequited love for Elena," she said. "Savelli was on the other side, Foscolo's enemy. Could they have had some encounter during the war? Some awfulness he blames Savelli for?"

"I doubt he is likely to tell us," Solomon said grimly. "We cannot question him, so we have to ask others, and I'm afraid—"

"Afraid we are running out of time," Constance finished when he broke off. She squeezed his fingers to get his attention and met his gaze.

There was a pregnant pause. "No," he said.

"Alvise," Constance called casually, "do you know where the

policeman Foscolo lives?"

ALTHOUGH IMPATIENT, CONSTANCE bowed to Solomon's sensible insistence on a light luncheon and rest before going to Foscolo's home. After all, despite his original refusal to consider her participation in any such visit, he had eventually given in to her argument that she would supply the innocence to the occasion.

"What man would take his sick wife to help break in anywhere, let alone to a policeman's house?" she had said blithely.

He'd thought it over for some time. "Our excuse to be there, if we need one, is that we are calling on him with the questions we could not ask him earlier in front of Signora Savelli. But we must time it correctly. In daylight, not long before he might reasonably be expected home, yet not so late that he actually *comes* home. But if there is difficulty, Constance, we leave. In fact, we don't even go in. Breaking and entering is not a charge any British consul could save us from."

As if trying to convince himself, he added, "We should be in and out so quickly that no one will know. At this stage, we need to discover if he is at least a collector of antiques. I can't believe we would be so lucky as to find the dagger in his house. It is more likely at the police office. But he might have Savelli's keys. And we might find some hint, some proof of what he did in the war, of why he hated Savelli."

"A reason more than Elena? I doubt Savelli beat her."

"Perhaps Foscolo knows otherwise," Solomon said.

She was uneasily aware that he was right. Elena bore none of the obvious signs of an abused wife. Nor did she seem to have the character of a victim, as Constance understood it. On the other hand, the widow was racked with guilt and confusion over Giusti, as if she deserved punishment.

The policeman had rooms in an old building that, according

to Alvise, had once belonged to his own family before it was sold off decades ago. Now it served as lodgings for several middling sorts of people.

It was not built at the side of a canal, but along a narrow passageway to a little square with a well at the center. On disembarking from their boat in their role as tourists, Constance and Solomon strolled arm in arm to the nearest bridge, where they paused for a few minutes to watch the gondolas and the supply boats sail beneath them. Then they walked on to the other side and down the passageway to the square and Foscolo's discreet building.

They had no idea which floor he lived on, and the side gate, presumably to a backyard, was bolted shut. Even in the dark and quiet, they would have had difficulty getting in. So Solomon knocked loudly on the door.

As it opened, he removed his hat and asked in his best Italian for Signor Foscolo.

The short, stout, middle-aged woman with the hard eyes shook her head emphatically, explaining that Signor Foscolo was not at home.

Solomon frowned. "He told us to come at this time," he said testily. "My wife is not well enough to walk around the streets… We will wait."

He took a step forward, and the woman almost rolled up her sleeves for a fight, only her gaze fell on Constance, who clearly did not yet look as well as she felt, for the woman stepped back again and addressed her directly.

"Come in, signora. I will find you a chair to wait."

Constance took a quick glance around the large, empty foyer. The door nearest the front stood open, revealing part of a small dwelling within—presumably this woman's.

"I am the caretaker," she said proudly. Concentrating hard, Constance picked up the gist of the rest. "I see when everyone comes in and out, so I know Signor Foscolo will not be home for—oh, at least half an hour, and probably longer."

"He would not mind our waiting in his rooms," Solomon assured her.

"That is not possible," the caretaker said with finality, toiling up the stairs with Constance and Solomon at her heels.

Constance remembered to walk slowly and to lean heavily on Solomon's arm. The snail's pace was eating into their half-hour, making her tense and impatient. Much to her relief, the caretaker paused on the first floor, outside the first door.

"Foscolo," she said. "Wait."

She waddled to the end of the passage and opened another door. Something scraped and bumped and scraped again, and she emerged, pulling a hard chair with her. Solomon strode forward and took it from her, which won a look of approval and a breathless *"Grazie."* But she obviously had her own, very strict ideas, for she waddled back to Constance and pointed to a precise place on the floor by the front door.

Obediently, Solomon placed the chair, and handed Constance into it. She sighed as if relieved and grateful, and thanked the caretaker in as weak a voice as she could manage.

The caretaker smiled at her. *"Bella, bella,"* she said wistfully, then swung again on Solomon. "Signor Foscolo is a very busy man."

"I know," Solomon said. "And much respected."

It was a good opening, but their hopes of learning about the policeman from his neighbor were dashed at once, for the caretaker merely waddled off toward the stairs again. "Half an hour," she repeated. "Or an hour or more. I cannot say."

Solomon crouched down beside Constance, as though still worried about her. "Can you wait that long?"

"I'll see," Constance said. "I will try."

Solomon's eyes began to dance. "My brave wife. Just say the word and I will take you home."

"Not yet. I will just rest here and then I'm sure all will be well."

Constance did not put it past the caretaker to begin mopping the foyer floor or finding some other task that would allow her to keep her eyes and ears on the foreign visitors. But much to her relief, the slow footsteps faded across the floor below, and she heard the click of the closing door.

From most of the foyer below, they could not be seen.

Solomon straightened and carefully tried Foscolo's door. Naturally, it was locked.

"Over to you, my dubiously talented wife," he murmured.

Constance opened her reticule and took out a couple of narrow steel tools. Talking idly, in case the caretaker or anyone else was listening, he moved to the balustrade and peered over, looking both up and down as Constance knelt by the lock and set to work.

Once, the lockpick slipped from her fingers and landed on the tiled floor with an unnaturally loud, echoing clatter.

"You dropped your scissors, my dear," Solomon said, again for the benefit of listeners. "Let me... Use my handkerchief while I pick these things up."

She cast him a lopsided smile, picked the tool up for herself, and got back to work. *I wish I were better at this...*

She smiled up at Solomon when the lock finally gave. He was already beside her, drawing her to her feet, and then he slid first into the space beyond.

TOWARD THE END of the afternoon, when Foscolo was considering going home early for once, Lampl strutted into his office without as much as a knock.

Foscolo regarded his superior with barely suppressed dislike. These days, he could hardly turn around without bumping into Lampl, whose mission appeared to be the sabotage of Foscolo's.

"Well?" Lampl barked.

"I have investigated all the servants, including the bodyguards," Foscolo said tonelessly. "As I told you, there is nothing against any of the servants in terms of character, and none of them were out of place when they rose in the morning. Even the bodyguards, who are a mix of brawlers, former soldiers, and one-time criminals, and sleep in a dormitory that the other male servants have to walk through to go anywhere, were all in their beds when the household woke."

"Then you have missed something," Lampl pronounced. "Look again. Someone is lying."

Foscolo barely retained his temper. "Very well," he managed.

"What of the consulate poisoning? Are you any further forward with that?"

"No, sir."

Lampl's gaze was sharp and unblinking, and Foscolo felt a sudden twinge of anxiety. Did the Austrian suspect him? If so, he was in trouble and liable to fall from the tightrope that had been his life over the last few years.

"Then what the devil have you been doing with your time?" Lampl asked.

"Investigating Savelli's servants, one by one, as you instructed me. It takes a long time to look at the entire life of one person. And now, you want me to repeat the process. As for the poisoning, I thought *you* were investigating that?"

It was a somewhat desperate attempt to turn the tables on Lampl, which had worked before to get the man off his back for a few hours at least. But Lampl must have grown wise to the tactic.

His eyes narrowed. "I said I would deal with the British officials. If you cannot manage a few cooks and cleaning girls, I question your fitness for your position. What have you been doing all day? All day yesterday?"

That, of course, was the question Foscolo could not answer, at least, not with any honesty.

"My duty," he said stolidly.

"And your duty took you to the house of Signora Savelli this morning?"

So Lampl did have a spy in the household. He had spies everywhere, including in this office, which made Foscolo's position somewhat precarious.

Foscolo raised his eyebrows. "Yes, sir. Investigating all these servants repeatedly takes me there quite often."

"So I hear," Lampl said deliberately. Oh yes, the man was suspicious. It was in his voice as well as in his eyes, and he wasn't even hiding it now. He took a step nearer, and Foscolo's fingers curled as though around the hilt of an imaginary dagger. "And you enjoy it, don't you? Harassing those who served Savelli. Harassing his widow."

"Who would you prefer me to harass?" Foscolo asked politely. "Giusti? The Englishman? Signor Premarin? The British consul, perhaps?"

"Your job is not to harass but to investigate, and you are obviously damned poor at that."

Foscolo itched to punch the Austrian in the face. He even sprang to his feet and, to give his hands something else to do, reached for his hat.

"Now where are you going?" Lampl demanded.

"To investigate," Foscolo snapped.

He wasn't, of course. He was getting away from Lampl, because if the man started questioning his every move, he was truly sunk. No, for once, Foscolo was going home early to rest, eat, and plan his next play of the game.

CHAPTER SEVENTEEN

T HE FIRST THING that Constance saw in Foscolo's home was a
small painting of a woman.

"Is he married?" she whispered to Solomon in surprise.

"Widowed, would be my guess."

And the painting would be the first thing *he* saw when he
came through the door. There was pathos in that, something
innately human and vulnerable and lonely. And yet they believed
he had killed a man and poisoned Constance. People were
complicated and *messy*.

Foscolo lived in a decent set of rooms. A kitchen to the right,
a dining room and a bedchamber on the left, and, facing the front
door, a pleasant sitting room with a rickety but tidy desk at which
he presumably worked.

Leaving Solomon to search in the sitting room, Constance
flitted back to the bedchamber and, listening out for any sounds
of approaching footsteps, began a quick, methodical search.

But there was very little here that was personal. Foscolo
appeared to be a tidy man, but he kept no letters in his room, no
keepsakes among his shirts or underwear. She found nothing
under his pillow except a nightshirt, and nothing beneath the
mattress. He had few ornaments and no jewelry. Apart from the
painting in the hall, she found no traces of a wife. A man who
lived for his work? Or a man perpetually in hiding from the
Austrian police, living down his past as a revolutionary?

She moved into the kitchen, which was equipped well

enough but was obviously little used. Too clean, too tidy. She had just opened the first drawer when she heard voices below in the foyer, and heavy footsteps mounting the stairs.

"Solomon!" she hissed, closing the drawer and bolting back into the hall, where she sat on a stool that was obviously used for standing on to reach the wall sconces.

After a tense moment, Solomon emerged, leaving the sitting room door in precisely the same position as they had found it, and loped silently down the passage to stand by her side. The footsteps paused an instant, as though their owner were surprised by the sight of the empty chair beside the front door. Constance held her breath, her heart beating loudly in her ears as she dredged up the story they'd hoped never to need.

"Signor Foscolo! Forgive us, but I was taken ill and the door opened, and Solomon was so anxious to speak to you. I do hope you don't mind…"

Thin. Damnably thin…

The footsteps moved on and continued along the passage and up the next flight of stairs.

Constance sagged.

Solomon touched her shoulder. "Anything?"

"Nothing. You?"

He shook his head. "A few family papers, a couple of bills. It's as if the man has no life."

"Or a life he is hiding from the Austrians."

"Precisely."

Then he'd taken even more of a risk killing the Austrian ally, Savelli. What had Savelli done that Foscolo should kill him at that moment? Was it part of a larger plan? Or were they right that it was all for Elena?

He stood no chance with her, Constance realized all over again, as Solomon returned to the sitting room and she went back into the kitchen. Why would she turn from one secretive man to another? She needed openness, honesty. And certainly not her husband's killer…

Constance searched the inside of the drawers and beneath them. She looked in all the cupboards, even inside the oven and in every empty pot and jar.

She had just stood on tiptoes to replace the last jar on the shelf when a shadow fell over her.

Not Solomon. She always knew his presence.

She turned her head slowly.

Foscolo stood in the doorway, watching her.

Her instinctive cry to Solomon died in her throat.

How the devil had he got in so silently? One thing was certain—her planned story if discovered had no chance at all now. He was not going to believe that she had collapsed against the door and it had opened... Wildly, she wondered how to warn Solomon without giving his presence away to Foscolo.

The man was alarmingly still. He had been a soldier. He had probably killed many men before Savelli, and had tried to kill Constance already.

"Signor Foscolo," she said loudly, and pushed the jar the rest of the way on to its shelf before turning fully to face him. "I was looking for tea, but of course I have no right and can only apologize for invading your home."

"Oh, I think you must do better than that," he said. "Explain it."

Very aware that he stood in the way of any possible escape to the front door, she said, "I wanted to talk to you. Did the caretaker not tell you I was here?"

"No. The chair in the passage warned me of that. I prefer to come and go without Signora Berini's surveillance."

Beyond Foscolo's shoulder, another shadow fell.

"You move very quietly," Solomon said.

"So do you," Foscolo replied without turning. "Since you came to talk, I advise you to begin."

"Perhaps we could sit and be comfortable?" Constance suggested.

Foscolo appeared to consider. "Perhaps I prefer to keep the

two of you apart."

"I wouldn't," Solomon said gently.

"But then, you have really lost any say in the matter by breaking into my home."

"Arrest me," Solomon said at once. "Take me to Lampl."

Foscolo turned slowly to look at him. "I'll give you his address, if you like. Which of you picked my lock?" Receiving no answer, the Venetian gave a crooked smile. "Very well. Let us discuss all accusations." He stood to one side and gestured exaggeratedly with one arm. "After you, signora."

Her heart thundering, Constance sailed past him to Solomon, who grasped her hand in a firm, welcome grip. They walked together to the sitting room. Constance did not hear Foscolo following then, but she *felt* him with every prickling hair on her nape.

Solomon handed her onto the sofa and sat beside her without invitation. To her surprise, Foscolo's lips twitched.

"You are a very cool and collected pair of housebreakers. Do I take it, my amateur sleuth-hounds, that you suspect me of something?"

"Actually, we are professional," Constance said, largely to give them thinking time. "We have an inquiry business in London."

Foscolo still looked amused. "Then I congratulate you again. Everyone else believes you, sir, are a great shipping magnate."

"Apparently, one can be both," Solomon said. "Why are you not investigating my wife's poisoning?"

"I am, in my own way."

"A way that covers your own tracks?"

"Yes," Foscolo said, "in a way. I gather that you have recovered, signora. I am glad of that, at least."

"I almost believe you," Constance said.

Foscolo leaned against the arm of the comfortable old chair opposite them. "What led you to suspect me?"

They could tiptoe around this for hours. Constance opened

her mouth, but Solomon said it for her.

"The murder weapon. Savelli's dagger is not missing. Lampl, the bureaucrat, might not have noticed that, but you are a policeman."

Foscolo inclined his head. "I did notice."

"Is the dagger found in Savelli's body still in the possession of the police?"

"No."

"Then either you did give it back to Signora Savelli, or someone else has it."

Again, Foscolo nodded. "And that someone else has to be a policeman, so here you are."

"And then you were at the consulate reception, standing close to my wife's glass when neither of us could see it."

"That is the one time it is unlikely to have been tampered with," Foscolo said unexpectedly. "Lampl and I watch each other like hawks."

A first twinge of doubt caused Constance's eyebrow to twitch. Foscolo did not sound like a guilty man.

"Then who took the dagger from police custody?" she demanded.

Foscolo smiled faintly.

Solomon threw himself against the back of the sofa. "Lampl. Lampl, who was Savelli's friend and must have seen his collection, who had plenty of time to fall in love with Elena, who could make himself the hero of the investigation into the murder, while executing whomever he chose."

"Savelli's prominence and the politics of the day gave him every excuse to personally oversee the case," Foscolo said, "and he does, largely by keeping me busy on futilities. But he suspects I already know too much. I am expecting the dagger to be planted among my possessions very soon, and then he will be home and free—though whether he wins Elena Savelli is another matter."

"She is a woman who inspires obsession," Constance said. "Not yours?"

A rueful smile tugged at the policeman's lips. "I am not dead. I notice her, as I notice you. And I pity her. I don't pity you, now that you are well. But Lampl is dangerous, and he has spies everywhere. You have to keep out of this."

"We can't," Solomon said briefly. "How did he get his hands on the twin dagger?"

"I'm not sure. I think he found it, pillaged it, during the war, from what I have learned from the Austrian garrison—which is vague, by the way, and even if it amounted to evidence, which it doesn't, the government would not allow it to be used. I cannot prove he ever had it. No one ever saw him with it. When he visited Savelli and saw he had a dagger exactly the same, he must have seen his chance and made his plan."

"That is a cold-blooded murder if was for love."

"Love. And the conditions of power and submission that exist here. He felt entitled to do what he wanted."

"Even though Savelli was his friend?"

"He was still a Venetian. A lower rank of friend."

"Surely all Austrians don't think like that," Constance said, appalled.

Foscolo rubbed his forehead wearily. "Of course not. Nor do they go around murdering the natives. Lampl is…flawed."

"And no one knows all this but you," Solomon said. He didn't quite trust Foscolo, and neither did Constance. They had been so sure they were right about him. Foscolo was surely the man with the opportunity, because he did the actual work of investigating and collating evidence. "I hesitate to ask how you worked it out."

"Prejudice," Foscolo said cynically. "I don't like him, so I was doubly careful. Especially when he identified the murder weapon at once as Savelli's own dagger. And then he never mentioned the presence of Savelli's dagger in the study and, in fact, removed *my* mention of it from my report that he passed up the chain of command. I might never have known that if I hadn't made it my business to read all of Lampl's reports on the subject. At first, I only really suspected him of trying to take credit for my work, probably to get me removed, but it was always more than that."

His face was bleak, and for a moment he seemed lost in unpleasant thought. Then he glanced up, his gaze bouncing from Solomon to Constance and back.

"You see, I am trusting you with the truth. You are at perfect liberty to go to Lampl and report everything I said. I hope you won't, for your sakes as well as mine. For the record, you won't find his house as easy to break into as this one. He doesn't have a gullible caretaker but a very large and sour servant who shuts the door in your face while he delivers a message."

"Would we find the murder weapon in his house?" Constance asked.

"I don't know. It could be anywhere by now."

"Not if he is a true collector," Solomon argued. They had come across several of those in London last year.

"I don't think he is. He knew Savelli before the revolution. He may have seen the dagger then, came across its twin during the war, and took it on impulse." Perhaps Foscolo saw something in their expressions, for he added almost defensively, "I am limited in what I can ask. I cannot be suspected of working against him or I will lose my job."

"Then if he is guilty, how do you expect to catch him?" Solomon demanded.

"By leaving the Austrians some way of covering it up," Foscolo said with genuine bitterness.

"Or getting privileged foreigners to make the accusation?" Constance suggested.

Foscolo smiled. "That's the other reason I chose to trust you. Either way, the Austrians must be able to brush Lampl's guilt under the carpet, because they will, whether or not he is punished, and he *must* be."

There was silence for a few moments.

Solomon shook his head in annoyance. "It makes no sense. I can understand if someone chose that particular weapon, and made it look as if the killer stole it from Savelli himself. It widens the list of suspects from the only person with access to the keys—namely Elena."

"Exactly," Constance agreed. "What would be the point of killing her husband and then watching her be arrested for murder?"

Solomon rounded on her. "Then why didn't he find some way to remove Savelli's own dagger from his collection? By leaving it there, he sabotaged his own plan. Anyone could have seen it there! Foscolo did. It was pure luck that Elena herself didn't notice it until today."

Constance leaned back on the sofa. "That is a good point."

They both gazed at Foscolo, who sighed.

"To be fair, I think he aimed to. He arrived that morning just after eight o'clock, and I heard him ask Signora Savelli for permission to use the study to conduct his initial investigation and interviews. Unfortunately, he found me already ensconced there. One of my men had wakened me, you see, almost as soon as the body was discovered, and I was at the Palazzo Savelli well before seven. He kept trying to send me off on trivial tasks, which was quite amusing, because I immediately sent my own men and sat back down. I was interviewing the staff—and yourself, Mr. Grey. It was Lampl who was unnecessary, and he knew it. But miraculously enough, no one noticed the dagger's presence in its case—except me, and I have a spiteful policy of telling Lampl nothing he does not ask me directly. I know he went back a couple of times, but Signora Savelli had herself better in hand by then. I doubt she allowed him to run tame about her house. And in any case, he had already got away with it, just by altering my report. And now everyone thinks Lampl returned the valuable weapon to the widow."

"*She* doesn't," Constance said.

Foscolo waved that aside. "A poor widow, shocked by grief and not remembering correctly."

"But isn't police evidence recorded?" Solomon asked.

"Signed in and out. I saw it shortly before I left the office. My name is beside the dagger's return, but I never took it."

"And the Austrians will not believe you over him," Constance murmured.

Foscolo inclined his head. "You see my predicament. But for now, you must go. You were seen entering the building and I can guarantee I will have to answer Lampl's questions on your visit tomorrow. I will tell him that you are impatient at the progress of the investigation and that I think I calmed you down. For your own sake, say nothing else to anyone. I'll find a way to talk to you tomorrow."

⟫⟫⟫⟩⟨⟨⟨⟨

"I FEEL AS if I've been hit over the head again," Constance said as they walked back toward the boat. "He makes a bizarre kind of sense, but do you believe him?"

"Mostly. But he's a subtle devil. He has had to be to survive."

Constance nodded, holding Solomon's arm closer to her side. "He didn't give a reason for Lampl poisoning me, and I can't think what either of us might have said to make us appear dangerous."

"Neither can I. We don't have quite all the pieces yet, but my feeling is we now have most of them."

"Unless Foscolo made it all up. He was very vague on how Lampl is supposed to have acquired the twin dagger, and we have no proof of any of it. It's Foscolo's name on the evidence book. He could easily be the one who returned the murder weapon to its case."

"Or failed to take the Savelli dagger away," Solomon said consideringly, "because he couldn't get hold of the case key from the safe. He was not an intimate of the Savellis, so he wouldn't know how it worked. I still think it's Lampl."

"Actually, so do I. Foscolo might admire Elena, but he's not a madman. He knows he stands no chance with her. Lampl, on the other hand, is an Austrian aristocrat. It would be a good match for her, in time. And he could take her away from Venice and gossip."

"Something is still wrong, though," Solomon said. "Why did he kill Savelli that particular night? Because, after the fight, Giusti could be blamed, thus removing another rival? Could he have known about it so soon?"

"Only Giusti has not been blamed," Constance pointed out. "Or not yet."

"Then there is your abduction. He could have heard about that too and decided I would make a good culprit."

"Yet if anything, he seems to have protected you, or at least ruled you out."

Solomon scowled. "Apart from poisoning you… And we still don't know why that happened. Alvise—take us to the back door of the Palazzo Savelli."

Although the light was beginning to fade, the palazzo was still clearly visible. The water rippled up the steps from the canal, leading straight to the stout, closed back door.

"Did the killer come by boat, like us?" Solomon murmured, looking up at the building. "Lampl, rowing himself, would surely have intrigued Savelli, and he would not have felt threatened. Did he see him from one of these windows?"

Constance followed his gaze. "Maybe. He certainly didn't have to be in the study at the time if he didn't take the dagger with him. Earlier, Elena saw Giusti from one of them." She pointed upward. "That partially open window has the brightest curtains. I suspect that is Elena's dressing room, where she stood when he rowed by. The windows next to it are surely Savelli's. They are definitely close to that part of the building, for I looked out when Elena showed us his rooms. We can ask her to confirm it…if it's important?"

"It's another oddity," Solomon said. "Was Lampl prepared to wait here, hour after hour, night after night, on the off chance that Savelli would look out of his window at the right time, see him, and come down to be murdered?"

"He would have been seen by someone," Constance said, "considering all the people who skulked around here that night. It must have been prearranged."

"Why would Savelli agree to anything so bizarre? Surely it would be unusual enough for him to alert the bodyguard."

Constance shivered, throwing off her sudden memory of the men who had abducted her and scared her so badly. She tried to concentrate. "Unless they just didn't turn up. And Savelli went out anyway."

"I suppose they could have covered that up," Solomon said doubtfully, "with the police and with the rest of the house—" He broke off. "The lowest window to the right of the door. The one without bars."

She saw it at once, not only because it was placed higher up in the wall than the other bottom windows, giving the row a pleasingly asymmetrical appearance, but because there was movement behind it. A face pressed up against it, grinning and sinister, and she couldn't look away. It was Pellini, one of her abductors.

Solomon went on with growing excitement. "It's almost directly below the window we think was Savelli's dressing room."

"It must be the bodyguards' dormitory." Somewhere, Constance could see that was important and tore her gaze from the terrible face at the window, which was surely more important, yet…

"Did one of them summon Savelli outside from that window?" Solomon continued. "Throw something up at his window to get his attention, wake him, if necessary, without the rest of the household being aware? A trick any schoolboy knows… Constance?" Solomon finished in a suddenly high, frightened voice she had never heard before. "Are you ill?"

"No. No, let's go home, I…"

She gazed at the back doorstep of the Savelli house where she had walked out of danger and into Solomon's arms—some time after being dragged inside by the owner of that face at the window. She hadn't seen it at the time, of course, only when Savelli had removed her hood. The face at the window had recognized her and still thought it was funny to frighten her…

Dragged away from Solomon while he was still in danger, blind and helpless and unable to call out… The rough, bruising hands of her captors and their alien voices babbling words she had not understood because she had been too afraid to think and hadn't known enough Italian.

Days later, she knew quite a lot more. She had grown almost used to conversing in a mixture of English and Italian—with Elena and Rossi and the Palazzo Zulian servants, particularly Maria during her illness, and before that, with some people at the reception. Perhaps more importantly, her ear was now more attuned to the rhythm and speed of the local accents. She could recognize some Venetian words, but her abductors had not used any. One of them—that one at the window, Pellini—was not Venetian, so they had spoken to each other in more universal Italian. The memory of those sounds was in her head, repeating and repeating until they made sense.

Solomon was holding her hand, leaning forward to gaze anxiously into her face. She squeezed his fingers in instinctive comfort.

"…*potremmo perdere i nostri comodi lavori per questo…*"
…could lose our comfortable jobs over this…
"*Starò bene. Potrei parlare con l'austriaco per te.*"
I will be fine. I might speak to the Austrian for you.

She blinked, refocusing all her attention on Solomon. "The Austrian. It *is* Lampl. And that *is* how it was done and why he needed rid of me. Pellini is Lampl's spy, his tool within the Savelli house."

CHAPTER EIGHTEEN

S OLOMON WAS SHAKEN by the sudden reminder of her recent illness. That right now her weakness was caused more by mental shock than physical exertion was not much comfort. His first priority was to get her home and safe and calm.

She paid no attention to what he was ordering and doing, until she seemed to notice quite suddenly that she was in bed, in her nightgown, with a tray of food on her knees and Solomon sprawled beside her, fully dressed, with a tray of his own.

"Oh, Solomon," she whispered. "Have I made a fool of myself?"

Though he could have wept, he merely gave her the gentlest of elbow nudges and spoke with deliberate calm. "Hardly. You are still weak, and I let you do too much. Yet still you solved the case."

She smiled a little. Perhaps she heard the glowing pride in his voice. "It was being there, seeing him at the window. Until then, I had only been asking myself what either of us could have said to Lampl to frighten him. But the bodyguards must have told him."

"We should have thought of it before. We know the Austrians have spies everywhere. But this is more than spying. This was using a government spy to plan a personal murder."

Of course, she had worked that out too. "Lampl *must* have known of Savelli's planned attack on Giusti and taken the opportunity to blacken him and Savelli further in Elena's eyes by abducting a woman off the street at the same time. Elena was meant to know about it. That's why that Pellini and the other went alone by boat while the others were on foot. It might have been bad luck that you and I were in the wrong place at the wrong time, but I doubt luck had much to do with taking *someone.*"

"And of course it provided more suspects to keep Foscolo busy and distracted from the truth."

They ate for a little in silence. Then she said abruptly, "Are we just speculating again? A few hours ago, we believed implicitly that Foscolo was the murderer."

"But this feels right. It fits."

She nodded and reached for her watered wine. "But we still have no actual evidence. How do we prove it?"

"We'll think of something. We have baited traps before."

"And we have an ally in Foscolo," she said more comfortably.

When her eyelids began to close, Solomon took the glass from her fingers and removed both the trays. As he returned to the bed, he saw that her eyes were open again, and smiling at him.

He rearranged her pillows so that she was lying more comfortably. Her fingertips skimmed across his cheek, and he paused. Her eyes were lethargic and clouded, her lips slightly parted. God, she was beautiful…

"It is terribly early to go sleep," she said huskily.

Her invitation was unmistakable, and when he kissed her, so was her desire. Aroused, he groaned into her mouth, only *almost* amused by the temptation. Since their wedding, he had grown so addicted to her body that the last few days of abstinence had felt like famine. Her passion battered at his resolve and came very close to defeating it.

Just a little, gentle love… Where is the harm?

He swallowed, closing his eyes. Because it was the comfort she needed in her exhaustion, not the exertion of passion. "Sleep first," he managed. "I will hold you. Only hold you."

It was not easy, but he managed it. And curiously, it soothed them both to sleep.

PAOLO PELLINI WAS restless and vaguely surprised to be still in the employ of Signora Savelli. It was not as if she feared to go out without her bodyguard, for though she did not go out often, she never took them with her when she did.

The bodyguards were bored and dealt with it in different ways. Some drank and played cards until they couldn't have dealt with an attacker except by falling on them by accident. Ugo paced constantly and threatened to find other work. Mario and Giovanni filled their days by helping the house staff and the boatman with his repairs.

Only Pellini was not bored, because he had his own tasks—reporting on the signora and her visitors. And tonight, he rather thought he had something to report. Accordingly, he made his excuses to his fellows, as he often did, and slipped out of the back door to the rougher steps where the smaller supply boats were tied up.

"Pellini," Ugo said from the doorway.

Pellini glanced at him with impatience to be on his way. He didn't like Venice. There was altogether too much water for a Tuscan who couldn't swim. It was unnatural to live like this, and he wanted to go home. But orders were orders.

"What?" he said grudgingly, climbing into the boat and reaching for the rope that tied it.

"Don't forget what you promised. Speak to the Austrian."

"Yes, yes," Pellini said, scowling with as much threat as he could manage. "If *you* keep *your* promise and shut your mouth on the subject."

He pushed off from the steps and began to row without looking back. He supposed he would have to speak for Ugo. Otherwise the fool would blab of Pellini's double loyalties to the others and his usefulness here would be over.

At least then I could go somewhere else. Preferably somewhere inland, with no larger stretches of water than the odd fishpond.

He rowed fast, for he was a little later than he meant to be and would not be let in after eleven.

The Austrian lived in an unobtrusive house, annoyingly on the water, and though it could be reached by foot, Lampl insisted that his minions use the back door, which, like the Palazzo Savelli, had to approached by boat.

As usual, the large, stony-faced servant opened the door before Pellini had the chance to rap it with his oar.

The man's nostrils flared with undisguised distaste. "What?"

Sometimes, Pellini fantasized about the canal flooding in the heavy rain and sweeping the large man's body away to the lagoon, where it would be eaten by fish. One day, he might help that fantasy along.

For now, he smiled with mock affability. "Oh, just thought I'd drop in for a chat. You're always such good company. Is he there?"

Without a word, the servant shut the door, but Pellini knew better than to leave. By the time he had tied up the boat, the door was open again. Pellini climbed the step and went in.

Lampl's windowless "office" reminded him of the little-used room at the Palazzo Savelli where they had taken the captive foreign woman. A comely wench she was, too, yet Savelli had thrown her back, which was a damned waste of a female.

Lampl sat at the solitary desk, busily writing. "Well?" he said, without looking up.

"They were there again, the Englishman and his wife."

Lampl sighed. "Where?"

"Outside the palazzo, at the back, looking."

The pen stilled. Lampl glanced up, removing the spectacles from his nose. "Looking at what?"

Pellini shrugged. "Just the back of the building."

"With what purpose?" Lampl sounded bored, yet Pellini knew instinctively that he wasn't.

"Who knows? They're obviously still poking about the murder scene."

"Where were you?"

"At the dormitory window."

"Did they see you?"

"*She* did," Pellini said with a satisfied grin. "Looked white as a sheet—petrified."

"Did she." It wasn't even a question. Lampl didn't believe him. "What did *he* do?"

"Nothing. Told the boatman to row on."

Lampl sat back in his chair, his eyes oddly chilling. In rare moments of honesty, Pellini admitted that this cold, correct gentleman, who never lifted a finger—physically—against a soul, scared him far more than the large servant with the fighter's poise.

"Wait," the Austrian said at last. "I might have instructions for you…"

⟫⟫⟩✕⟨⟪⟪

IN THE CIRCUMSTANCES, it was not surprising that Solomon dreamed of his wife's warm, soft body, of her hair falling against his chest as her lips traced sensuous patterns on his skin, and her hands swept delicately across his hips. He almost purred with pleasure. And when, smiling, he opened his eyes and wrapped his arms around her to hold her closer, her weight was suddenly real and fiercely arousing.

"Solomon," she whispered, raising her head, though only to move and kiss his mouth. "Love me now," she whispered against his lips, and gave him no choice.

He might not have been able to hold back the storm, but at least he kept some kind of rein on his starving desires, holding on to tenderness until the final, shattering conclusion.

Afterward, sprawled across him, she murmured lethargically, "Positively the best start to the morning."

Solomon could not disagree, though he gently, half anxiously, pushed her hair off her face to see if he had hurt her or tired her unbearably.

She was smiling with contentment, the shadows beneath her eyes faint now, and her eyes themselves brilliant and happy. "I'm better," she said.

He stroked her hair. "I believe you are. I am all the better for that myself."

It meant that when they rose and dressed and went sedately downstairs for breakfast, he felt capable of anything. He even felt optimistic about bringing Lampl down.

Beyond the dining room window, the sky was cloudy yet did not remind him of home.

"When do you suppose Foscolo will come?" Constance asked when the servants had left them alone. She was risking a cup of coffee for the first time since she was poisoned. Solomon noticed but did not comment.

"I don't think he will. If there are spies everywhere…"

She set down her coffee. "Then why not in a house rented to foreigners?" she finished for him. "I don't believe I like that idea."

Solomon, having been through the same thought process himself, said, "Look on them as gossips. They are not really there to control us but the local population. The Austrians got a huge fright in 1848. They are not about to let it happen again if they can avoid it. And local people are poor enough and desperate to enough to take payment for harmless information."

"Like the Venetian policeman calling on us?" She frowned. "Who do you think—"

"Don't," he said. "Not if you want to stay sane and enjoy our time here."

She stared at him, then a smile began to form. "I never realized you were quite so pragmatic. And wise."

Or stupid.

"So we should just go out and hope he comes upon us by accident?" she said.

"If you are up to it."

Her eyes were suddenly wicked. "Oh, I am up to anything now."

Fortunately, perhaps, a servant returned bearing a sealed letter on a tray, which he presented to Solomon, then bowed and departed.

Solomon broke the seal and caught his breath. It was in English and written by a fine hand.

My dear Mr. Grey,

It is imperative that we meet where we will not be seen or over-heard. I dare not be seen helping you, but please know that you and your wife are in danger. Her illness was no accident and I can provide you with proof of her would-be murderer. You, sir, must present this proof, not I, for I should not be believed and would end up like poor Savelli. You must take this chance and bring all to justice.

Come to the Rialto Bridge tomorrow at dawn. Tell no one and burn this letter immediately.

Yours in desperation,
Rudolf von Lampl.

"I think," Solomon said thoughtfully, "your theory is about to be tested."

"What theory?" she asked.

"That you are up to anything. This is from Lampl. He wants to meet tomorrow at dawn. And he wants me to burn this letter."

She leapt up from her chair, snatching the letter and reading its carefully phrased English. "He has signed it to make you think he is genuine," she said, her voice high with sudden fright. "But he isn't, Solomon. It's a trap."

"He does seem to have baited his first."

GIUSTI HAD NEVER lacked courage. But as he marched boldly up to the front door of the Palazzo Savelli, he wondered if he was being the most arrant coward, for he would not even ask to see her. He couldn't.

He rapped confidently on the door while his heart quailed.

As soon as the door opened, he thrust his parcel into the surprised hands of the servant. "For Signora Savelli, with the compliments of Ludovico Giusti. Please give it to her immediately."

He was already turning away on the last word when the servant stood back, opening the door wide to reveal Elena herself, halfway across the foyer. She seemed to be frozen in mid-stride, as though she had heard his voice. She looked...stricken.

His throat closed up. He could not speak.

But his paralysis seemed to release hers. Her expression smoothed and she walked gracefully toward him. He would have bolted, if he could.

"Signor Giusti."

It was formal, but better than "Leave."

He bowed and forced his tongue to move. "Signora. I did not mean to disturb you."

The servant offered her the package, and she took it, her unreadable gaze still on Giusti.

"I am not disturbed. Come in."

Oh dear God, help me... He could not refuse, did not want to, although this meeting was what he had been trying to avoid.

He stepped inside, heard the door close behind him as he followed Elena through the charming foyer and up the staircase to her drawing room. It all looked different since he had last been here. Not faded and empty like his own place, but fresh and splendid and curiously comfortable. Homely. It had never been homely before.

She sat in one of the chairs grouped by the window and, at her invitation, took one at a respectful distance. She put the parcel on the table between them as another servant appeared with wine and cicchetti.

She waited until they were served and the servant departed before she again picked up the parcel.

"How are you?" he blurted, though whether he was trying to distract her or himself with such a stupid question, he didn't know.

"Bored," she said. "The house feels empty. Now that everyone has presented their dutiful condolences, they leave me respectfully—and with some relief—in peace. Patriotic Venetians despise me anyway, and Angelo's friends suspect I killed him."

He had forgotten her blunt, humorous way of speaking, the honest, brave way she faced everything. But she had unwrapped the parcel while talking and now spilled the jewels into her lap.

She regarded them in silence, unmoving except to stop her father's ring from rolling off onto the floor.

He could not bear the quiet and rushed again into speech. "I did not mean to be here when you received them. It felt like rudeness and pressure, which I do not at all mean to inflict—"

"Why now?" she interrupted. "Because he is dead?"

"Yes," he said miserably. Slowly, her gaze lifted to his and he couldn't bear it. "Not because I imagine he left you destitute. Not even because there is no point if I can't annoy him. Just because they are yours."

She placed her father's ring on the table beside her glass, which reflected the intense blue of the stone, and waved her hand over the little pile in her lap. "They were always mine."

"And I should have returned them long ago. I meant to—except when he annoyed me with his demands—but..." He reached rather wildly for his glass and took a sizeable gulp.

"But what?" she asked, and he knew she would not leave it alone.

He met her gaze. "I was afraid that once I returned them, I would no longer have any excuse to see you."

"You weren't exactly using them as an opportunity. Have you decided you don't want to see me after all?"

He shook his head. "It just all seemed so silly, so pointless. So…dishonest." And God help him, the truth would out. "You broke my heart, Elena."

She swallowed. "I think you broke mine too, over a longer period. During the siege, I stopped feeling. I felt I couldn't and still survive. You and I caused all that. Angelo stopped it. He was safe, and I did love him."

He closed his eyes, then opened them again because he couldn't bear not to see her. "Safe love. I was never safe. I'm still not. But I am constant."

"I wished you would find someone else and then you would stop all this." She waved her hand over the jewels in her lap again.

"I'm sorry."

"So am I," she whispered. Her eyes were wet, and she let her eyelids fall to cover it. "Damn you, Ludo, don't make me *feel*."

"Feeling is the point, Elena. All of it."

Her gaze flew back to his, outraged and accusing.

He smiled crookedly. "You see?"

To his surprise—and unspeakable relief—she let out a breath of laughter. Once, he would have stayed to try to build on that instant of empathy, pushing his luck. Older and wiser, he rose to his feet.

"Thank you," he said. He didn't mean for the wine. He meant for that moment, for receiving him in the first place.

She did not stand with him, merely swiped something off the table beside her and held it out to him. Slowly, he stretched out his hand, and she dropped her father's ring into his palm. "This is yours. It was my gift. Unless you are returning it."

Although she spoke carelessly, without emphasis, he saw the vulnerability in her eyes. She was afraid he would refuse. Exactly what this meant, he did not know yet. He suspected neither did she. But it was a beginning, a renewal, an opportunity.

He put the ring in his pocket. *"Arrivederci." Until we meet again.*

He felt he was walking on air. He reached his own house, it

seemed, without engaging his brain, simply by his body's memory. But once there, reality arrived back with a thump.

Foscolo was waiting for him.

IN THE AFTERNOON, Solomon and Constance wandered into an old building with an open door and a large bill advertising an exhibition of paintings. It was a pleasingly normal thing to do after their "accidental" meeting with Foscolo at a coffeehouse, where he sat with them for ten minutes in casual conversation that was anything but.

Constance almost jumped at the paintings to distract herself from a plan she could not like, but which Solomon had already agreed to. Even so, she was not entirely surprised to see Domenico Rossi's face beaming at them from the center of the room.

He detached himself from the group of obvious fellow artists around him and hurried toward them. He seemed to be sober, possibly because Adriana was in charge of distributing wine to the visitors. In spite of everything, the sight of the girl with bottles and glasses sent a shiver down Constance's spine.

"You are out and about, signora!" Rossi greeted them. "I am honored this should be one of your first calls."

"It's an accidental call," Solomon confessed, "but no less welcome for that. You never mentioned an exhibition."

"It was a sudden decision. Adriana arranged it and wheedled another few artists to join us—which brings in more people," Rossi added, his eyes twinkling, "even if the other artists are not as good as me."

"Then you won't be working on our portrait for a few days?" Solomon said.

"I give Signora Grey time to convalesce. But I can come tomorrow afternoon, if you like. Adriana and the others will look after things for me here."

"Yes," Constance said firmly, before Solomon could answer. "Come tomorrow afternoon." She needed to believe it would happen, that by tomorrow afternoon, Solomon would be back, alive, at the Palazzo Zulian, and they would all be safe.

CHAPTER NINETEEN

SOLOMON HAD HOPED Constance would sleep through the dawn and not wake until he was back. But he should have known better. She was already awake and watching him when he slid from the bed.

Deliberately, he concentrated on what lay ahead, not on her, but somehow he was not surprised to find her washing and dressing beside him in the pale light of one candle. She said nothing until his shoes were fastened and he reached for his coat.

"Let me come, Solomon. I'll keep out of sight and do nothing."

"Then there is no point in your being there, is there?" With his coat on, he went back to her, placing his hands on her shoulders. "I will be fine. And you must stay here and remain safe."

"But you have no one to watch your back."

"One of Foscolo's men will be there. And I will have Alvise."

"And how many will be with Lampl? Any number of police and spies, including Savelli's bodyguard."

"If he means to attack me, he can't allow so many people to know," Solomon said patiently. They had had this discussion already. Twice. "I can take care of myself, Constance. I always have."

She caught his wrists. "Don't despise him as a pampered aristocrat, Solomon. Lots of them are vicious."

"So am I." He bent and kissed her. "I need to know you are

safe. Otherwise, I may not be sharp enough."

It was a low blow, and he could see her hating him for it. But she released his wrists and let him go.

"I love you," he said gently.

She tried to smile, and if anything had convinced him to stay, that failed attempt would have been it. "I will love you when you come home."

Solomon kissed her again, and her mouth clung to his for a moment before she stepped back. He left the room without turning back and made his way carefully down the darkened stairs to the front door, which he unlocked and relocked behind him.

Alvise awaited him in the boat, nodding a greeting as Solomon climbed in. Then he began to row toward the Grand Canal, apparently untroubled by the lack of light.

Solomon hoped it would not occur to Constance that Alvise could be Lampl's spy in their household. Solomon had considered it himself before recruiting the gondolier's help. But Alvise had already defended him in a scrap, and Solomon, who still regarded himself as a decent judge of character, had decided that even if Alvise did spy, he would not attack him.

So much depended on what Lampl did, on how he attacked. Would he provoke Solomon into attacking him so that he felt obliged to shoot in self-defense? Would he entice him close enough to try to slide a knife between his ribs, meaning to then heave him into the canal?

He just had to observe closely and react with speed. Solomon was not a brawler by nature, but life had taught him to be constantly aware, and he knew his own strengths. He was quietly confident.

Dawn was just beginning to break as Alvise tied up where they had agreed and they walked the rest of the way to the Rialto Bridge by quiet streets. Alvise kept his distance in case Lampl saw him, but in the quiet, Solomon could just hear the faint footfalls, comforting, allowing him to concentrate on his immediate surroundings, the buildings he was passing, the corners he was approaching.

Even so, when he turned wide around a church-like building, the shadow detaching itself from the doorway took him by complete surprise. His fingers curled, poised, as a man fell into step beside him.

"Good morning," said Ludovico Giusti.

You should not be here. Solomon's skin crawled with sudden, unthinkable suspicion. Had they been wrong all along? Was Giusti, the great Italian patriot, a spy and traitor after all? Had he murdered Savelli for his own ends but on Lampl's orders? Poisoned Constance? The possibilities rushed upon Solomon, trying to scramble his brain while he poised for an attack.

Did Lampl even write that letter?

He must have done. Foscolo had recognized the writing.

Somehow, Solomon kept walking.

"You are abroad early," he managed, every nerve ending aware, his gaze searching constantly for other threats that could finish him before he even got to the Rialto. Surely no one could have known he would come by this particular route...? Had Giusti been watching him, seen him tie up the boat? If so, then he knew about Alvise. And Alvise did not know about him.

Unless Alvise...

God help me, I wish I were alone. The thought flitted through his brain, and he discarded it at once, for at this stage, it didn't matter. He had to deal with *this* reality. Whatever it was.

Giusti said quietly, "Foscolo sent me. He said you might be suspicious. I'm to watch your back."

"You're to go home. It's not about suspicion. Your presence will scare off Lampl." *Or complete the ambush.* He could not allow Giusti onto the bridge.

With every tiny hair standing on end, Solomon turned the final corner, and the Rialto Bridge stood silhouetted against the lightening sky, directly in front of him, arched and ageless and deceptively simple, spanning the splendor of the Grand Canal.

"Wait here," Solomon instructed Giusti. Whether or not the man was on his side, that much was vital—though, of course, he could not force him to obey. "Don't let him see you."

Without pause, he kept walking, tensing for the immediate attack from behind, from right or left. None came. Giusti remained where he was. Solomon could no longer hear Alvise's footsteps and had no idea if that was good or bad. He climbed the steps onto the empty bridge. It looked oddly naked without its usual covering of scurrying and admiring people. But every arch hid a possible threat, a possible enemy.

No one stood at the other end. No one approached it. Even this, the busiest of the canals, was quiet. Only a couple of boats in either direction seemed to be moving in the still water, like dots in the distance.

His footsteps sounded on the bridge, echoing in his ears so that he could not be sure what moved behind him. It recalled an incident in Jamaica when he had been alone and followed stealthily for some purpose he had never discovered. He had missed David's presence then, for, like now, ambush had seemed inevitable.

Ruthlessly, he pushed the memory out. He could not afford to let the smallest part of his attention wander. Foscolo had said he would have a man watching, but if he had, Solomon could not see him. He could see no enemy either, which surprised him. He had expected Lampl to be here first, lying in wait.

He stopped in the middle of the bridge and faced the water. He could not see Giusti to his right. Nor Alvise. And he heard no footsteps. No one approached the bridge from either side of the water. He turned to face the other direction and leaned as casually as he could muster, as though he had come to watch the sun rise. He found the right angle to lounge, with his back half against the side of the bridge, from which he could see all approaches, and waited for someone to emerge from the arches, or from one end of the bridge or the other. The air felt unnaturally still. The water below barely moved.

The two men appeared quite openly from a side street some yards to the left of the bridge, on the opposite bank to where Solomon had left Giusti and, presumably, Alvise. They moved smartly through the gray dawn light, one very much larger than the other.

The smaller man was Lampl, and he had clearly brought his bodyguard. Nevertheless, Solomon maintained his lounging position and kept observing the bridge and all approaches to it. He only straightened when Lampl had climbed the steps, and even then, he made sure he could see both sides of the bridge.

The large man—much more brutal in appearance now that he was nearer—waited at the top of the bridge steps. Lampl advanced alone, wearing a long, dark overcoat against the damp chill of dawn. He looked neither scared nor triumphant, just serious.

He inclined his head with normal civility and spoke in English. "Mr. Grey."

"Herr von Lampl."

The Austrian came to a halt a foot or so away, an unthreatening distance. "Thank you for coming. We do not have long."

"You say you have proof of who poisoned my wife."

"I do. But I need some assurances from you."

Solomon was more than happy to listen. The longer he kept Lampl here, the longer he was giving Foscolo to find the real proof. "Go on."

"You must tell no one except the British consul."

Solomon blinked. "What on earth does the British consul have to do with justice in Venice?"

"Nothing except influence," Lampl said vaguely. "Leave this proof with him and then you must flee Venice immediately. Never return."

"I don't understand," Solomon said flatly. At the far side of the bridge, the large man hadn't moved. Nor, as far as could tell, had Giusti. Where was Alvise? And Foscolo's man?

"I don't have time to explain it to you."

"Make the time," Solomon said, hiding his alarm at this hurry.

Lampl whisked open his overcoat and Solomon tensed, but the quick, slender hand diving into the coat's inside pocket only produced a small glass phial. "Take it."

"What is it?"

"The poison given to your wife."

"By whom? Where did you get it?"

"You know," Lampl said, and, of course, he did. "Take it. Give it to the British consul, and all will be well."

Solomon raised a skeptical eyebrow. "Well for me? I doubt it. Because it is in my possession, I will be arrested for my wife's attempted murder. And Savelli's."

For the first time, a gleam entered Lampl's eye that might have been amusement, or even admiration. "You have a suspicious mind, Mr. Grey. I have tried to save you and your wife, but if you will not accept the help..."

With astonishing speed, Lampl flicked the little phial over the side of the bridge. Solomon was not gullible enough to follow it with his eyes, but he heard it splash into the water below. Lampl's coat swung open with the movement of his arm, revealing the other, larger inner pocket on the opposite side to the first.

Solomon caught only the tiniest glimpse—a distinctive shape, a glint of metal, a flash of color—but it was enough to know that their careful scheme had failed.

Constance was right. It was a stupid plan.

HIDING AT THE bottom of a boat on the other side of the canal at Lampl's back door, Foscolo breathed a sigh of relief. Berndt, the big man, had followed his master out of the house by the back door and now climbed into the boat with Lampl. Of course, Berndt was there to do the rowing as well as the protecting.

Berndt seemed to be the one man that Lampl trusted, and normally one of them always remained in the house. Foscolo had recognized this as the weak part of his plan. Had Berndt stayed behind, most of the men would have been needed to subdue the brute, and that would have meant they were not searching the house.

And they wouldn't have long before someone fetched the soldiers, when they would all be sunk. This was their one risk, and it seemed fortune favored them. Foscolo spared a sympathetic thought for Grey and his own man Guiseppe at the Rialto, who would now have to deal with Berndt instead. He thanked God he had thought to recruit Giusti to the cause.

But speed was still of the essence. As soon as they found the dagger, they would have to rush to the bridge to aid Grey. The longer the Englishman could keep Lampl there and quiet, the better, but they were all prepared for an instant attack. It was an appalling risk, but one Foscolo had felt obliged to take, for Lampl *had* to be brought down. As quietly as possible.

Foscolo stretched one cramped leg. He waited until Lampl's boat turned the first bend, then sat up. Instantly, so did his companion, who reached for the oars.

A massive thump on the back door caused it, eventually, to open a crack. It was a child's dirty face that appeared there—another stroke of luck—and Foscolo leapt past him into the house.

A woman stood frozen by the kitchen table, gaping at them, her fist clenched as though she were about to pound the dough in front of her.

"Police," Foscolo said. "Wait there and don't move."

His man stayed by the back door, pistol in hand, while Foscolo barged through the kitchen to the stark office beyond. As he had suspected, there was nothing there but a few sheets of blank paper, a pen, a letter knife, and a bottle of ink. A quick stamp around the room revealed no obviously loose floorboards.

He moved swiftly on to the front door of the house and

yanked it open. His men swarmed silently inside, closed and locked the door, and threw the key to Foscolo, who was already partway up to the next floor. As previously instructed, his men spread out and the search began.

It was not a large house, and Lampl kept surprisingly few servants. Those who did stumble upon them were too sleepy and astonished to interfere. Foscolo and his men tore through the house with speed and thoroughness, breaking locks, going through drawers and cabinets and cupboards. It was not easy to miss a long-bladed dagger with a hilt encrusted with jewels.

Lampl's bedroom had always been the likeliest place, for it was the most private. Foscolo searched it with gusto, muttering to himself, "Come on, come on, where do you keep it, you bastard? You would never throw anything so valuable away..."

There was always the possibility, of course, that Lampl had sold it, probably to buy Elena Savelli expensive gifts. But Foscolo would not think of that. Even a hoard of money would be something...

But it was not in any of the drawers. The only thing of interest he found, beneath Lampl's cuff links, was a small lace handkerchief, embroidered *E*. Clearly stolen from Elena. Foscolo pocketed it with a brief return of elation and turned to the mattress.

Five minutes later, he dragged his hand through his hair and glared at his shuffling men. "Nothing," he uttered through his teeth. "How can there be nothing? It *must* be here!"

His men would think he was mad. Lampl would crucify him and go on unhindered, crushing and killing and doing exactly as he pleased to Venice, and then, no doubt, in other places, growing always in confidence and cruelty.

"I cannot allow it," Foscolo fumed. "Why the hell is it not here?"

Because he was wrong, horribly, unforgivably wrong?

Or... "Oh dear God," he whispered. "He took it with him!" He raised his voice, yelling, "He took it with him! To the Rialto!"

Unforgivable stupidity... Please, God, let us be in time to save Grey...

CONSTANCE PACED HER bedchamber, the coffee Maria had brought to her untouched. Sometimes she strode to the sitting room and paced there. When that grew unbearable, she marched downstairs and sat at the dining room table. Here at last, she sipped some coffee and nibbled at bread, but could not remain still for long.

Abandoning the remains of her coffee, she gazed out of the window, knowing it was far too early to expect Solomon back. It was not even properly light... And yet all the servants were up. How did they know? Had Solomon instructed them to protect her? Or had they just heard her relentless pacing and, like the good servants they were, risen early to serve?

She walked through to the drawing room, which, being much larger, offered more satisfying opportunities for an anxious pacer.

It felt all wrong, letting Solomon face the culprit without her. They had always confronted the foe together, and somehow, despite a few near misses, it had always worked out. Admittedly she was weak now, and Solomon faced a specific kind of threat where she could not help and would only distract him, as he had pointed out. This was the only reason she was not now on the Rialto Bridge, or at least watching it, watching his back...

She wished she had not promised. She could go now, hide and watch in case there was anything she could do. Only, she *had* promised. And Alvise and one of Foscolo's policemen were watching over him instead. Surely, he was safe.

The plan was sensible on the face of it. They were using Lampl's own bait to bait their trap with Solomon. While Foscolo collected the evidence from Lampl's house. But it was not an official raid—that would never have been sanctioned. Foscolo was risking everything to find the twin dagger in Lampl's possession, and if he failed, he fell, and Lampl won, even if Solomon survived.

If Solomon survived.

Dear God…

She hurled herself across the room, unable to bear such possibilities, and gazed out of the window across the canal. It was daybreak. The sun was rising, pale and promising.

It will be fine. It is always fine in the end.

The door opened behind her, and she swung around eagerly, in the suddenly wild, desperate hope that it was Solomon, early and triumphant.

It wasn't.

It was Pellini, Savelli's thuggish bodyguard who worked in reality for Lampl.

The man who had abducted her at the beginning of all this trouble walked into her drawing room, closed the door, and turned the key.

She didn't even need to ask how he had got into the palazzo, for she knew. They did indeed have a spy in the house.

SOLOMON HAD ALREADY seen how fast the apparently stolid Lampl could move, when he threw the rejected phial into the canal. So as the Austrian whipped the dagger from his swinging coat, Solomon leapt swiftly out of range. Even so, he was only just in time, for in the same quick, fluid movement, Lampl lunged with deadly accuracy for Solomon's heart.

Lampl moved his feet to compensate for Solomon's defense, and the dagger thrust on. It would still have inflicted vicious damage had Solomon not seized Lampl's wrist in his left hand and wrenched it downward.

He tried to squeeze hard enough to pry Lampl's fingers loose, but a blow to the chest sent him staggering backward. Then the Austrian was upon him, shoving him against the side of the bridge, his left forearm across his neck, while his right rose and plunged the blade downward.

Solomon fought desperately with both hands to dislodge the arm at his throat, while raising his elbow to block the worst of the dagger's blow. At the same time, he kicked with all his might, aiming for Lampl's knee. With a satisfying and somewhat sickening crack, Lampl grunted and stumbled, flailing his arms to keep his balance.

Solomon desperately needed people, witnesses. Where the devil was Foscolo's man? To his left loomed Lampl's charging brute, who didn't need a knife to finish Solomon.

But Lampl was not finished either. With a silent snarl of pain, he lunged at Solomon once more. Solomon lashed out with his right fist, landing a decent blow to the Austrian's jaw, while with his left he aimed for his stomach and sliced his fingers against the blade. He followed it up with a savage kick between the legs, which doubled his opponent over.

Lampl sank to his knees, his mouth open in silent agony, but Solomon had no time for triumph. A huge hand closed around his nape.

The powerful fingers of Lampl's bodyguard reached all the way around to his windpipe. Solomon drove both his elbows backward into unyielding flesh and bone, but the large man didn't even seem to feel it.

There was, Solomon felt grimly, a certain inevitability about this now. His ears rang, and it took a moment to realize it was men yelling. From what he thought of as his own end of the bridge came a bloodcurdling battle cry as Giusti and Alvise charged into the fray—God knew on what side.

From the other, an entirely different man seemed to have materialized from nowhere, bending over the half-collapsed figure of Lampl and plucking from his fingers the dagger that had killed Savelli.

The unbearable pressure on Solomon's neck released abruptly and he was shoved, gasping, against the side of the bridge. Giusti and Alvise rocketed into the big man with such force that they knocked him backward. His feet slipped on Solomon's blood, and he went down under them with force.

"Hold that," said the man with the dagger to Solomon, who grasped it like the hand of a best friend, and produced iron manacles from his bulging pockets.

Lampl moved at last, hauling himself to his feet. Blood trickled from his mouth where Solomon had hit him. He was panting and clearly in considerable pain, and yet his eyes were bright as they sought and held Solomon's.

The rest of the noise around Solomon, those chaining the big man, and the curious workers and boatmen trailing onto the bridge from both sides, seemed to fade. He could hear only Lampl.

"It seems we underestimated each other."

"I didn't underestimate you," Solomon said with contempt. The rat had almost killed Constance.

Lampl laughed, showing the gaping redness of his mouth. "You see? You still think you won."

It seemed he could still move quickly. He hurled himself at Solomon, who lashed out with the dagger. But Lampl barged straight past him and tumbled over the side of the bridge into the canal below.

Solomon was left staring at the reddened blade of the dagger, the murderer's words ringing in his head, chilling his blood.

"You still think you've won."

"Constance," he said hoarsely, and began to run.

~❦~

CHAPTER TWENTY

CONSTANCE FILLED HER lungs to scream.

"Don't," Pellini said casually. He was pointing a pistol at her heart.

For a moment, she stared at it, her mouth closing, a sense of unreality washing over her. After the first jolt, she didn't even seem to be frightened.

"So you have come to kill me," she said in Italian. "Why?"

The question seemed to surprise him, but in fact, she really wanted to know, although keeping him talking was also a reasonable tactic to extend her life. He advanced upon her, the pistol steady in his right hand.

"You don't know, do you?" she said pityingly. "You just do what Lampl says, regardless. He won't even care that you hang for it. You are a loose end he will need to tie off for his own safety. If he survives. Do you want to die? Because you will, if you shoot me. Whoever let you in, my other servants will break down the door so fast that you will never escape."

That didn't trouble him. He shrugged. "I leave by the window."

So he would talk. That was good. "But how long would you remain free? A hunted man? Neither the Venetians nor the Austrians will stand for blatant murder. It is idiocy to shoot me."

"I don't want to shoot you," he admitted, and the first, dangerous sparks of real hope ignited within her.

Too soon, as it happened, for he was taking something else

from inside his coat. She remembered the feel, the smell of that coat when he had dragged her through the streets, his powerful fingers crushing her arm…

She blinked at the flask in his left hand. *What on earth…?*

Understanding iced her blood, even as he grinned at her, and she took an involuntary step backward.

"You are right," he said. "I don't want to shoot you, though I will. I want to have a drink with you."

Somehow, she recovered her dignity and curled her lip. "Don't be his dupe. Everyone knows I was poisoned before. If I die now, they will know it was murder. Let Lampl do his own dirty work. As he did before."

"You'll feel different once you drink," he mocked. In a practiced movement, he unstopped the flask one handed and closed the distance between them.

Pride kept her still, her chin tilted in supreme contempt. "I will not drink."

"You will," he said with chilling certainty, and seized her round the neck with his left arm, the flask bumping against her jaw, while the pistol was pressed to her head, paralyzing her. "Face it, signora. One way or the other, you die, and I don't care which. The drink is easier on everyone, and that's my instruction, but…"

Is this it? Is this where it ends? Without Solomon… Oh, my poor Solomon…

While the wild, pointless thoughts flashed through her mind, she had shut her mouth tight, like a child refusing food, her whole body stiff with resistance, straining against him. It wasn't bravery, it was mere instinct, and if it caused her to be shot—surely that was no less messy than dying from whatever filthy poison he would force down her throat…

And suddenly she didn't care. If she had to die, she would do it fighting to the end so that Solomon was proud of her, so that he would know she'd tried to stay alive, for him.

Her resistance irritated Pellini. Despite his somewhat terrifying strength, he had too many things to hold on to—her wriggling head, the flask, the pistol. He needed two hands to force the contents of the flask on her with any efficiency. He hadn't thought this through, she realized, but relied on fear of the gun to make her compliant. In fact, her fear of the poison was probably greater, though her body was certainly reacting without her permission.

And there were footsteps, voices outside the drawing room. Someone knocked.

Pellini swore beneath his breath, and the pistol slid off her temple while he tried to wrestle the lip of the flask back on to her mouth. The pistol didn't fire. No projectile ended her life in an instant.

Quite suddenly, she realized the pistol was *only* a threat. He needed her to drink.

"Signora!" called a servant from behind the door. The handle turned and rattled and the voices grew frightened.

But Constance knew she had to save herself. She struggled and strained even harder—but only for an instant. She went suddenly limp in Pellini's hold, forcing him to support her entire weight, and as he desperately adjusted his grip, she snatched the flask from his fingers and wrenched herself free.

She staggered backward away from him, just as something crashed against the door and hurtled inside to the distinctive sound of splintering wood.

Inevitably, Pellini turned to face the new threat. Constance whipped back her arm and hurled the flask with all her might.

It struck Pellini somewhere near his right ear. Liquid splashed over him and over the carpet as the flask fell and bounced on the floor. Pellini stumbled. One knee buckled, and the pistol fell from suddenly nerveless fingers. Several people rushed on him at once.

Constance blinked. They were her manservants. All of them. And straightening from among them, Sebastian Kellar met her gaze and gave a wry yet satisfied smile.

"So sorry to intrude upon you at this hour," he said politely, sidestepping the scramble between them. "I saw you from my boat, at the window, and had the feeling something was amiss."

Constance had the insane desire to laugh.

Below, the front door slammed, and more footsteps clattered across the tiled foyer.

"Constance!" Solomon shouted, and stupidly, unforgivably, though at least silently, she began to cry.

She blundered past everyone, and abruptly he appeared in the doorway, disheveled and panting. In one bloody hand, he carried a jeweled, long-bladed dagger. None of that mattered because the chest she threw herself against was solid and strong. Fear was still fading from his face as she gripped it, gasping, between her hands to be sure. His arms enfolded her in warmth and reality, and just for an instant, nothing else mattered.

"WHAT AN EYE," Kellar said, his face alight with amusement and admiration as he gazed upon Constance. "Quite deadly accuracy, I assure you."

It was an hour after Pellini's capture, and the would-be assassin had been taken away by Foscolo's men, who had turned up very shortly after Solomon. Solomon had washed and changed, and Constance had dressed his wounds. The cut to his fingers was long, but not deep enough to need stitches, so he now sat beside her on their favorite sofa looking more or less his usual, elegant self. His bandaged hand added a touch of dash.

Whatever had been in Pellini's flask, it had been well scrubbed from the carpet and a chair it had sprayed over on its way down. Constance could no longer smell it, possibly because the windows were wide open and she was desperately interested in all everyone had to say. Giusti, who had arrived with Foscolo, had told his tale, and so had Solomon, partially, at least. Kellar had just finished his.

Foscolo eyed Solomon. "You should be careful." He was only half jesting.

"Oh, I am."

"I'm sorry," Foscolo said abruptly. "It never entered my head he would try to use *that* to kill you too." The dagger lay on the low table between them, winking in the splashes of sunlight that came and went through the clouds. "Perhaps it should have. I think it was symbolic."

"The way he ran at me," Solomon said, speaking for the first time about the fight, "I thought he meant to impale himself on it. That would have been symbolic, too."

"I received word while you were changing," Foscolo said. "Lampl's body was pulled out of the Grand Canal. He is indeed dead. It will all be covered up, of course, and there will be someone else to take his place. But his guilt is known now, all over Venice. The Austrians will not deny it, just make the point that he acted alone and against their law."

"So you will be safe?" Giusti asked.

"Yes, I think so. Anything else would be too much of an embarrassment for the government." Foscolo turned to Constance. "How did Pellini get in here?"

"I think we have a spy in the household who let him in—possibly with reluctance, for *all* the servants helped capture him in the end."

Foscolo sighed. "It was not a great plan, was it?"

"It did what we intended," Constance said, prepared to be kind now that the danger was past. "If not quite *how* we intended it."

"You are generous," Foscolo said moodily.

"She is," Solomon agreed.

Foscolo rose to his feet and lifted the dagger from the table. He wrapped it in the cloth Constance had found for the purpose and hid it beneath his coat. "A less public progress through the streets, this time."

Solomon's face darkened along the blades of his cheekbones,

and Constance realized with astonishment that he was blushing. He must, in fact, have looked a demented and terrifying figure, rampaging through the streets, quite unaware of the dagger still clutched in his bloody hand.

"I thought I might show it to Signora Savelli," Foscolo said. "She deserves to know the outcome of all this."

Giusti glanced up. "Are you going there now?"

"On my way back to the office."

Giusti stood up, almost but not quite casual. "I'll come with you," he said.

Constance smiled.

When they had gone, Kellar picked up his wine glass, twisting the stem absently in his fingers. "What will you do now? Shake the dust—or the water!—of Venice from your feet and move on?"

Solomon's good fingers wrapped around Constance's hand, and she smiled because she understood. Somehow, the magic was still there, and they would not waste it. "Oh no. It is too soon to leave."

Kellar's lips quirked. "You are a rare and brave couple. Don't get into any more mischief while I am gone."

"You are leaving Venice?"

"I am required in Rome. At the Vatican. I depart tomorrow." He finished his wine and set down the glass in a decisive sort of way. Still, he hesitated, before speaking with unusual diffidence. "After that, I shall be on leave. I had thought of a visit to England. I wanted to ask you—would it be…advisable to call upon your mother?"

How to answer that? He was the first man Constance had encountered who had ever looked on her mother through a lens of romance and respectability. How would he face the reality of Juliet, colorful and unbowed but nevertheless damaged by drink and by men? More to the point, how would Juliet face him? Constance's instinct told her it would be cruel to inflict such painful humiliation on her mother. But that was not really her decision to make.

Solomon took several visiting cards from his pocket and selected one, which he passed to Kellar. "Why don't you call on us? Whatever Juliet decides, we will be delighted to see you again."

Constance regarded him with considerable respect, as Kellar inclined his head before taking his leave.

"You really are wonderful," she said to her husband as they stood on the balcony, waving to Kellar in his boat. "I didn't know what to say to him."

"Oh, I am wonderful in so many ways," he said with light self-mockery.

She gripped his hand. "You are. But no more plans that keep me *safe*."

"It does seem that you are only safe under my eye," Solomon agreed.

"I would not go that far."

He smiled and leaned on the balcony rail. She leaned on him.

"Do you think Elena will marry Giusti in the end?" she asked.

"Probably. If they learn to put each other first at least some of the time."

"I think they will. I think they have. Like us old married people."

Beneath them, the water rippled and shone, and boats glided by in the sunshine. In the distance, a gondolier broke into song. Closer by, a shopkeeper and a tradesman were quarrelling and gesticulating. Tranquil and vital, Venice endured. And so did they.

ABOUT THE AUTHOR

Mary Lancaster lives in Scotland with her husband, three mostly grown-up kids and a small, crazy dog.

Her first literary love was historical fiction, a genre which she relishes mixing up with romance and adventure in her own writing. Her most recent books are light, fun Regency romances written for Dragonblade Publishing: *The Imperial Season* series set at the Congress of Vienna; and the popular *Blackhaven Brides* series, which is set in a fashionable English spa town frequented by the great and the bad of Regency society.

Connect with Mary on-line – she loves to hear from readers:

Email Mary:
Mary@MaryLancaster.com

Website:
www.MaryLancaster.com

Newsletter sign-up:
http://eepurl.com/b4Xoif

Facebook:
facebook.com/mary.lancaster.1656

Facebook Author Page:
facebook.com/MaryLancasterNovelist

Twitter:
@MaryLancNovels

Amazon Author Page:
amazon.com/Mary-Lancaster/e/B00DJ5IACI

Bookbub:
bookbub.com/profile/mary-lancaster